The soft denim molded to a fantastic specimen of a man that she missed as soon as he was around the corner.

Time to get on with her day and just move forward. Last night, her thoughts had taken her into dreams that had been mixed with murder and lovemaking and decaying bodies and excellent bodies. She was exhausted from sleeping. That was a fact.

How was this supposed to work? Did she really think she could just calmly take care of business? As if being chased by a serial killer/assassin wasn't enough, she had to be partnered with a man totally oblivious to her attraction.

"I'm in so much trouble."

SHOTGUN JUSTICE

Angi Morgan

There is never a book without my pals Jan and Robin. Thanks for the crazy cabin inspiration, Nicki, JoAnna and Lizbeth. Ruth…thanks for the idea for my "pal" Snake Eyes. And a special shout-out to Julie for helping me at the beginning and end of this book.

ISBN-13: 978-0-373-69893-6

Shotgun Justice

Copyright © 2016 by Angela Platt

Recycling programs for this product may not exist in your area.

The publisher acknowledges the copyright holder of the additional work:

What Happens on the Ranch
Copyright © 2016 by Delores Fossen

Printed in U.S.A.

CONTENTS

Angi Morgan writes Harlequin Intrigue novels "where honor and danger collide with love." She combines actual Texas settings with characters who are in realistic and dangerous situations. Angi and her husband live in north Texas, with only the four-legged "kids" left in the house to interrupt her writing. They recently began volunteering for a local Labrador retriever foster program. Visit her website, angimorgan.com, or hang out with her on Facebook.

Books by Angi Morgan

Harlequin Intrigue

Texas Rangers: Elite Troop

Bulletproof Badge
Shotgun Justice

West Texas Watchmen

The Sheriff
The Cattleman
The Ranger

Texas Family Reckoning

Navy SEAL Surrender
The Renegade Rancher

Hill Country Holdup
.38 Caliber Cover-Up
Dangerous Memories
Protecting Their Child
The Marine's Last Defense

Visit the Author Profile page at Harlequin.com for more titles.

SHOTGUN JUSTICE

ANGI MORGAN

CAST OF CHARACTERS

Jesse Ryder—Lieutenant with the Texas Rangers assigned to protect Avery and capture the assassin chasing her. When he goes all save-the-day on Avery, she's stunned. An assassin's attack leads these best friends to a place where love is as dangerous as the killer stalking them.

Avery Travis—Deputy Sheriff in Dallam County. Currently the target of an assassin who wants the location of her brother, Garrison, and his witness to the Tenoreno murder.

Snake Eyes—A serial assassin who replaces the eyes of his victims with river rocks painted like snake eyes.

Julie Oden—Dallam County Sheriff Department's dispatcher and receptionist.

Josh Parker—Major in the Texas Rangers, in charge of Company F based in Waco.

Bryce Johnson—Lieutenant in the Texas Rangers, Company F's authority on Texas organized crime.

Tenoreno Family—Texas organized crime family. Isabella Tenoreno has been murdered. Her husband, Paul, awaits trial.

Garrison Travis—Twin brother to Avery. He's a Texas Ranger currently on protection detail to a witness to Isabella Tenoreno's murder.

Kenderly Tyler—A cosmetologist who witnessed the Tenoreno murder, currently under the protection of the Texas Rangers.

Prologue

"My twin brother is the one wanted for murder. You have no right to lock me up, Dan." Avery Travis was experiencing insane fury. She'd been disappointed, been angry, had even been fighting mad, but this was worse. Her head just might explode.

Jesse Ryder had absolutely no right to suggest she be thrown in jail for her own safety. When she got out she might…she might just… Well, she knew how to hurt him.

"Dan, you know Garrison needs help to get him out of this mess and clear his name." She could help him. Just as soon as she sweet-talked her way out of this holding cell.

"What I know is that you're upset and have a reason to be." The older sheriff of Dallam County locked the cell and gestured for her to back up to the bars—just like he did to every common prisoner.

"Okay, you win, Dan. I'll give you my word as a deputy that I won't take off to Austin." She crossed her fingers. "You know you can't spare me right now. Who's going to answer to keep the reckless juveniles in line?"

"I'm not arguing about you being the best deputy I

have. I'm only doing what that Texas Ranger friend of yours suggested."

She walked to the cell doors for him to remove the handcuffs, her fingers definitely uncrossed. "You didn't have to cuff me."

"Now, darlin', you know that's not true." Dan drew another circle in the air and Avery turned around. "If I hadn't surprised you, then you wouldn't be here."

He removed the cuffs and she rubbed her wrists, glad to be free. Well, almost free. She looked at the three walls of the small county jail. "You can't be serious about keeping me here. How long?"

"Until the Rangers have everything under control. It shouldn't take long. They're very capable men who know what they're doing."

Right. *Men.*

"He didn't do it, you know." She stated the fact without having spoken to her brother. He hadn't called her or their mom during all the confusion, but she knew it was true. She knew that he'd been framed. And she knew that she could find out the person responsible—if she was allowed to help. But the Texas Rangers were on top of it and didn't need her.

"I haven't met him, but I've never thought he murdered those two women. He's your brother." Dan turned to leave. "But that makes no never mind. If he were here, I'd have to take him in. Since I don't believe it and a criminal family is involved, I tend to agree with your friend—I mean Lieutenant Ryder. You need to stay safe and won't be if you go traipsing off to Austin trying to help your brother from this predicament."

"I promise to stay out of trouble," she said with crossed fingers.

"I tend not to believe you, Avery. Don't get me wrong. You're a blasted good deputy and can take over this office in a New York minute. But staying out of trouble when your brother's being hunted for murder?" Dan shook his head and pursed his lips, rubbing the graying whiskers on his chin. "No, missy, I just don't believe you'll stay in Dalhart voluntarily. So this is the best solution."

"I can't believe you are seriously going to keep me locked up." She threw her hands in the air and walked over to the very visible toilet. "Are you really going to make me stay here while my fellow deputies watch me tinkle on a video screen?"

"Avery, we'll make it work and find a way to keep your privacy. But I guarantee you one thing… I like you being alive more than I'm worried about any of that." Dan waved his hand in the air toward the toilet area. "I'll have someone bring your standing order from the Dairy Barn for dinner. You can have the bag you packed as soon as Julie goes through it for weapons."

"What weapons?"

"Anything sharp or heavy you can use to hurt Bo and Derek." He laughed over his shoulder as he walked away. Probably because he used her movie-reference nicknames for his two perfect-ten deputies.

She'd packed too fast to think about a heavy object that could be used to hit anyone over the head. She'd had no idea that she'd need anything sturdier than extra undies, socks and a toothbrush. Carrying her service weapon would have been enough for what she'd intended.

Well, then again, it wouldn't take much to get the jump on the two young men. She'd put both of them on the training mat right after she arrived. At least she could do that six months ago. After the first training workout, they wouldn't come with her again. They were afraid to hurt her. Big laugh. She predicted their moves as soon as they faced her because they thought of her as a woman. She'd practiced with Jesse her entire life.

Jesse. The man behind all her problems.

None of that mattered at the moment unless it would help her get free of this place. This was all Jesse's fault. She plopped down on the thin mattress and right back up. They'd forgotten to take her cell out of her back pocket. She tapped a number still on speed dial and waited.

"Hey, Avery. Been a long time. Like your new job?"

Oh, that voice. She'd missed it. Even being embarrassed beyond anything she could have imagined, she'd still missed him. "Jesse Ryder, if anything happens to my brother because you won't let me help..."

"Whoa, whoa, whoa, Avery. You know me better than that. I'm doing everything I can. We all are."

She recognized his sincerity. He believed the best of the best were on the case. And she hadn't been good enough to be a part of *the best*. "I need you to make a call to my boss and get me out of here."

"Where's 'here,' babe?"

Oh man, there had been a time when she yearned for him to use that endearment. Now was not it. "Exactly where you suggested Dan hold me until my brother's problem is over."

Laughter. Lots of laughter. And then a little more laughter. "Are you serious? I made a tiny suggestion and he put you behind bars? How did anybody get the drop on you?"

"Your sweet-talking won't work this time. I'm going to stay angry forever. Especially now. I am not one of those girls who hangs on your every word. So you make that call and get me out of here."

She'd been exactly one of those girls. From the time she could run, she'd followed her brother and his best friend everywhere. She'd pined for Jesse and gone unnoticed when they were teens. And for just a short period of three months last year, she'd been the happiest girl on the planet.

"There's nothing to be done, Avery. I'll be a pal and call in a couple of days to update you. Even that's against the rules and you know it."

"I wouldn't call you a pal at this particular moment."

He cleared his throat. She could tell he was about to mention that horrible night when they'd almost made love. That sounded pathetic and she wasn't even saying it out loud. If he apologized for walking out on her...

"I haven't had a chance to explain—"

"I don't want to hear it. It's done. Over. I've moved on. Moved to the far northwest of Texas, in fact."

Living in Austin after the guys had been promoted had become impossible. Everywhere she'd gone there had been a memory of one of them. She might have been able to handle missing her brother—eventually.

But Jesse? She'd been head over heels in love with him her entire life. One day out of the blue last year, she'd caught him looking at her differently. Then it was three months of clandestine, sexy kisses. Three months of sensual foreplay. And one night they'd almost made love. Whatever she'd done wrong, it had scared Jesse into walking out.

"I grew up next door to you, too. Remember? It

doesn't sound like you've moved on. So when are you going to let me explain?"

She pressed the disconnect button. She was angry and needed to stay that way. Focusing on her job was the only thing keeping her sane in this little town. There wasn't anything to really worry about. Right? Seriously, this was her brother. Of course she was worried. It was the first time they hadn't been together for a crisis.

Dan might have turned the key in the lock, but Jesse was responsible. She could focus her anger on that man. He deserved it for putting the idea into Dan's head.

"Oh yeah. The next time I see Jesse Ryder...I'm definitely going to kill him."

Chapter One

Late April, the South Texas Desert

"Please, please. I beg you. I...I have money. Lots of money. I can pay you more than Tenoreno."

Rosco had awakened from the drug and would soon become annoying. The drive was almost over. The first part of his assignment almost complete.

"Sorry, man. It's nothing personal. Just a job," he answered, trying to prevent the inevitable. He still had to make a decision on how to kill this man.

Gun. Knife. Swizzle stick. He chuckled at the idea. Of course, he could do the job with anything. He was that good. The swizzle stick he chewed on, however, would retain his DNA and he'd never be that stupid.

The perfect set of gloves sat on the seat next to him along with the rest of his tools. Some killers went so far as to shave their bodies so as not to drop a single hair. For him, the diving suit worked just as well. He'd changed a few minutes ago before continuing down Texas 349 to find just the right abandoned spot.

There were no witnesses on this stretch of deserted road. No cameras. No recording devices of any type. Rarely a car or driver that would think twice about seeing his ordinary vehicle. He'd deliberately left the burner phone at the Kerrville hotel. An automatic text message would be sent to indicate he was hundreds of miles away on Interstate 10. Not that anyone would call, but it was there in any case. No one in the nearby town would notice a plain blue rental car that looked black on this moonless night.

No one ever noticed. As he'd said many times—at least to himself—he was very good at his job.

He didn't tire at becoming better, striving for more. He was a professional, after all. Thomas Rosco kicked his seat.

"Stop that. What do you hope to accomplish by annoying me?"

"I want you to see reason. Let me go."

"Mr. Rosco, don't you know who I am?"

"I haven't seen your face. You could leave me here and I'd never be able to identify you."

Pulling onto a dirt road leading under an old faded gate, the single windmill made him feel lonesome. That was ridiculous. He was completely at ease in this desolate country and never tired of his work. The fun was just about to begin.

"I'm hurt that you thought Tenoreno would hire anyone other than myself."

"You…you…you're Snake Eyes?"

"It seems an appropriate name." He turned around to stare directly at his prey. "Don't you think?"

He knew what the crime boss saw. Almost glowing eyes, slanted and the color of a reptile's. The contacts added a dimension to his persona that made his victims quake. He laughed, the sound deliberately sinister. It normally put fear in his victims' eyes.

Rosco wasn't any different than the other men. A sad example of a tough guy. Tough men bled just like the rest. Their bodies rotted under the sun just like that of a man with a good soul.

The gloves slid over his hands, and then he helped Rosco stand from the car. No rough stuff was necessary.

The man was about to die. The fear rushed through Rosco's veins. The poor fellow might get a burst of adrenaline. Might make a run for it. Whatever. It didn't matter.

"You should make peace with your God, if you have one. Maybe ask forgiveness for all the men and women you're responsible for killing."

"Do you tell that to all the people you're about to murder?"

"Let's get moving."

The answer was yes. It was his thing. He believed in a higher power and that he'd be punished accordingly. But he had a calling to be the best at his work as he could.

They walked into the field. The knee-high tobosa grass crackled under their feet as they shuffled through. Near the dried-out gully was the perfect place to leave a body. He doubted anyone would find Rosco for months. Not until the hunters returned for wild turkey or deer in the fall.

"No wailing? No more pleading?" he asked, curious.

"I know you get the job done. That's why we employed your services so often. I... There is nothing I can say?" Rosco sank to his knees near some mesquite scrub. "Nothing you'll accept in payment over what Tenoreno is paying you?"

"No. This is a waste. I wish I had time to play, but sometimes work comes first."

With one stroke he pulled his knife and sliced left to right across the windpipe before him. Rosco's eyes widened as he realized he couldn't take a breath. The gurgling sound of him choking wasn't unpleasant. It was satisfying to Snake Eyes that he'd completed the job. Rosco fell forward, hands secured behind him, twitching as his lifeblood soaked the parched earth.

Slicing easily through the plastic handcuffs, he gathered the remnants and shoved them inside the diver's bag at his side.

Now the fun really began.

He flipped Rosco to his back, not bothering to wait for the body to grow cold. He methodically removed the lifeless eyes in Rosco's face. He wouldn't keep them. He wasn't sentimental and didn't need a souvenir, just a way to identify himself as the killer.

He'd studied serial killers, read up on them. If it had been possible, he could have shared his checklists of how to get away without a trace. But then…if everyone knew his methods, he wouldn't be in such high demand.

Laughing, he withdrew the artificial snakelike eyes, using a cleaning solution and a polishing cloth to make them shine. Then he meticulously placed the stones in Rosco's face, leaving him staring at the heavens.

The eyes would be anonymously shipped to his employer. Proof of the completion of his task. He popped them into the jewelry case he carried in his bag.

Many of his victims had never been found. Some never would. But those who were…the eyes were an eerie sight when his handiwork was discovered. As a calling card, they were unique and rarely reported to the press.

But they knew. He was precise and unique. He methodically went through his mental list. Then he opened the notebook and verified he'd performed everything on the list again. He would not get sloppy and make a mistake.

Or bored.

Admitting that he was bored was why he took on the next challenge. Keeping a captive alive long enough to extract information. A definite challenge that needed a new notebook of lists. He flipped the pocket spiral closed, satisfied that he'd covered everything.

Now it was time to discover the details of his next victim. How she lived her mundane life. What drove her to make a mistake. He had a short time to get to know Avery Travis. His new commission would be a test case. Careful planning would be the key to a successful kill.

Chapter Two

"Thomas Rosco is dead. His throat was slit by the Snake Eyes Killer."

Texas Ranger Lieutenant Jesse Ryder had to replay the words in his mind to verify that he'd heard the major correctly. There really wasn't another interpretation of *Thomas Rosco is dead*. Everyone in the room quieted, probably replaying the same words.

Rosco was a crime boss, rumored to have been partnered with Paul Tenoreno—brought to justice earlier that year. The Rangers received the credit, but the man mainly responsible had been his best friend, Garrison Travis, and his witness, Kenderly Tyler, a beautician. They'd witnessed a double homicide orchestrated by Tenoreno. Her courage, along with detailed files left by the murder victims, provided the prosecution with an excellent case.

Then they'd turned Rosco to testify against his partner, but he'd been missing for the past week. Tenoreno had one play left…eliminating the witnesses. Rosco was just the first. He'd be after Garrison and Kenderly next.

Major Josh Parker stood at his office door to make the

announcement. If he expected a response, there wasn't one. It looked as though the other rangers in the room were just as dumbfounded.

Tenoreno had hired an assassin who left no trace of evidence. He was a virtual ghost. Law-enforcement agencies across the country hadn't collected more than a page of notes on the man. Or woman, whatever the case may be, since they had no DNA to prove either.

So far, Snake Eyes was known for killing bad guys. The bodies found had all been those of people wanted for other crimes. If there had been more evidence, maybe someone would look harder.

"Property owners came across the body off of Texas 349 south of Sheffield," the major finally continued. "The medical examiner estimates he's been dead six days. Pure luck on our part that the owners were dropping off a hunting blind."

"His death blows a huge chunk of the case against Tenoreno." Bryce Johnson hadn't realized what he'd said until the sputters grew in number around the room. "Okay, okay. Huge chunks. Got it. Ha-ha. We all know that it has to be Tenoreno pulling the strings from his jail cell to order something like this."

Bryce was the resident expert on Texas organized crime. He knew better than any of them how much the state's prosecutor was depending on the rival crime family's testimony.

"Tenoreno's been in solitary. No visitors. No communication other than his lawyer." The major might have been waiting on answers or ideas, but none came forth. "No apparent connection to Rosco's murder. No one believes that to be true."

"How was he killed?" someone behind him asked.

"What does that do for Garrison's detail?" It was no secret that Jesse was more concerned about his best friend's safety than putting Tenoreno away. One couldn't happen without the other, but Jesse knew what his priority would be.

"Who's taking the lead on the investigation?" Bryce asked.

The major gestured for the two of them to come to his office. Jesse followed Bryce, ready to work with him, ready to get some real action instead of tracking criminal activity through the internet.

"The murder of Thomas Rosco will be handled by the local PD with the aid of Company A. Headquarters is ready to roll if they think there's a problem. They've got it covered and don't need our help. Before you begin objecting, the two of you are needed other places."

Jesse was ready to object anyway, but his commanding officer turned his back as he walked around his desk. He sat and propped his feet on the corner, taking his thinking position.

"Prosecutors have asked for your help, Bryce," he continued. "They have a lead that needs your knowledge and expertise. Vivian has the information. Hand over anything you're working on to her and we'll get it taken care of."

Bryce didn't hesitate. He was out the door and gathering his things after a hurried "Yes, sir." Jesse's nerves began twitching. Whatever was about to come, he didn't get the feeling that Major Parker felt comfortable, either.

"What's happened? Did they discover the location of Garrison's detail?"

"No, nothing like that. But while Tenoreno was at the pretrial, he plainly stated that no one close to Garrison would be safe. It's a threat most criminals make. That's nothing new. But we have intel that someone accepted a contract on Garrison's sister."

"Avery's a deputy in the Panhandle. Has she been made aware of the situation? Have you alerted Sheriff Myers?"

"Headquarters believes this could be another nail in Tenoreno's coffin if we can capture the assassin and get him to turn state's evidence."

"That would mean they're using Avery as bait. Did anyone tell her?"

"It's been handled. Her participation, on the other hand... Well, Jesse, the attorneys think it would be better coming from you when you arrive in Dalhart."

"Then they should think about that again, sir. I'm the last person Avery wants to see. The title's mine with Garrison a close second."

He actually missed Avery. They'd grown up together, gone to the same schools, same concentration of studies. He'd made the Rangers and she hadn't. She quit everything, packed up, left and hadn't spoken to him since. Of course, the real reason for not talking to him was a little more involved.

"Our information is credible, Jesse. The hit is happening soon, so you don't have much time." Major Parker wasn't pondering any longer. He had both feet on the floor and leaned forward on his desk. "It's already been decided, Lieutenant. Already in motion. This isn't a debate."

"I had her thrown in jail to protect her the last time this happened, sir. She's not going to listen to me. And I doubt I can get her near the county lockup again."

"Make her listen. The last thing we need is for Garrison Travis to be lured from the safe house and be killed. Take care of his sister or you'll be searching for her murderer instead."

The two choices hit him between the eyes like the baseball Avery had thrown when they were nine. His head was whirring just as badly as back then. Murdered?

No one else would try as hard as him. That was a certainty. And if something happened to her, he'd never forgive himself. Neither would Garrison.

"We call. Now. She needs to be warned." *And Garrison needs to be kept in the dark.*

"The state's attorney informed the sheriff as soon as we knew about the threat."

"Who else is on the protection detail?"

"Did I mention a detail? One riot, one ranger. That's our motto. Right?" Parker stood, looking ready to dismiss Jesse. "You'll be coordinating with the county sheriff. Keep the element of surprise on your side. You know the hit man is coming. He doesn't know about you. Handle it."

"Of course, sir. I'll catch the next available flight."

"Vivian arranged a private flight to Amarillo that leaves as soon as you arrive. Then a rental car. We've got Tenoreno on lockdown, but somehow he's getting directives to his men." Josh Parker picked up a stack of papers and tapped them into a neat pile. "Did I ever tell you why you have Garrison as a partner here?"

"We both knew it was improbable." The suspicions he'd had for eight months were going to be confirmed. The major waited. "You mean why it's me and Garrison. Not me and Avery."

"Exactly. You've had a relationship with her. A close

one, from what I gathered. You didn't lie to cover it up. If you had…"

"If I had, sir, none of us would be rangers."

"That's true." He nodded his agreement.

It was a fact. *He* was the reason Avery hadn't become a Texas Ranger. Somewhere while they were being secret, kissing in corners, or sneaking glances at each other… Someone had seen them.

When asked about it at the end of their training, he'd come clean. Avery had discovered she wasn't selected, then said the Texas Rangers was an old-boy organization and would never consider her good enough. Well, he'd known she'd never forgive him for what he'd said in the interview.

Of course, she didn't know and she'd left anyway.

"This isn't the time to rebuild bridges. There's no evidence that will help you pick out the Snake Eyes Killer. He's good at what he does. Killing. You're there to protect Deputy Avery Travis. It's not going to be easy. If it were, a ranger wouldn't be needed. Go on. Vivian's waving information for you on the other side of the door." Parker opened the first file, ready to get to work. "And, Jesse, remember, we want to interrogate the man hired to kill her. Try not to kill him."

"Always up for the challenge, sir."

If he survived the assault of the green-eyed deputy he was being sent to protect, he might be able to capture Snake Eyes.

Definite challenge.

Dalhart, Texas

AVERY TRAVIS IGNORED the readout on her radar gun. Five miles over the speed limit was forgivable in her opinion.

She'd told herself for months that sitting here wasn't a speed trap. Drivers had enough time to slow down before they reached her spot at the tractor store.

Or they slowed down as soon as they spotted her. It was the ones who ignored both that she'd stop for a ticket.

Midweek shifts were easy to hate. Especially in the middle of the night on a Texas Panhandle road. But it was her turn. Life was totally different here as a Dalhart deputy after four wasted years trying to become a Texas Ranger.

Her brother was the one fighting real criminals. He'd uncovered evidence against one of the biggest crime bosses in the state. Garrison rescued witnesses, saved the day and who knew what else. The anger was building up again. It was definitely easier to tap it back into place, buried under the surface of everything job related.

Safe zone. Find a safe place to park all this emotion.

Knowing what to do and accomplishing it were definitely different, but she'd manage. Her self-improvement tapes would be easier to understand the second time through. But if she began listening to one tonight, she'd fall asleep.

This. Is. Boring. With a capital *B*, boring after being posted in Austin. No, after working anywhere.

An occasional flat tire. Watch a lot of shooting stars. Watch a lot of dust. Watch a lot of snow. Watch a lot of grass grow. Did she mention giving a ride to an occasional driver with a flat? Yep. Boring in every sense of the word.

"Car two-twenty-two. You around, Avery?" Julie Dunks's perky voice broke the silence. "Are you still out on Highway 385 at the Supply Company?"

"Where else would I be, Julie? I always tell you when I go on break or move locations."

"Oh good. But you know Bo sometimes doesn't bother to tell me. Sheriff Dan always takes a break when his coffee kicks in—if you know what I mean. So it'd be understandable if you did the same while you're out and about. I know you drink coffee."

"You switched me to tea." She yawned, wishing for some coffee.

"Did I tell you what Miss Wags did this morning? That terrorizing little diva wouldn't let me leave the house today without feeding her a bacon treat. Isn't that just too cute?"

"Julie, was there a reason you needed me?"

"Why, yes, there is."

"And…"

"Oh. Right. You had a visitor here looking for you. He said he was a family friend. Pretty nice lookin,' if you ask me. Of course, you didn't ask, but I didn't think that would matter."

A good-looking family friend could mean only one person. Jesse Ryder. Avery was forced to listen. She couldn't interrupt Julie on a two-way radio. Besides, what else did she have to do?

As Julie kept being her natural chatty self, Avery tuned her out and wondered what had gone wrong. What or who would force Lieutenant Jesse Ryder to come barging into her life? Barging all the way up here to the Texas Panhandle?

It wasn't fair. She'd left Austin and Waco behind because she'd been upset for being passed over. But it was also because everywhere she looked there was a memory of her with the man. Memories she no longer wanted to think about. If he was coming to see her…there would be images of him at the café to haunt her mind every time she ate there.

Then at the Main Street Motel—where he would definitely spend the night, because he wasn't staying with her. Each time she passed it, she would imagine seeing his car return for another visit.

"No way he's staying with me." She released the talk button and sank in her seat, knowing that Julie had heard her.

"What was that, Avery? Actually, he said he was on his way to find you. Isn't that excitin'? He couldn't wait until the morning when your shift ends."

"Thanks for letting me know, Julie. Over and out."

Jesse was on his way? To her? Right here at her favorite spot? Well, she wouldn't be here. Her future would not be parking here night after night and picturing him sitting on the hood of her patrol car.

Nope. No way. No how.

She'd arrest him. Throw him in jail. He'd had her boss do it to her three months ago when Garrison got in trouble. Now, that was a good place she could picture Jesse…behind bars.

The second favorite place to park and wait for speeders was a little over two miles down the road. If she hurried, she could be waiting on Jesse as he sped past. This was going to be a blast.

A few minutes later she parked and took out the radar gun, pointing it toward town. It wouldn't take him long if he'd left right before Julie checked in with her. But she waited and kept waiting. Maybe he'd changed his mind.

No headlights. It was more likely that he'd stopped

at the motel first. And less likely that Jesse would get caught in her speed trap.

Disappointment. Plain and simple disappointment. Maybe she could give him a ticket for jaywalking tomorrow. Or maybe vagrancy. Something obscure where he'd never agree to pay the fine. Then off to jail he'd go.

Before Avery cut the engine, she lowered the window, letting the fresh summer air into the car. She leaned her head back after readying the radar gun on the dash. The stars were sparkling on a blanket of black. Her plan about limiting where Jesse created memories was completely shot now.

She'd remember him here because she thought about him here. In the jail, in the back of her patrol car and the same places she always thought of him. Just about everywhere.

"What I need more than anything else is to learn how to live with Jesse around. As long as he's Garrison's best friend, he's going to be in my life." She closed her eyes and let out a long soulful sigh, continuing her lonely conversation. "This is my life. I've worked hard to become independent, but I refuse to live in isolation any longer, because I'm petulant. I can be an adult about this."

On a clear night like this, she could see a vehicle miles away. Out of nowhere, headlights were on the highway from the opposite direction. A local heading to town for an emergency?

She pointed the radar, placed her foot on the brake and shifted the car into Drive—ready to perform her duty. Ninety-two flashed in red. High school kids on a dare or a rancher in serious need of an escort to Keen Hospital in town. Either way required her deputy services.

The car lurched forward, the radar gun dropped to the

seat and she flipped the lights on in one smooth motion as she raced after the speeder. She followed less than a minute when the car pulled onto the shoulder. The tags were obscured by mud.

It might not be Jesse, but it was a little bit of work. Anything was better than being bored.

Chapter Three

The car pulled over well onto the grass at the side of the road. Plenty of blacktop was to their left as her vehicle lit up the area in red, white and blue. Avery ran the tag number, found it was a rental and got out of her truck.

What were the odds of two visitors in separate cars showing up in Dalhart within the same hour? Extremely high. If something had happened to Garrison, Jesse would come to take her home. But two cars?

The tiny hairs on the back of her neck were prickling. Avery unsnapped the thumb break on her sidearm holster. The door opened and a man swung one leg and then the other from the vehicle.

How pathetic of her...she recognized his boots. Relaxing a little during the seconds it took Jesse Ryder to unfold his tall body from the sports car, she snapped the thumb break back into place. Why hadn't he phoned? It still irritated her that she didn't know why he'd come in person.

Irritated or scared. The feelings caused similar nerves to gurgle in her stomach. Or maybe anticipation because...

Lord have mercy, he looks good. Bo and Derek were attractive young men. But they had nothing on Jesse.

Six foot two, dark walnut hair that was neat and close to his head. She'd looked into those mischievous brown eyes before. Looking again wasn't going to resolve any problem. He was lean, with shoulders wide enough to make her feel small. And she wasn't.

At six feet minus an inch—as her mother referred to her—she was not small by any means. Not as tall as her brother, but she'd learned to be as strong as possible. Jesse got partial credit for that. They'd always gone toe-to-toe in wrestling or racing or even at the shooting range.

"Do you know how fast you were going?"

He wrinkled his brow, looking concerned. His eyes were searching the landscape. Didn't he know there was nothing around? Maybe a couple of cows or deer, but no threats.

"I think it was close to eighty or eighty-five. What are you doing out here without backup, Avery?"

The ice around her heart melted a little at the sound of her name. It was so good to see him. And so embarrassing. "That's well over the speed limit." She took a defensive stance, stabilizing her shaking knees. "What are *you* doing here?"

Her heart shook a little at the possibilities. He didn't look as though he was bearing bad news. But if he wasn't, then why had he come?

"Can't a guy visit a friend?"

He was lying. She'd known him too long not to hear the warble in his voice. The one she'd recognized as he said being with her was great.

"We're not friends anymore. I haven't returned any of your calls. A Texas Ranger like yourself would be able to pick up on that clue. So why are you here?"

"Vacation?"

"Are you asking me if you're on vacation? Like I'd ever believe that. You've never taken a vacation. And your first wouldn't be to Dallam County."

"Okay, you got me." The smile left his face and his demeanor changed. "Enough kidding around. You seriously don't have backup? We need to get you secured."

"Secured? What's happened?"

"I'd rather talk about it at the sheriff's office. Let's go." He extended his hand her direction and she flinched. He looked shocked. She didn't have a memory of that expression on his face before.

Had she really never surprised him by following her own mind? *Wow, I really was desperate if I never disagreed with him about anything.*

"I asked you a question, Mr. Ryder. What business do you have in Dalhart?"

His handsomely chiseled face searched the road both directions. "I'd rather talk to you in private back at county."

"In case you didn't notice…" She expanded her arms into the darkness lit by only her patrol lights. "This is pretty private. If you refuse to cooperate, I'm going to have to take you in."

Okay, she knew it was a stretch and she really didn't have any reason to haul his backside to jail. But he deserved it. She remembered the three days of no privacy behind bars. Three days of trying to occupy the time by pretending to read a book. But most of all, the three days of being worried sick about her twin.

The moonlight made her rarely used handcuffs sparkle when she pulled them from their pouch. "Turn around and put your hands on the car."

"You're not arresting me." He laughed, throwing back

his head. Then he focused on her and squinted when she took a step forward. "Wait a minute… You *are* arresting me?" He took a step back, something on his belt clinking when it hit the rental. "What did I do? I'm here in an official capacity, Avery. You know I am."

Avery hadn't heard Jesse's voice this high-pitched since it changed in the seventh grade. She covered the laugh, trying to escape by clearing her throat as she pulled his left hand down and snapped the handcuffs around his wrist. "You're refusing to cooperate. I don't see that you've given me any choice."

"I've done nothing *but* cooperate. I didn't have to stop, you know. I only did because I thought it might be you." He slipped around to face her. "No one's going to believe that I didn't cooperate."

"This—" she pointed to him facing her instead of remaining where he was against the car "—this is not cooperating, Ranger Ryder."

"I can understand if you're still angry about the last time we saw each other. We've never really gotten a chance to talk about what happened. Unfortunately, we don't have time now except for an apology. You would have had one sooner if you'd returned my calls." Jesse placed his hands on either side of her waist and began to lean closer.

"That's it." She knocked his hand away, stepped to the side, whipped his arm behind him and forced him to kneel. "Nobody goes for my weapon and doesn't go straight to a cell."

"I wasn't going for your weapon and you know it."

"Well, we'll just see what the judge has to say. Your word against mine. And I live here."

"Avery, I'm a Texas Ranger, for gosh sakes. This ludicrous charge will never stick. It's not going to keep me from doing my job while I'm here. As soon as Sheriff Myers finds out I've arrived—"

"Oh, don't give me that, Jesse. Julie told me you were asking about me at the office."

His body stiffened. Something changed in his posture. He seemed worried or anxious. "Let go, Avery. This has gone far enough. I don't want to hurt you, but I will if I have to." The playfulness was gone from his voice. "Didn't you get the message about Rosco and the threat?"

She reached for his other hand, but he jerked it away, twisting out of her grasp. "No one's given me a message and you're not talking...your way...out of this." She stuck a knee in the small of his back, taking his chest to the ground.

He was halfway struggling with her now. Only halfway, since she was familiar with what he could do if he put his strength into a shove or his elbow into her gut.

"I'm serious, Avery. Tenoreno put—" Jesse twisted to his back under her. "He hired someone to take you— Ow. Dammit, that hurts."

"Stop struggling and the cuffs won't pinch you." She still had hold of his arm that he'd pulled above his head. She was pulling it back to her when he got very still. It hit her just where she sat—straddled across his lap. She scrambled off. "Get up."

"Are you still going to arrest me?"

"I owe you a night in jail. Two, actually, if I'm getting technical."

"I'm serious. Call it in, Avery. I haven't been to Dalhart yet."

"Julie said a family friend asked where I was. You're the only person that could be."

"Don't you see? It's the hit man. We can get a description—"

"Oh, good grief. This is too much, Jesse. You don't have to lie."

"They said they called, spoke to the sheriff and explained everything." He remained on the ground. "I'm going to kill a state official."

She watched him, aware of his every move. He was tense, waiting for her to make a mistake. Maybe move the wrong way.

"Tenoreno doesn't care about me. I'm not a witness." All the anger that she'd been suppressing seemed to bubble up to the surface. "I can't believe you'd come up here and…and what? What could you possibly want to do? Sabotage my new career?"

"Okay now." He raised his hands above his chest. "I think you need to calm down."

Acting like a cop with a perp at her feet, she used her boot to flip him downhill to his chest, swiped his arm behind him and flicked the second handcuff onto his wrist before he could work his way free. "Do. Not. Tell me to calm down."

AVERY GROUND HER knee into his kidney as she forced her words between her locked jaws. She was furious, and if he reacted, she'd get hurt.

Deliberate or by mistake, it didn't matter. He resisted the temptation to buck her onto the road behind them. Her pride had been hurt enough. It probably would be again. But not by him.

"I knew this was a bad idea." He'd never live this story down if it got out.

"You think?"

"Look, Elf Face— "

"Come on, Jesse. You can't call me that. Your face is the one in the dirt. I'm in my uniform, for crying out loud. Using my nickname stopped working on me ages ago."

He didn't believe that for a minute. She'd already removed her knee and her voice had spunk again instead of anger. So, yeah, using the name worked.

With her knee gone, he rolled uncomfortably to his back. Her voice might have calmed, but the look on her face hadn't. Intense. Jaded. The anger made her eyes narrow. Of course, they'd been narrowed and upset like that each time she looked at him since they'd slept— well, didn't sleep—together.

If he explained everything, she wouldn't listen. He should have called her before he got on the plane. He dialed when he was waiting on the rental car. Somehow telling her over the phone just didn't seem like a good idea. He'd gone through the pros and cons of telling her.

The cons won out. He simply didn't trust her not to take matters into her own hands. He'd driven like a race-car driver to get to her side before something happened. Or before she led Snake Eyes into a trap of her own.

"You're seriously going to put me in jail?"

Her lips turned up in a smile. It was easier to give in. At least she'd be indoors and protected, not running around searching for the man who'd asked about her at the desk. Once he spoke with the sheriff, they could work together to set the ground rules for Avery.

"Let's get this over with." He rolled onto the grass

again. Loose gravel from the side of the road stuck in his knees as he tried to get up without his hands. "You'll have to help."

"It's pretty funny watching you."

"Come on, Avery. If our man was at the sheriff's office, we should get out of here. He might be stalking you right now." He cursed under his breath for bringing attention to the man bold enough to walk into the county jail. It didn't matter. Avery ignored the warning and stood strong.

Acting as if it was against her better judgment to touch him, she helped him stand. Hands on the cuffs, she guided him to the patrol car, shoving him inside and locking the doors.

She opened her own and dropped her hat on the passenger seat.

"Will you at least get my stuff? There's a bag in the trunk. Maybe lock the car, grab the keys. It's a rental."

She stood and tapped the roof. Slow taps. One fingernail. He recognized the signal of the internal debate she was having. He remembered when that action became a habit right after her dad had been killed.

Tap. Tap. Tap.

That was when she stopped arguing as much. The more her brother's feeling had been disguised with charm, the more hers had been pushed down deep. He hadn't realized it until years later. Way past the point of return. He'd always been in the middle between her and her brother. Their parents called him the peacekeeper.

Some peacekeeper.

Tap. Tap. Tap.

Avery and Garrison had been inseparable twins before their father was killed in the line of duty. Afterward, they became fierce competitors. She'd even tried out for the football team with them.

It wasn't pleasant around the neighborhood when she was forced by her mother to play volleyball. Even if she had been their star player for four years. She was so damn tall it was a given. Didn't hurt that she could actually spike the ball and scare the other girls from the net.

The fingernail against the metal roof stopped. He heard her feet crunching gravel, then the click of the radio as she walked away. The duffel he'd packed was lifted from the trunk and dropped to the ground.

"Check inside," he told her. If she did, she'd see his weapons. She'd know he was telling the truth.

She ignored his command to look, locked the car and engaged the alarm. There wasn't anything else he could do at this point. He had to wait to have his story verified by Sheriff Myers.

And he had to keep his mouth shut. He couldn't afford to tick her off any more—as evidenced by her fast and false arrest. She needed him whether she liked it or not.

"Julie, I'm coming in with a… ETA is six minutes. Out."

"That's great. I'll let everybody know."

"Could you ask her to have the sheriff meet us there? I'm sure he'll be able to straighten out this whole mess."

"No."

"Dammit, Avery. Enough is enough. I've got a job to do."

"It's not up to me. Dan's in Dallas. His daughter just had a baby. He won't be back for another four days."

"When did he leave?"

"Three days ago."

No one from the State's Attorney's Office had explained the situation to the Dallam County Sheriff's Department. Hell. He was on his own.

"Elf Face?"

"Stop calling me that." She shifted back and forth uncomfortably in her seat as she buckled up.

"You're not really going to put me in jail. Are you?"

"You bet your last dollar I'm going to. Of course, the cell isn't as comfy as Dan made mine, but it's not bad. Hardly any privacy, but that shouldn't bother you. Right?" She pulled onto the deserted highway and pushed the gas to the floor. "I mean, you don't care for anyone's privacy. Or their private life. Or things like suggesting their boss incarcerate them for their own good. Things like that are second nature to you. They don't bother you at all."

Jesse closed his eyes and let her rip into him, knowing he was the only person around who could save her life. She was going to force him to take that night in jail. He'd be lucky if he didn't receive life in prison for wanting to hug a deputy.

Chapter Four

There she was… Avery Travis had returned early to process a prisoner. A Texas Ranger prisoner. How fun was that?

The foot traffic in and out of the county jail was higher than Snake Eyes had anticipated. A point in his favor that his employer hadn't put a rush on the job. He'd have to get creative with this one…a deputy and the additional bonus of a real Texas Ranger.

He couldn't take one without the other. If he did, there would be too many complications. Both were quite competent. He was aware of their history, of them growing up as neighbors. He had expected that Jesse Ryder would come when Avery went missing.

This was better. Much better.

Now he could widen his plan to include them both and not be bothered with searches. How convenient.

Finding out the prisoner was Jesse Ryder took no skill. Walking in the shadows across the street from the jail, he'd overheard Jesse as they'd gone inside. Not all the conversation, just what had bounced between the buildings.

It was time to go. There was no longer a need to discover vulnerable extraction points. Unfortunately, Jesse's arrival would delay the extraction while he fortified his plan. If the Rangers were involved, then it meant they knew about his contract. Maybe not the details, or his name—

Well, no one knew his name, as he was very careful not to be identified. He'd taken precautions. Lots of precautions. Even the criminals who employed him didn't know. Frustrated officers referred to him as the Snake Eyes Killer.

Assassin was the more accurate description. After he'd successfully completed his third murder, he let himself be hired. Then proof of a completed assignment had been needed.

The first pair of replacement eyes had been simple marbles. The next had been fashioned after the venomous creature his victims called him. He rather liked it. Kept it. Made it easy for the police to identify him.

If they found the body.

He pulled away, leaving the jail and sheriff's office behind. He had work today. Lists to make. A new plan would require a new spiral.

Did their argument indicate they were more than close friends?

The arguing would work to his advantage. He snapped a couple of pictures of back doors and guards on cigarette breaks, noting the time. But he already knew how he'd take Avery Travis. He knew exactly what he was going to do with her and where it would happen.

Smaller towns created a challenge to blend in and not be noticed. He'd handled them before. The extra element of this job required him to obtain information. A nice challenge. A new string of contingencies. He must be detailed. Thorough.

His camper was in Clayton, New Mexico. He'd develop his plan during the ninety-minute return drive.

The ranger needed further study. Killing Jesse was too common. Too predictable. Patience equaled reward. Yes, life would be interesting for the next several days.

The Snake Eyes Killer deserved some fun.

Chapter Five

"This has gone far enough, Avery. You've had your fun, now unlock the door. You can't leave me here even overnight. We need to call the state's attorney."

Did she really want Jesse to spend the night in jail? It wasn't as if he'd really broken the law or anything. She was exacting her revenge the best way she could. The only way she could, really. So, yes, he would.

She smiled, doing an about-face straight into Martha Coburn. She'd followed them through the booking area asking why they'd bypassed it. "Jesse Ryder is definitely staying the night with us."

He cursed. Martha jerked at the profanity.

"Sorry, ma'am. When I get out of here, Avery, I'm going to paddle your behind like I used to in junior high," he shouted.

She shut the hall door on the loud clang of his boot kicking the bars. She recognized the sound well, having made the same gesture once or twice herself during her stay. "I think he needs to calm down a bit before we do any paperwork."

"You know that's not protocol, Avery. Is there something wrong with him?" Martha asked, tapping her temple. "I mean, he's claiming to be a Texas Ranger."

"How do we go about getting a psych evaluation?" She tried to be serious. If Martha's reaction was an indicator, Avery had been successful. "Oh, I'm just kidding. We knew each other a long time ago and he..." She raised her hand to whisper behind it even though no one else was there. "He got a little fresh, if you know what I mean. I'm just teaching him a lesson."

"I see." Martha crossed her arms, looking completely like an old-fashioned schoolmarm. "Dan's done that a time or two in his day. I'm not one for telling stories that aren't mine to tell, but he has a couple of doozies."

"I can't wait to hear those. I better get back out there. Never can tell who's breaking the law before dawn on the weeknight." She did look forward to those stories about Dan setting someone straight. Maybe it would lessen the rampage she already expected when he found out what she'd done.

Or maybe it would lessen the concern her boss had about her safety when he discovered she'd taken care of herself. It didn't really matter. The satisfaction of keeping Jesse in jail was worth the chiding she'd receive from Dan.

Now that her heart wasn't racing ninety to nothing, it bothered her that Jesse would come up with a wild tale about an assassin...or was it? After Garrison had volunteered to spend his time until trial in a safe house, she'd done her own investigation into the Tenoreno family. She'd taken extra precautions.

Just because she was on her own didn't mean she was an idiot. She'd installed extra locks on the windows and doors of her rental house. Installed security lights to the point her neighbors had raised their concerns with Dan. She'd even spent a day trimming back the hedge and trees so she had line of sight to the road and sidewalks. Her landlord nearly had a cow, but admitted it was safer for a single woman—even if that woman carried a gun.

Maybe she was an idiot after all. Jesse wouldn't lie about his concerns for her safety. He was the one guy she'd known who just didn't lie. And he wouldn't take off work and come all this way for...for what?

Just because Paul Tenoreno was in jail didn't mean that the crime family's money and influence would be stopped. She sat in her truck and waited, watching the jail instead of heading back to the highway. Some of that Texas Mafia money could have prevented the warning Jesse claimed the State's Attorney's Office should have made. But what if...?

She jumped from the truck, locking it on her run across the street to the office. "Julie?" She raised her voice to get their dispatcher's attention in the back.

"Oh, hi, Avery." She poked her head around the corner. Her cute wireless headset still sat on top of her head. "I thought you said you were—"

"Did Dan have any messages you were keeping until he got back?"

"Avery, you told me to keep all his messages. Remember? You said the big guy deserved time with his family." She thumbed through a pad of sticky notes. "This is everything that's come in since he's been gone. Well, his calls, that is. All three of us are keeping them in the same place."

"May I take a look?"

"Sure." Julie passed the notes.

Each page of the lined pad that had been used was folded back, easy to thumb through. One had a scribble about teenagers shooting beer bottles and a note that it had been passed on to Derek to check out. Another from an unfamiliar number. The last on the list that afternoon was from a 512 area code and marked urgent.

"What about this one? Did they leave a message?"

Julie looked closely. "I bet Mrs. Lena took that. She said they asked for Dan and wouldn't talk with anyone else. Was it important? Should I call him now and pass on the number?"

"No. It's okay. I'll take care of it." An Austin area code, asking for Dan and no one else meant... "Shoot. Jesse's telling the truth. You mentioned a man came in to see me. What did he look like? How was he dressed?"

"Oh, I don't know, Avery. Nice looking enough, about late thirties or early forties. Sort of stylish in a Western kind of way. Hair hung below his collar. It was the only thing that just didn't seem to match the rest of him."

"That's not Jesse. Man alive, I've messed up." She pushed the pads of her hands into the corners of her eyes, blocking all the light, wishing she could block the image of Jesse's face when she'd mentioned this stranger. "Does Dan ever need a forensic artist?"

"I can ask Mrs. Lena when she gets here in the morning. Why?"

"I have a feeling that the man avoided the camera and we'll need a drawing from your description. I'll check the video, but I'd like a name to call if I'm correct."

"You mean a criminal came in here tonight? I was talking to a genuine criminal?" Julie's face lit up in a smile.

There was no way Avery was going to tell Julie the truth. But she'd need someone to stay with her until this man was caught. If she could identify him, then she was in danger.

"I'd just like to know who was claiming to be a close family friend."

Hopefully that would quiet Julie's curiosity. And unfortunately, she'd have to let Jesse out. Or maybe not. Perhaps the safest way to talk to him was with steel bars between them. It might become very public, though. And once she was mad enough, she might just ask about their fated night.

The night she thought things were changing between them. She'd changed clothes and he'd changed locations. *Think of something calming.*

So maybe a nonconfrontational approach to his release was a better idea. She'd send word to release Jesse with the shift change, leave instructions to take him to his rental car and give him directions to her house. She'd apologize first thing.

Privately apologize for not listening more carefully about the possible assassin. But for sticking him in jail... never. He deserved that. When the yelling began, they'd be in the privacy of her home. Then they could work out a plan to catch whoever the Tenorenos had hired.

Yes, she believed him. Now that she was calm and could reason without his Texas-size smile in her face. But she wouldn't leave her job. Nope. She had responsibilities. Dan was counting on her to keep things under control while he was gone. She couldn't pick up and run every time someone threatened her brother.

Or threatened her pride.

Logically, that meant releasing Jesse and getting started immediately on whatever he'd come to do. They shouldn't wait for morning. She should face him and get everything done.

"Julie, can you get Tosh and Tolbert Jennings out

here to go pick up a car on 287?" She dug in her pocket and placed the rental keys on the counter. "Have them leave the car here and leave you the invoice and keys. I'll pay for it."

"Sure thing." Julie raised a finger, paused in thought. "The county usually tows, but you know that, so this must be different."

"Yeah. There's one person who gets under my skin and, well…he did. Let Martha know when it's back, please."

"I can do that."

Avery walked back to her truck, changed her mind and went inside the county jail. "No loud banging. That's a good sign."

Martha tossed her head back, looking up from her paperwork. "At the moment. That is one angry gent in there. Keeps ranting that you're in danger. You back to process him?"

"Yeah, about that." Her choice was a private conversation. It didn't mean she was a coward. Facing Jesse and exposing their complicated past just wasn't an option. "The Jennings boys are going to bring his car here. Julie will call when it's back. Do you mind letting him out?"

Martha closed her eyes and shook her head. "Well, it won't be the first and I doubt it's the last. Should I direct him to the nearest motel or tell him they're all full?"

"I'm sure he has my address. You could tell him I should be there. If he asks." Tapping the counter, she was hesitant to place Jesse's wrath on Martha's shoulders. Private or not, it was definitely the cowardly way out. "Thanks. I owe you."

"Two margaritas at Consuelo's. There's no doubt in my mind that this man is a handful. He's really a Texas Ranger?"

Avery nodded. "My brother's partner and best friend. He's also the guy who grew up next door to me and felt that it was his job to persecute me until the day I left for college. Oh, wait…it didn't stop, because we all went to Baylor. My social life was horrible with not one, but two, men claiming to be my brother."

"Whew. I don't know what went wrong out there tonight, but I'm glad I'm not hanging around you when he gets out." Martha laughed. "Really, really glad."

"Yeah. I better get going. Lots to do before the big confrontation."

"I have faith in you, Avery. And, hon?"

Confidence wasn't one of the feelings overwhelming her at the moment. "Yes, ma'am?"

"I trust that you'll let the rest of us help you with whatever is going on as soon as you can. And you might consider calling Dan—even if he is on vacation. He won't like it that you're in danger and kept him out of the loop."

"Sure thing. As soon as I know what's what." She stepped onto the covered porch just outside the door, noticing the Jennings truck across the street.

Trying not to be obvious, she looked without moving her head. Nothing was moving accept Tosh's dog. He barked a couple of times at her until she closed the door to her truck and sat inside. Tosh waved at her as he came out of the county building.

A couple of cars were heading north on the business route through town. Other than that, nothing was moving besides a southwest breeze.

It wouldn't take long for them to bring back Jesse's rental. She needed to check the videotape. Whether the man had hidden his face or not would determine how she moved forward.

She had about an hour before Jesse would be waiting on her porch, waiting for answers. And an apology.

JESSE KNEW AVERY almost as well as he knew himself... maybe better. Predictable, a woman with efficient routines that worked, and a woman who did not like him at the moment.

Moment? It would be days. Months that might add up to the rest of his life. The reaction to him on the highway proved she wouldn't work with him. Now or in the future. Walking out on her that night without an explanation was a relationship destroyer. There was no coming back from something like that. He'd known it before he'd seen her cry the next day.

He'd messed up. Hell...she'd left him in jail.

An hour alone, behind bars, was plenty of time to think himself into every possible corner. Or not think his way out of any. Major Parker needed information from him to find whoever said the county sheriff had been notified of this threat. They should know who had screwed up or been bought off by the Tenoreno family.

He had to convince Avery's coworkers that she was in danger and to let him go. So far they'd left him alone. He wanted to see a confident, satisfied Avery waltz through and tease him. He'd imagined her barely speaking to him. Maybe making him beg to be released. Or putting her hands on her hips while stating dramatically to get out of town.

Okay, that was a little on the Clint Eastwood side. She'd try to tell him she could take care of herself. He knew that much and had his argument ready.

The door at the end of the hall opened, and a young deputy with a couple of bottles of water in one hand and cell keys in the other approached him. He began reformulating his arguments.

Jesse had studied a lot of people. When you were best friends with a man as outgoing as Garrison, you weren't required to say much to fit in.

Garrison thought of what to say faster and usually better. Jesse required time to think things through. Then react. Which, admittedly, he could have and should have done better when Avery pulled him over.

The deputy's body movements indicated he didn't know if he could trust Jesse. He dangled freedom from one finger as if he wanted to be convinced, then dropped the keys in his pocket.

"Mind telling me who you are?" the deputy asked, extending a water bottle through the bars. "No one logged you into the system."

"Lieutenant Jesse Ryder, Texas Rangers. My ID's in that duffel you're holding, unless Avery took it with her." He gulped the water, letting it cool not only his parched throat but his temper. "And you?"

"Deputy Bo Jackson. Why are you here?"

"Where's Avery?"

"Good question." He shifted his weight to his other foot, attempting to look casual. He didn't succeed. "We're hoping you could tell us if she's not coming back here because of you. Or if you're here because something's up with that thing her brother's involved in."

Jesse's heart rate sped out of control. He lost his grip on the plastic, then watched the bottle bounce and roll, spilling cold water across the old tile. *He has her.* His gut and mind were in sync. *Snake Eyes has her already.* "Get me out of here. Now."

The deputy jumped back a little. Maybe from the spilling water but more likely because of the animalism Jesse barely recognized in his own voice.

"Just hold on a minute and don't get worked up again. Nothing's happened to her, but I think you answered my first question. This is about her brother, but you're here because of you. She's been tight-lipped for the past hour and I wanted some answers."

"Deputy Jackson, you're smarter than I gave you credit."

"Thanks. I think. Easy mistake. I'm a lot older than I look." The deputy retrieved the key and swung the door open. "Avery had your car brought to the office. Keys are across the street."

"You aren't going to keep me here till I spill what's going on?" Jesse slid through the water on the floor and darted through the door before the deputy could change his mind.

"Smarter. You should remember that later." He smiled, making himself look younger than before. Then he handed over the blue duffel. "Go inside the office across the street and collect your keys. Avery wanted to know if you needed directions to her house."

"I got it, thanks."

Keys. Paperwork. A short drive down unfamiliar streets. Jesse's mind was blank following the directions on the map he'd printed out. He hadn't thought of what he was going to say this time. As he pulled into a driveway, a motion detector flooded the yard with light. His eyes adjusted and he saw her sitting casually on the front porch.

Relief coursed through him like dousing a sunbaked

body in a cool stream. She was safe. Exposed. Beer in one hand. Shotgun lying next to her bare thigh.

Very short shorts. But who was he to complain? She was safe. Avery had long, terrific legs that he'd admired for most of his life. Sand volleyball at Baylor had been eye-opening when he was eighteen.

"Sorry for losing my head on the highway." She took a short sip from the bottle, never taking her eyes from him. Her short pixie cut—and he knew that only because of his mother telling him years ago—was under a black hat.

"Sorry that I didn't give you a heads-up before arriving." He took a couple of steps closer, wondering if that shotgun was for him or Tenoreno's hired man. "Got another one of those?"

"Didn't you bring your own weapons?" She sipped, then set her bottle on top of the water ring already on the old porch. "Oh, you meant a beer. Sure."

The amber bottle had been sitting behind her for a while. Evidenced by the moisture dripping from its surface. He didn't care if the beer inside was hotter than hell; he'd guzzle the peace offering he recognized being offered to him.

"Nice hat." They tapped the bottle bottoms together and each drew a long drink.

"I bought it when I moved here. Symbolic. Rangers wear white, et cetera."

Crickets chirped, the floodlight went off. It was a calm he could be thankful for. No words were necessary. In spite of their differences, they could work together. Old friends, falling into sync with...

"Your assassin waltzed into the sheriff's office this evening." Avery tipped the bottle for another swallow. "Want to see his picture?"

Chapter Six

Warm beer shot from Jesse's mouth and up through his nose. Avery remained on the step, calmly finishing her last swallow. Her eyes sparkled from the porch light but mainly with laughter. Or maybe it was satisfaction.

No one had caught a picture of the Snake Eyes Killer. If they had, they didn't know it. Completely at home with her, he untucked his shirttail and used it to dry his face. "You're lucky I wasn't facing you when you shared that news."

"It's all about the timing. Have a seat." She patted the space on the far side of her daddy's shotgun.

He recognized the initials carved into the wood. *A.T.* Hers. He'd helped her do it when they were ten. They'd both been grounded two weeks for ruining it, according to their dads. He took his seat and tried to be patient.

She pulled a folded piece of paper from her back pocket and flipped it on top of the gun. "I'm not convinced. Too easy for someone who's never left a trace."

"You know?"

"I'm not helpless, Jesse. I already admitted that I lost it on the highway. But honestly, when have you ever known me to lose the good sense God gave me during a case? I called Major Parker. I got all the details you didn't tell me." She spun sideways, leaning against the porch rail. "You sort of buried the most important part of your story when you got out of the car."

"I apologized."

"Yes, you did. So, moving on." She leaned forward and tapped the paper with a short nail. "Professional hit men don't curiously face a video camera like this guy did. He smiled at it, for crying out loud."

"I agree. Probably not our man, but—"

"It's someone who's met him," she finished with him.

Jesse unfolded the picture of a guy who looked normal enough. Looking directly at the camera with a big grin. "Did you send it to Major Parker?"

"Yes. He has someone working on facial recognition. I issued an all-points bulletin." She shook her head. "We both know that's just busywork. Why do you think this Snake Eyes character would show his hand, letting us know that he's here?"

"To draw you out? Think he was waiting for you at the jail?"

"If he was…then he knows you're here." Her palms covered her eyes. An old habit she'd had since a kid. "There goes that bit of surprise."

"I may be wrong."

"I doubt it. Makes too much sense."

"So I guess you're on board with flushing this guy out. No way to talk you out of it?"

"I said yes to Parker. He explained why it's important and asked that I remind you to take Snake Eyes alive. I don't understand why he thinks you'd shoot him. I mean, you haven't killed anyone in the line of duty."

Jesse knew. Watching her, he'd kept an eye on her legs, her waist, the curve of her lips. There wasn't a night that went by that he didn't wish his hands were stroking her silky skin. He remembered how she'd felt against his flesh, how she'd eagerly responded to his kisses.

He'd defend her with his life. He'd rather shoot the other guy first. Yeah, he knew why his commander needed to remind him.

"You know he's not going to approach me if you're around."

"Probably won't be tonight, then." He chugged the rest of his beer, listening to her small pretend gasp. "I'm not heading anywhere."

"I put sheets and a pillow on the couch. I don't have a guest room."

The security light popped on. They both went for the shotgun. Both realized it was just a tree branch blowing in front of the sensor. No one stood in the driveway ready to kill them. She slid the gun across her lap anyway.

"You're not going to like the couch," she added with a grin.

"It's okay. I didn't plan on getting much sleep."

Avery stood on the step, shotgun resting on her arm as she looked up and down the street. He understood that she was silently waiting on him to gather his things and come inside. He did, watching as intently as her.

Once inside, he dropped his bag and laptop, then began checking window locks.

"They haven't been open since I was locked up."

Focus. They'd apologized. No need to go back and dredge up another hurt. If they were going to do that, he'd talk about their last night together. Explain how things had seemed different.

Later. Now was the time to talk strategy.

"When's your shift start tomorrow? How much do

you plan to tell your staff?" He checked the back door and paused for her answers back in the living area.

"Are you even curious why I didn't get the message that Rosco was dead?"

"You said Sheriff Myers is out of town and you released me before daylight." He returned from the small bedroom that was just big enough for her queen mattress sitting without a frame in the corner. "We both have deductive skills that we utilize fairly well. All the windows are secured. You spoke to Parker. If there's a problem, he'll find it."

"Glad nothing's changed in the last ten minutes. I checked them when I got home."

"Just making sure."

"Well, you could have asked."

"Come on, Avery. We both need to be on our toes. We can't get emotional about this situation." He dug through his bag, removed weapons and ammo. Unzipped carrying cases, setting a rifle and three handguns on the coffee table.

She placed the shotgun between the door and porch window. Easy access. Then she huffed to the kitchen. "I suppose some things will never change."

"I'm the same man I was before. I'm not changing who that is for this assignment. It's the reason they sent me." It sounded as if a metal pot hit the floor. "I never wanted to let you down, Avery."

"Ha."

They were there. Emotional. A night of mistakes between them. "There's no way to avoid this conversation. Is there?"

"You seem to have done a good job avoiding it for at

least eight months," she said, not quite shouting from behind a wall.

"I'm sorry."

Half her body appeared at the kitchen entrance. She pointed a wooden spoon at him. He would have ducked if it had been in her throwing hand.

"For what part? Not speaking to me? Not making love to me? Leaving me embarrassed in my apartment without a word of explanation? Why are you apologizing?"

"All of the above?"

"That's what Garrison would say." She left him alone.

If she was using the spoon, she used it silently. He barely heard a sound for several minutes. The microwave beeped and a pretty good aroma wafted into the living area.

"I want to ask if any of that is for me. Then again, I believe it is. We might be arguing, but we're family and you wouldn't leave me hungry." He was joking, trying to lighten the mood. It always worked for Garrison.

"Come get your plate. I'm not waiting on you."

He joined her in the kitchen, where she was filling two plates—one more than the other. She shoved his plate complete with a fork into his chest.

"Jesse Thomas Ryder, we are not family. You're my brother's best friend and a Texas Ranger who I'm being forced to work with. But we are not family." That answer was loud and through gritted teeth. "My brother hasn't seen me naked since we were four years old." She had her head down, looking a little embarrassed at what she'd implied.

And I have seen her beautifully naked. "You're right, of course. Avery, about that night—"

She nodded to the refrigerator. "There's soda." She left him standing there.

He followed, shoveling a forkful of some sort of cheesy casserole into his mouth. It wasn't bad. "Did you start cooking? I don't think it's restaurant quality and doesn't taste store bought. Did you start watching food shows?" He looked around the house. "You know, this is pretty cozy, with the exception of the mattress on the floor."

"Fully furnished," she said while setting her plate down. "I needed a bigger bed and haven't found a frame yet."

The confident woman sitting in front of him was gorgeous. Even more so than when he'd taken her to his bed. The smoldering in her eyes and the slight arch of her eyebrow would have implied sexy reasons why she'd needed a bigger bed. He'd believe that look from anyone other than Avery.

If she'd been seeing someone, not only would Garrison have spilled his guts, but their mom would probably have asked for a background check. Things had changed, though. So was she...?

"You're teasing me?"

She jumped up and tapped his shoulder as she passed with her plate. "Good grief, Jesse. You aren't the only guy around. And it's none of your business."

"Yeah, I know. I just thought—"

"You thought that because you wouldn't have sex with me, no one would? Or did you think I was still upset about it?" She hugged him from behind. Her arms wrapped around his chest.

He could feel her warm breath through his shirt as she pressed her cheek to his back. His hands were occupied with a half-eaten plate of the mystery casserole or he would have hugged her in return.

"Get serious. I'm not upset because you were drunk and obviously had some…um…problems. I'm totally angry because you suggested that I spend three days in jail and my boss listened to you over me. Is that misunderstanding all cleared up?"

Forgiven as if their embarrassing encounter meant nothing? Or it hadn't caused her to quit the Highway Patrol and move hundreds of miles away? He couldn't tell if she was lying. Not without looking straight into her eyes. If she was, they always opened wider. Or she'd accidentally wink, forcing them not to open. She knew that he would know.

"Yeah, we're good. Let's get started." He pushed the last three bites into his mouth and took his plate to the kitchen.

She grabbed a laptop from the bedroom and sat crosslegged on the couch. He took an uncomfortable chair across from her. If Avery was lying about how she felt, she'd learned how to fake it. She didn't seem fazed in the least that he was there. He couldn't say the same from his view and those legs.

"Major Parker said he'd email you the research they'd gathered on Snake Eyes and possible homicides he's linked to. Do you have them?" She never looked up from the keyboard.

Whatever she was doing…she kept at it with that same sexy upturn to her lips. He opened his laptop and she told him how to access her network. A loaded question that he ignored.

"Got it. We should probably print these. Looks like there's a dozen possible matches."

"The printer is wireless. Same password." She let him know but kept typing.

"Why Snake Eyes?" She tipped the lid toward her and looked at him as the printer zinged to life. "I mean, the rocks are polished like flattened marbles, hand-painted with reptile-like features. Why snakes? Why not human eyes?"

"Something in his past maybe?"

"Or present."

"These bodies all have one thing in common—they were found in wilderness. Doesn't matter what state, they're miles from the closest town. Nothing else around them except nature."

"Is there a profile?"

"No. He hasn't been considered a serial killer. More like an assassin for Mafia or gangs. These deaths weren't all connected until today." He thumbed through the photos. They almost all showed the same scene.

"So we know he likes snakes. He's comfortable in the outdoors. He has money." Avery typed her list.

"By the looks of these pictures, he doesn't care if the bodies are found. He probably *wants* them found. The decomposition and the fact that he's in the middle of nowhere would cover any DNA mistakes he might make." Jesse pointed to different remains that used to be humans.

"Do you think he's proud of his work?"

"He took the real eyes and left fakes for a reason. He wouldn't have if he didn't want to connect all the murders." What kind of man were they facing?

"True." Her eyes dropped to the keyboard. The familiar *click click click* began. "A lot of serial killers are eventually caught because of their egos. Oh, I know you said Snake Eyes hasn't been classified as that. He might be getting paid, but he has all the markings of a serial."

"Agreed. The person who did this..." He paused, flipped a photo of a corpse toward her so she could take a good look. "He would still be killing if he wasn't getting paid."

"Elements, animals or him?" She reached for the paper.

They'd analyzed cases before. Shoulder to shoulder, for years studying to become better than the best. He could do his job and protect her.

"Jesse?"

"What?"

"I asked if there was anything in those files that indicated how the victims disappeared."

"Sorry. I must have drifted. It's been a long day." He wasn't lying, just not admitting how worried this guy made him.

"Oh man, don't I know it? Covering for Dan is exhausting." If that wasn't the complete truth, she hid it well. "So we'll leave it for the morning and have something to discuss for polite breakfast conversation."

She picked up the shotgun as she went to the bedroom. "If you need to use the facilities, better do it now. I'm taking a shower in about three minutes."

He nodded his confirmation before she shut the door.

Polite conversation discussing the motives of a deranged serial killer. Why did the prospect of more than one such breakfast discussion turn him on and give him hope for the future?

Chapter Seven

The smell of strong coffee woke Avery. She wasn't startled or frightened. Jesse had slept in the front room, insisting the door to the hall remain open. She was cool with that.

Stretching her arms wide, she patted where her daddy's favorite weapon rested next to her. "Better protection than any man."

She giggled, something that just didn't happen anymore. It was her joke. Not that Jesse—whether she was upset with him or not—was close by. And he'd already made coffee.

"What's so funny? Want a cup?"

Jesse extended a mug. The steam encouraged her to sit first before accepting his morning gift. She had to blink a couple of times to make her eyes work as she blew across the coffee's surface to cool it a bit.

The fact that Jesse had his shirt off shouldn't have disturbed her. She'd seen that rock-hard chest before. Her view from the floor gave her a more in-depth view of the contours of his muscles. Nothing had changed except that she knew what was below the snug fit of his jeans.

She sipped, forgetting to cool the coffee first. "Shoot."

She reached across and set the cup on the old wood floor. "I should get up. Do you need something?"

She should have been grateful. More polite. Her mother had raised her better. His bare chest was just so...so...

"I came for the copies you slept on—literally. I couldn't get them out from under you. Thought I'd give them a once-over before I showered. We eating in or going to a drive-through?"

He'd already been in her room? She glanced down at her chest, verifying she'd slept in full pajamas and was still covered up. "I usually just have a protein bar."

"Mind if I take a couple of eggs, then?"

"Go right ahead."

"Come on, Elf Face. Time's a wastin'." He hooked a thumb over his shoulder.

"I'd forgotten you were a morning person," she called out, watching his backside leave her bedroom. The faded tight jeans were different than the dark black he'd worn the day before.

The soft denim molded to a fantastic specimen of a man that she missed as soon as he was around the corner.

Time to get on with her day and just flat move forward. Her thoughts had taken her to dreams mixed with murder and lovemaking and decaying bodies and excellent bodies. She was exhausted from sleeping. That was a fact.

How was this supposed to work? Did she really think she could take care of county business while Dan was out of town? As if being chased by a serial killer/assassin wasn't enough, she had to be partnered with a man totally oblivious of her attraction.

"Oh Lord, I'm in so much trouble." She tossed back

the covers, changing her mind about being alone with Jesse. "Hey! On second thought, let's go to the diner."

"Sure. Give me your word you won't leave the house and make me follow you. I need a shower, but I'm not wet behind the ears." He wandered in front of the door, two eggs balanced in one hand, a frying pan in the other.

Very conscious of rolling her lip between her teeth, she stopped herself by biting it. Then stopped again at the first brush of her tongue to wet them. She'd be professional. Especially with him. Even if he was shirtless, abs abounding naked in front of her.

"I'm not going anywhere alone until we have a plan," she finally admitted, knowing he'd get his way. And knowing it was the smart thing to do. If she was being watched, it only made sense to stick close to Jesse.

"I sort of need to hear the words, Avery."

"All right. I promise." She did the childish symbol of crossing her heart. "Do I need to pinkie swear or something?"

Half of his mouth turned up in a grin. "Next time."

She heard noise in the kitchen and had to mumble to herself, "I wonder if he knows how sexy that makes him look?"

Yes, she said it out loud for her ears only. It was just a true statement that she needed to remember. Jesse was sexy. That particular thought had floated around in her head since sex education.

She'd never understood why girls flocked to Garrison and left Jesse alone. It seemed that he was always out with girls, but never anyone steady. Garrison seemed to have a girlfriend every other week. It had been worse in college. They'd go to Austin and her best friend would insist to her twin that she'd be okay. They'd sit in the background and watch Garrison do his thing. Without a doubt, her brother was charming.

So yes, there always seemed to be girls around. Thinking back, they were leftovers. So what was it about Jesse she wasn't seeing?

The shower started and she got dressed quickly. Gathering papers and straightening the linens on the couch, she left them there. It was no use to ask him to stay at a hotel. He wouldn't. At least not until Snake Eyes was apprehended.

Just as he'd had to hear the words, sometimes talking through ideas made them more real for her. The past eight months here, she'd done a lot of talking to herself. It stopped her from picking up the phone to ask Jesse why he'd left. And it stopped her from calling her mom to see how Jesse was doing.

"Yes, Jesse is sexy. But… He's off-limits. He's out of your league. He's your brother's best friend. He stood you up—that's a nice way of putting that traumatic night. He's a professional colleague, a partner, even." She wagged her finger into the mirror at herself. "No fraternizing with partners."

Oh man, I spend way too much time alone.

Sweeping her short—massively tangled after a sleepless night—hair away from her face, she dabbed on some eye makeup and stuck her tongue out at the image. The same eyes that gave her brother such a carefree, bright-eyed friendly look… Well, they made her look weird in her opinion. Jade. A bright green that people accused her of wearing contacts to create.

No color change required. They were even greener today wearing her Kiss Me I'm Irish T-shirt. Soft, stretched out and comfy. Along with her favorite pair of jeans with worn spots in the knees that showed white threads. Fashionable in the real way—not that store-bought look with frayed edges. It was her day off.

His bag was gone. He'd taken it into the bath with him so he'd come out fully dressed. She wanted to be completely ready to walk out the door. Her small satchel held her laptop and the paperwork. Her service weapon was in its holster on her belt. And her pink toenails peeked out under the very worn edges of her jeans.

"Shoot. Shoes."

She'd grown up wearing Western boots and had half a dozen pairs on the floor of her closet. Along with a backup Glock in the pair reserved for dancing. *Like that has happened recently.* She sat on the couch and tapped her feet into her everyday boots.

The bathroom door opened, steam billowing to the ceiling.

"Whoa. You're…um…ready." He sounded genuinely surprised.

Thank God he wasn't wrapped in only a towel. The realization that she just couldn't have handled that came with the desire to pull his dark T-shirt over his head.

It's the danger of the unknown. It has my adrenaline pumping and doing crazy things with my hormones.

"I've collected the paperwork. We can use Dan's office to spread out and make some real notes about the homicides."

"Sounds good. Can we run the sirens to wherever we're eating? I'm starved." He laughed, but he meant it.

The diner wasn't far. It was a converted old storefront in the historic district. She ate there all the time, since it was between her house and the sheriff's office.

"This place fast? I am seriously hungry." Jesse pulled the door open for her.

"Is there a time you're not famished?"

"As a matter of fact—"

"Oh, don't bother saying that in a public place."

His grin and wink told her that his mind had gone to the same scenario hers had raced to. *Sex.*

"One day, Elf Face."

"You blew that chance." She left him behind her and found the rear booth, placing her back to the wall. He shook his head at leaving himself in a vulnerable position and slid into the booth next to her, pushing her over with his hip.

"Have you lost your mind? You can't sit next to me."

"I'm sure as hell not sitting with a window and the door behind me," he whispered firmly.

Curious looks were expected. Avery was still considered new. This morning there were double takes from the customers and waitress. She was the new kid in town and had been working her butt off to prove she was capable. There had been no time to make friends or form any real relationships other than at work.

But even the cook sneaked a quick look by strolling past to collect a syrup bottle in the next booth.

"Now look at what you've done. Everybody's going to think you're something special."

"I'm not?"

She ignored him.

The restaurant had limited seating, since it was open for only breakfast and lunch. Half the chairs were bar stools that kids loved to spin around on until they were dizzy. Jesse placed a huge order as a tall, lanky man entered. Avery hadn't seen him around before. He sat on the first stool and looked around anxiously.

Funny because he was looking at the ceiling and stopped his gaze on the security camera pointing at the register. Older... Longish hair over his collar...

"Is that the guy who claims to be my old family friend? Come on." She shoved at Jesse's rib cage to get him out of the booth. "He ordered coffee to go."

Jesse began moving, but slower than she wanted. "Couldn't we get Bo to follow him while we eat?" He joked because he already had his weapon drawn and resting at the back of his thigh, pointing at the floor. He waved at her to stay put as he quickened his pace.

Avery shooed the customers back. Jesse stood next to the man they'd barely begun searching for. The front glass shattered. A split second later, the man slumped and fell to Jesse's feet.

"Everybody down." Jesse lunged toward her, tackling her backward to the floor and covering her with his body. "Call 911."

The window was pierced again. Then a coffee carafe burst.

"Crawl behind the counter! Get to the kitchen!" Jesse shouted into the room, then gave her a shove under him. "You, too."

"What do you have planned?" she asked him as the customers belly crawled around the end.

"To keep you alive."

"But we can get this guy. He's right across the street."

Jesse shook his head. "He'll be gone before we decide which building."

"We're wasting time. There's an exit by the restrooms." They were far enough away from the window front that

Snake Eyes couldn't see them. Not from the roof. So she stood and ran.

"Avery. Stop!"

THE GIRL HE'D grown up next door to had always been fearless. The officer she'd grown up to be wasn't afraid, but she wasn't foolish, either. He was out the door two seconds after, following in her footsteps, crouching behind her, waiting for the next shot to hit.

"You know he could have help, a partner." He tried to catch her before she darted along the back of the buildings. At least it wasn't the most direct route to Snake Eyes. Jesse didn't have any doubts about who was firing.

"Not this guy. He just killed the man working for him."

He heard a car speeding up. Avery jumped out, waving her arms before he reached her. A deputy stopped the vehicle and began asking what was going on. Avery explained as she holstered her weapon and took a pump-action shotgun from the trunk. "I don't miss with this."

The deputy followed Avery's lead, staying to her right. Jesse followed on the left. "I've heard four rifle shots since we left the diner, but not in the past two minutes. He's probably on the move."

"You take the south side." She pointed. "I'll take Spencer around the north."

There was no time to argue or make a different decision. He had to trust her direction and the man who worked with Avery to have her back. He ran under the sidewalk awning. People should have stayed indoors at the sound of a sniper. But he yelled at them to get inside and lock their doors.

Stealthily arriving wasn't going to happen. So he got

louder, shouting, waving his gun. People cleared faster and perhaps he drew attention away from Avery's approach.

Jesse rounded the corner. No vehicles sped away from the block of buildings. He continued and spotted the deputy he hadn't met. "Where's Avery?"

The older man pointed up. "I gave her a boost."

"Dammit! I thought she was staying with you."

"Have you tried telling that *chica* anything?" He pointed his weapon where he scanned behind him.

"It's all clear," Avery stated from the roof, shotgun on her hip. "He got away and I have no clue how. I'm coming down."

The deputy caught Avery's shotgun and she propelled her legs over the faded red brick. She had a couple of handholds before she dropped to a covered Dumpster, then slid off the top to the ground.

"I could see the streets from there and no one was running or driving away. I'm not certain how he escaped so easily."

"He planned it. Like everything else he's done."

A few people joined them from the main street through town. One with a rifle in hand. Jesse pulled his badge and hooked it on his belt. "Texas Ranger, folks."

"Call the funeral home for me, Spencer."

"Who?"

"Not sure yet. I don't think he's from around here, but there are a lot of seasonal guys who fill up the hotels this time of year who I'm unfamiliar with."

"I'll take care of the scene." Spencer shuffled off. A handful of people followed along with Avery.

"Hey." Jesse stopped the deputy with a hand on her

upper arm, but immediately released her with the narrowed gaze he received. "Don't—"

"Let me save you the trouble, Lieutenant Ryder. You're in my town by my invitation. I get to say what I do and don't do. I was safe."

"Not hardly."

"You said it yourself. Neither of us expected Snake Eyes to be there."

"Do you have a forensics team to see...?"

"You're looking at her. It's one of the reasons I was hired, because of my training. But there's nothing up there. No casings. No cigarettes. Nothing except evidence of a bit of drinking over spring break. We need to get to the diner."

He admired her quick decision making, but it might just get her killed if she moved around in the open. His job was to protect her, and he meant to do it. "Look, before we assess the scene, I've got to remind both of us that this killer isn't what we're used to dealing with. We need to be as smart as him, which is going to be hard."

"I know, Jesse. We'll be careful." She patted his cheek and left.

Snake Eyes scared him. He admitted it.

Simply put, the man was complicated and dangerous. He had everything to lose—whatever everything was. This killer wasn't going to make mistakes like the average drug dealer.

Snake Eyes needed Avery alive or she'd already be dead. He'd been waiting on John Doe to walk into the diner. Probably sent him there in order to eliminate a witness.

Jesse took a long look, gauging the trajectory of the

bullets. He could have shot either one of them when they'd parked. This stunt was to prove he was in charge.

Snake Eyes knew it. He wanted Jesse and Avery to know it.

Chapter Eight

Dan's office walls were covered in copies of crime-scene photos, sticky notes and autopsy reports. It had started on his bulletin board and just kept spreading both directions. The back of the door and window were covered in one piece of tape at a time.

"Looking at the photos and sheer volume of information, I can't believe some of these victims weren't linked together sooner." Or as Jesse had pointed out the night before, law enforcement wasn't as concerned because the dead bodies were criminals.

Her partner nodded as he finished off the last bite of a hamburger Spencer had picked up for him. He tossed the wrapper in the trash can and ceremoniously gave himself two points. Avery didn't know how the man could put away as much food as he did. She'd never noticed just how much before she was constantly ordering it for him.

"Leonard Nelson was working with one of the harvesting crews. Did we find out what motel? And did he have a vehicle?" he asked, looking up from his constant internet searches.

"Yes to the first, no to the second." Her stomach growled. "In fact, the motel is over a mile to the diner. And there's a twenty-four-hour restaurant across the street. So it wasn't a coincidence that he came to the place I frequent."

Each time Jesse had eaten, she'd been a little put off by the thought of food. An empty stomach was catching up with her. She had to admit that one particular photo was making her a bit queasy.

"Snake Eyes told him to be there."

"Yes. But how did he know *we* would be there? *I* didn't even know." She stared at the tire tracks at one scene. *Duh.* "He had Nelson with him and followed us. He killed him to make a point."

Jesse acknowledged her with a "right." Meaning he'd come to that conclusion much earlier but let her get to it on her own with the evidence. It made an impact. Probably more than if he'd told her they were being followed. It also made sense now that they'd returned to her house, retrieved his weapons and car, then come straight back to the office.

"I've been through all the evidence collected. The only strange thing is a wet-suit fragment found close to the third victim. Strange because the body was discovered in the desert and the wet suit was over thirty years old. No DNA." He leaned back in the chair, rocking a bit, deep in thought with the pen tapping his lip.

She wrote the info on another sticky note and stuck it to the picture.

Was it horrible that her brain was a mishmash of emotions and thoughts? Every other one involved the case. The window made her think that she was freaked out about a serial killer stalking her. Each crime-scene photo made her think about each missing victim and their families, sending her right back to her dad's death.

Then she'd glance at Jesse and feel the support he'd

been all through her life with the exception of one lone night. And he was here now. Working next to her even after she'd thrown him in jail. Or he'd let her throw him in jail because he could have overpowered her and stopped it.

But he hadn't.

So even now, amid a room full of horror, he was her source of comfort and confidence. She could manage, but it was so much nicer working the case with her best friend.

"There really is nothing connecting these murders except the fake eyes." He hit the laptop keys a little harder. Frustration showed in his compressed lips and furrowed brow. "He has to be making them himself. The police from several of these cities canvassed hobbyists with rock polishers. But nothing."

"Polished river rocks. Hand-painted to look like eyes of reptiles."

Jesse tossed the ballpoint onto the desk. They both watched it bounce to the floor and roll to the wall. "There's got to be a connection."

"Are these just snakes? They look different."

He stood and went to the far side of the room. "These are gray. Brown. More detailed gray. In fact, these get progressively more detailed. Solid black."

She followed him back to his laptop, where he started searching for pictures of snake eyes.

"Each of these pictures matches a variety of snake." Jesse put in another search, then slapped the desk. "He's going through a damn alphabetical list. Each of the replacement eyes seems to be increasing in detail. He's obsessed with getting better each time."

"Or he's proud about his work. There are a dozen victims here. How long do you think he's been killing?"

"No way to tell from his calling card. I thought he might be connected with snakes somehow. You know, like a zookeeper or have them for pets or something. The different types just means he's looking at a book or online."

"In other words, it's another dead end with no way to connect him to a place." She pressed her palms into her eyes, completely and totally discouraged.

"Why don't we take a break from this and look at something—"

"Everything we've accomplished can be filed right next to a likely place where he lives. Nowhere." She couldn't bottle up the frustration any longer. "He's all over the country. Arizona. Texas three times. New York. Pennsylvania. And half a dozen more. Even Florida— that's such a lovely picture, by the way. Makes me want to throw up."

Jesse was out of the chair, pulling her into his arms. She let him. She might be trying to keep her distance, but the fruitlessness of the situation hit her hard. She felt like…like a girl.

The tears surprised her. She sniffed, raised her hand to wipe one away, and Jesse beat her to it. The back of his knuckle was gentle under her eye. Instead of drying up the rest, his caring opened a flood.

"Hey, it's going to be okay." Jesse held her tighter.

"There's… No… We can't…" She couldn't suppress the hopelessness of the situation. She also couldn't finish a sentence, so she stopped trying.

Jesse held her. They swayed and she heard the lock on the door being pushed. It really didn't help that he was such a nice, thoughtful man. She cried until his T-shirt was wet.

"We can catch this sick bastard, Avery." He gently tugged her face from his shoulder, looking in her eyes. He filled her with confidence. "It may not seem like this is giving us much to go on. But even a lack of anything is something. You're smarter than me. You can do this."

As she was about to step out of the intimate circle, Jesse pulled her back to him and leaned forward. Cheek to cheek. It seemed natural for them. Just a kiss between friends. Turned out as anything but…

Their lips gravitated to each other, locked together and struggled to come apart. It wasn't just her. She opened her eyes to see what Jesse was doing. His eyes were open, checking out her reaction.

They held each other's shoulders, keeping each other in place with little pressure from their hands. Just a whisper of their bodies touched. It was the weirdest moment.

Jesse's eyes closed. The pressure of his hands holding her in place eased, but his arms swooped around her, pulling her to conform to the mold of him. Her arms stretched around him, helping the process.

His tongue pierced between her lips, seeking what she wanted to give. Or filling a void she had known was there but wanted to ignore. It seemed inappropriate. Bad timing. Impossible.

Yet perfect, replenishing, just what she needed.

They drifted apart.

The grin was back on his face. "You going to knock me into the next room or pull out those handcuffs again? Your shirt does say to kiss you, even if I know you're not Irish."

She could only shake her head. She'd participated.

He wasn't alone in avoiding the problem of Snake Eyes. "I'm guilty this time."

"Guess we should…" They broke apart and went back to their respective corners. Jesse unlocked the door as he passed.

Avery wiped any makeup residue from under her eyes and took a peek using the reflective surface on her cell.

"I didn't mean to fall to pieces," she said softly. "Sorry about that."

He shuffled, raising a hand mimicking a schoolkid with something to say. He thought too hard on his word choice. "Not a problem. It's frustrating. What if we set this aside and see what we can come up with as far as trapping this guy instead of the other way around?"

"What do you have in mind?"

"He's told us that he's here. He thinks there's nothing we can do. All of this—" he pointed to the papers hanging on the walls "—tells us that he's meticulous. He's a planner. The longer he waits, the better his plan will seem."

"That's partly what I'm afraid of."

"You can call this off, Avery. We can get you a protective detail or you can stay in a safe house."

"That might be exactly what he's looking for us to do. Retreat like Garrison. It might give him a clue where my brother is located." She picked up the pen Jesse had tossed earlier and gave it back to him. "Could we trap him that way? Make him think I was being escorted to a secure location?"

"It might work. I need to call Major Parker."

"What's going on out there?" She could hear noises. Telephones. Chairs scraping the linoleum. Frantic tones. A couple of shouts. She had her hand wrapped around the doorknob to see for herself and take charge if necessary.

"Don't!" Jesse shouted. "Let me confirm what's going on."

A frantic knock decided things. She opened the door and found Julie. It must be late if she was already on duty.

"There's been an explosion north of town, Avery. We've dispatched the guys, but now there's been a second and third explosion east and west. All grain silos. People are freaking out."

"You can't go," Jesse said behind her.

"I have to. There's not enough of us. You'll just have to follow me." She swiped the address from Julie's hand before she left to answer another call, but turned to him. "You understand, right?"

"Be careful. You'll be completely exposed."

AVERY STOPPED LONG enough to put on a windbreaker marked Sheriff across the back. They needed everyone possible.

"Are you calling all off-duty personnel?"

"Yes. I've sent the men on duty to all three sites. A fourth was just called in, so I'll be changing where Bo's headed. The off-duty officers are headed at the first three to help out local PD. This is crazy."

"It's a trap. Call in surrounding volunteer firefighters. You're going to need all the help you can get."

"That's not—"

"Trust me on this, Julie. Call Amarillo for anyone they can spare."

"But they haven't evaluated the fires yet," the receptionist said, her worried expression indicating that she wasn't comfortable.

"They're going to be big and keep everyone pinned down and spread out. He's after Avery and just might get her. Here's my cell number. Keep me informed."

"Okay, but I think I need to check with Avery about all this."

"You need to hurry." He pushed open the door, stopping to ask, "Where the hell is Avery going?"

Julie looked overwhelmed, but handed him an address. He tapped it into his phone, calling up a map before he left a coverage zone. Avery had a head start. Every minute she was alone, she'd be more vulnerable.

Map on his phone, he sped behind her in the rental. Out past the city limits, he could see a fire on the horizon. He didn't need a map to see where he wanted to go.

Taking a turn onto a dirt road, he fishtailed a bit, straightened up, and the car sputtered. Then it lost momentum, cruising to a stop. The engine light was on. He had no idea what might have happened. Except...

He hit the steering wheel. "That son of a bitch!"

Chapter Nine

Avery was sliding her truck around corners, taking them as fast as possible without rolling it. If she caught the drop-off on the edge of the road, she was sure to lose control. Yet there was a set of headlights in her mirror, gaining speed. Her first thought was that it was Jesse catching up.

As the vehicle got closer, she wondered if it could be Snake Eyes. His logical move was at the fire. Catch her in a vulnerable spot and drag her into the darkness. He was methodical. The fire was the best bet that he'd approach to abduct her. She'd keep herself safe. She wouldn't stand alone, especially on the perimeter of the scene. Jesse would be there, focused on locating Snake Eyes.

The car kept gaining and the blinker indicated whoever it was wanted to pass.

"Are you crazy? Slow down."

Maybe it was a volunteer firefighter? Another officer? She slowed and drove on the side of the road as far over as it was safe. The car never slowed, just gained more speed until it disappeared around the next curve.

No other car headlights were visible. "Where is Jesse?"

She tried calling him. There was no answer on his cell that went straight to voice mail.

The open country let her see a flash of lights ahead of her. Then she rounded the corner and saw the disabled car that had just passed. "I had a feeling that was going to happen."

"Dispatch. Julie?" she called before she pulled to a stop.

"Something wrong, Avery?"

"There's been a single-vehicle accident on 3212 just past 807 toward the fire. They were going pretty fast. I'm checking for injuries. Redirect someone to the fire."

"Bo's the only one still in his car. You want me to send him as backup?" Julie was very professional for once.

"I got this. The car's blocking the road, so tell Bo to take another route and you send a tow truck out here."

"Copy that, Avery."

Blaze in the distance. Lights flashing around her. Smoke poured from the front of the vehicle. She approached the car with caution, running quickly through different scenarios in her head. Each time, she came back to a volunteer rushing to the fire. A hired murderer wouldn't want her approaching his stolen vehicle with her weapon drawn.

"Hello? Are you all right?" She looked at the mirror, which was pointing oddly toward the ground. She drew her gun, stood in line with the back door, leaning forward to tap on the window. It descended.

"I think I'm...having a heart attack. Officer?" A man's voice. Pleasant. Adult. "I know I was going a little fast. I think I blacked out for a minute. Can you help me? Am I going to die?"

Once again she ran through scenarios. Would the Snake Eyes Killer actually have an accident? Would he know which fire she'd be headed to?

"I'm a volunteer firefighter at home…thought I could help."

"Is anyone else in the car with you?"

He did nothing to make her on edge. She needed to holster her weapon to check out his injuries, but her experience working as a state trooper kept her ready for anything.

No, it was the situation with Jesse that had her on edge. The fact that an unidentified man was threatening to kill her. She kept her weapon drawn, ready to do business. "Stay calm. Are you injured?"

"I…can't breathe… It hurts," he cried out.

Oh God, what if he dies while I play frightened schoolgirl?

She holstered her gun and reached out to take his pulse. As quick as the flicking tongue of a lizard, he pierced the back of her hand with a needle. The hypodermic swayed back and forth, almost hypnotizing her with the surprise.

She knew she collapsed to the ground, but barely felt the impact. Her thoughts got fuzzy as the door opened and a black snakelike man stepped from it. *Shoot the poisonous snake.* She tried. He kicked her gun away.

A man. A snake man all in black except his glowing green snake eyes.

Fade to black took on a whole new meaning. She tried to hang on to consciousness. She could feel the gravel pressed into her cheek. It couldn't end this way. She'd promised her mom she'd be careful. She heard a man speaking to her, but the words didn't make sense.

Then the darkness grew more real. More frightening. She was about to die on the side of the road…just like her dad.

Comprehension shifted from logic to dreamland as her body floated and curled into a shadowy, bumpy place. She couldn't wake up.

Chased. Stung. Falling. The green-slit eyes of a snake monster kept coming for her, pushing her deeper into nightmare land.

Chapter Ten

"I was supposed to meet Deputy Travis here. I was delayed with car trouble, but I hitched a ride. I can't get her on her cell. Have you seen her?" Jesse asked a firefighter coming away from the fire.

"Only county guy I saw was over by the car. Other side of the fire."

The deputy by the car was Bo. *Keep it real. She would be busy.*

"Where's Avery?" he asked once within shouting distance.

Bo met him halfway, raising his radio to his mouth. "Julie? Has Avery cleared that vehicle yet?"

"She's not there? I got a garbled message that everything was okay."

Recognition hit the deputy's eyes. "How long since the first message?"

"Half an hour, Bo. After she sent you to the fire, I got the other message about six minutes later. I've been pretty busy. Everything okay?"

"Is that normal for her?" Jesse knew instantly it wasn't. "Where was the accident?"

Avery's father had been killed in a routine traffic stop and found by a stranger on the side of the highway. Her mother had worked for months to find out what happened when the papers accused him of not following procedure. Avery had always been a fanatic about following protocol. She wouldn't change that habit no matter how laid-back her county coworkers were.

Jesse could feel the blood rushing in his ears. He was a couple of minutes from panic mode. "She's in danger, man. You gotta listen to me. Tell me where she is."

"Bo?" Julie's voice called through the deputy's radio. "There's a call for Jesse Ryder. They say it's important. Should I put it through?"

Jesse took the hand radio from the stunned young man. "It could be him. Don't let him hang up," he shouted after pushing the talk button.

Julie was unaware of who it might be. Bo dialed his cell. He'd make certain she knew that the situation was serious. There were a couple of clicks. "You should be able to talk now."

"What have you done with her?"

"You sound out of breath, Jesse."

Jesse locked eyes with Bo and mouthed, "It's him."

Bo removed the radio from his shoulder, pulled his cell from his pocket and walked away. Jesse could hardly catch his breath. Snake Eyes was right about that. "What have you done with her?"

"I know all about you, Ranger. If you want Garrison's sister alive, you give me his location and let him take his chances. He comes out of hiding, sissy gets a pass."

"Where is she?" Jesse asked too late. The call ended before he finished. He looked to Bo. "Anything?"

"We barely got on the call. Did you recognize the voice? Man? Woman?"

"Disguised." The young men and women in Avery's

department would be unprepared to face a killer like Snake Eyes. "I need a phone with reception. You need to call Dan Myers and get him up here pronto."

"What's going on? Is Avery in trouble?" Julie asked through the radio.

The staff would be spooked, but there was only one way to deal with this…truthfully. "Yes. This is what I need from—"

Everybody spoke over the other. Donny Ray broke in on the radio, panicked. Jesse let them have their minute. Everything was still in his bag that he'd tossed in the backseat of Bo's vehicle when he'd found him. He was about to leave the deputy stranded at the fire. But he was needed here and Jesse needed to check out the scene where Avery disappeared.

His commanding officer answered on the first ring. "Parker."

"It's Ryder, sir. We were outsmarted. He's got her and wants the location of Travis." He pulled away from the fire. No one took off after him.

"Hang tight. I'll get you backup from Company C."

"He wants this to go public, sir. If it does, it's a sure way to let Garrison know his sister's in trouble. You know him. He won't trust us to take care of this without his help."

"Witnesses don't have access to the news or social media. But I'll verify no one slips up with Travis. Don't do anything foolish, Ryder."

"No, sir."

Jesse took a deep breath to keep his voice calm in spite of the apprehension rising in his chest. The odds of finding Avery alive were… He was ready to find Avery, but something caught his eye.

Movement at the corner of an outbuilding. Someone was creeping in the shadows.

Stopping the car, he fought with himself. He took a couple of paces onto the gravel, hesitating. Backup in the form of a nervous Bo, who might shoot the person watching? Or approach the shadowy figure on his own. It didn't matter what was in the dark. It wouldn't help Avery if anybody got shot.

He did an about-face, heading back to the car.

There wasn't time to react to the two-by-four that hit his head. He fell onto the trunk, then to the ground. He was pulled by his feet into the dark, and his blurred vision prevented him from seeing much, but not from kicking weakly at his attacker.

His boot connected with something solid that let go. Released, he flipped over, ignoring the pain, struggling to get to his feet.

"You're bleeding," a man's voice said behind his ear.

He felt the sting of a needle. Felt the thick liquid enter his body and travel to his limbs. He was helpless to respond.

The glow got closer to his face. Green horizontal slits in a sea of black. He was pretty much paralyzed.

This was it. The end. He didn't want his final thought to be of failure. Instead, he chose to remember Avery's face just at the moment he kissed her that afternoon.

Then there was the first kiss that seemed so long ago. Second in their lifetime, but the first as adults. Her sweet eyes lit up like a fragile dogwood blossom. Easy to remember because that was how she'd smelled. All sweet and sumptuous.

It was a good last thought.

Chapter Eleven

"Wake up, silly." A sweet singsong voice penetrated Jesse's dreams.

"Avery?" Jesse pushed his face from the dirt. He wasn't dead. Neither was the girl he'd been dreaming about. He was in her arms, skin to skin. No secrets in their way. "It's still dark. Let me sleep."

"To misquote one of your favorite movies, this is a hell of a rescue." When his eyes focused, he could see that her hands were secured around a fence post.

"Drugs?"

"Yeah. Fast-acting, too. Son of a B must have been following me and faked an accident. He got me while reaching to take his pulse."

"Edge of the fire…then took a board to my head." He rubbed the wound that felt like the size of a golf ball. Wait. His hands were free.

"That's right. Snake Eyes didn't secure your hands. Can you untie me? Soon?" she asked.

"Sure."

Strange that he was free to move and not Avery. He took in their surroundings. Nothing close. Not a fence to go with the post in the ground. Which after his eyes focused a little he could tell was the end of a picnic table.

"I imagine you've got a whopper of a hangover. I do. And you know I never get hangovers from drinking. If this is what it feels like, I'll pass. I am sort of light-headed."

"You didn't eat anything all day." He struggled to pull himself upright.

Blurred vision and a sicker-than-he-could-remember gut had him moving slower than a slug. He hauled himself across the dirt to get close enough to work on the knots around her wrists, slowly getting her free.

For a second, Jesse thought Avery was stretching to get life back in her arms. Then those arms dropped around his shoulders to hug him. He remained barely upright, she was on her knees and all he wanted was to stay there awhile to be thankful neither of them was dead.

"What the heck's around your neck?" They both got to their bare feet and she began tugging.

"Whatever it is, it won't come off."

He ran his hands around the entire metal collar and couldn't find a release button or catch, just a lock. "Does it hurt?"

"It's snug, heavy and feels huge. It makes me want to swallow."

He'd never seen anything like what was clamped tightly around her throat. Whatever it was, it couldn't be good. "Any idea where we are? Or how long we've been here?"

"I think it's still Saturday night. I can see smoke on the horizon from the fires. Based on that, I think it's been four or five hours. That's just a guess, since he took my watch. But I know where we are. This is Thompson Grove Recreation Area. It's about an hour or so north of Dalhart. Not far by car. Might take us a while to walk to the nearest house with no shoes."

"I agree on the timeline." He shook his head, trying to free himself from the emotion of the moment. Drugs. Relief. He didn't know which, but it was doing a number on his head. And his gut was objecting to any fast change in any direction, especially up and down. "You don't know how relieved I am that you're still alive. Think I'll sit for a minute until we decide what we're doing."

"I'll join you."

The moon was rising high in the sky, reflecting off the picnic tables and structures across a small white gravel parking lot. As his vision cleared, he could see well, considering the circumstances. Moonlight seemed to bounce off everything.

"I have no idea why he'd dump us here." He laced his fingers with hers. "It doesn't fit his MO at all."

"I'm sort of relieved that something's happened. But totally confused over what he plans. Do you think someone scared him off or that he's hiding close by?"

"Honestly, Avery, anything's possible with this killer. We're not certain that the victims were killed where the bodies were found. This might be how he does things." Jesse scratched the scalp under his short cropped hair.

"So keeping victims out in the open like this might be his thing," she agreed with a long sigh and another tug on her metal collar.

"You don't think he's going to hunt us or something? There are a lot of farms and houses close by. Plenty of possibilities for an escape."

"It might not be that easy." He had a feeling they were being watched. The moon might be keeping their surroundings from being pitch-black, but it didn't permeate every corner of Thompson Grove.

"Ready to get moving? We have a long way back to

town and can talk about this dude's crazy motives all you want." She jumped up and he caught her upper arm, gently pulling her to a stop.

"We have to work together on this, Avery."

"All we're doing is walking. Unless you know something I don't." Her eyes narrowed and she visibly clenched her jaw. She twisted her arm free and fisted her fingers. "I suppose you're wishing you'd thrown me in jail this time, too."

"You know, I didn't think he'd lock you up, Avery."

"It was humiliating."

"I hope it wasn't too insulting. And your people don't think anything about it. They respect and care about you." He wanted to regret the suggestion of putting her behind bars. He didn't, though. She'd been kept safely out of the picture while the state searched for her brother.

He'd keep that opinion to himself. He could see the similarities to her twin brother when she was in deep concentration. But nothing could make him picture Garrison.

Not right now. This situation had everything to do with Avery. He was haunted with the last drugged memory he'd kept in his head. The sexy dreams had left him wanting to pull her into his arms as soon as he'd seen her face. Holding her hand reassured him she was really alive and unharmed.

"You shouldn't butt into my business. I know it's difficult for you to understand. I'm all grown up." She patted his hand politely and started toward the parking lot. "I won't hide just because Garrison's in trouble."

"We're probably in more trouble than he ever was."

It wasn't his fault she was so damn stubborn. Or that she hadn't listened to him when she pulled him over for speeding. But he kept his mouth shut. They needed to work together like partners even if they weren't.

The only words coming to his mind would make their situation worse. He had to ignore the urge to respond. If they were ever going to move past arguing and work together, that was what he had to do.

He shook his head, determined to bite his tongue in half before he argued with her. "I thought Dalhart was south of here?"

"If we walk due east we'll hit 385 if no one comes along before that." She was about twenty feet from him, still tugging on the silver collar around her neck.

"Wait—" He heard an electronic beep. A red light glowed from the back of the collar by the lock. "Do you hear that? Avery? Stop."

"We really need…" Her body convulsed and she fell to the ground.

Jesse ran to her. Whatever had just happened, she was still breathing. "Do me a favor and wake up, Avery. You've got to be okay."

Jesse smoothed back her hair, wiped away a few beads of sweat and worried about her clammy cheeks. There was nothing outwardly wrong with her. He'd seen the light, heard a beep—not a gunshot.

"And I thought…I had a headache before," she whispered as she came around. "What happened?"

"This thing around your neck is a…a shock collar. I don't know how—"

Avery's eyes fluttered closed again as she fainted. Jesse picked her up and placed her on the picnic table. Why put a collar and shock Avery? How would that get what Snake Eyes wanted?

Because Jesse knew the location of Garrison's safe

house. The Snake Eyes Killer had found where he was vulnerable. He couldn't watch Avery suffer like this and didn't know how many times she could be shocked without it disrupting her heart.

He wanted to be strong.

Wanted to keep his oath as a Texas Ranger.

But Avery was more than a colleague or family. He wouldn't let her die.

AVERY SLOWLY OPENED her eyes. Every muscle ached like it never had before. She turned her head cautiously, uncertain what the heavy weight was at her waist. Pretty sure a man had hold of her hand.

She recognized the back of his head. "Jesse?"

He popped upright, quickly taking in their surroundings, which were completely strange. Her back was stiff from whatever she was lying on. Trees swayed overhead. The beginning streaks of a sunrise peeked through the trees in front of her. The grasslands to her right. A cow mooed somewhere close by.

"How do you feel?" he whispered.

"I don't understand. What's going on?" She should probably remove her hand from his, since they weren't on really good terms at the moment. But her body felt chilled and his fingers were warm. He didn't seem in a hurry to let go, either.

"What do you remember?"

The outline of his features were worried expressions or frowns—but not because of something she'd done. No, this was different and frightened her. Her stomach tightened.

She couldn't let him see her scared, so she reacted the only way allowed in this new phase of their relationship.

"Throwing you in jail. How did you get out and where the heck have you brought me?"

"Thompson Grove Recreation Area. You said it's not far from Dalhart."

"What? Why?"

Glowing reptile eyes.

The image was so vivid it jump-started the memories that flooded back in one fast whack. "Shoot. Wow. For a minute there I lost a full day. Snake Eyes drugged you, too?"

"Yeah. You…um…you don't remember waking up before?"

"Why are you acting this way?" She shooed his hand from her side and swung her legs over the edge of the picnic table, sitting up, feet next to him on the bench. Sort of woozy, but determined not to let Jesse see. "You look worried about…me. And I know that's not what you should be thinking about. We need to get out of here before Snake Eyes returns."

"I guess we need to go over the details again." He shoved away from her and the table, cursing the hodge-podge of dirt, twigs and stones that he walked across without his shoes.

"Again?" She wiggled her toes…also free of shoes.

He cursed and pulled up his foot, brushing aside something that caused him pain. Facing the sun, she stared as he bent in half and grabbed the back of his head. When he straightened, he faced her with so much worry and concern in his eyes it scared her. "Dammit, Avery. It doesn't matter. Nothing does. I thought you were dead."

Dead?

Confused, she took a deep breath, noticing for the first time that her chest hurt. Swallowing hard, she felt the tightness inside her throat and out. Her fingers touched cool metal like a tight choker. "What is this thing? And what do you mean by 'dead'?"

"A shock collar."

"Like for a dog?" She tugged at it, barely able to get her fingers between it and her skin. "Get it off."

"I can't. He'll zap you again if I touch it. You've been unconscious most of the night. I can't believe you're standing up."

"He who?"

"Snake Eyes wants me to divulge information about your brother. Info I don't have, by the way. If I don't..."

"He plans to shock me to death? Is that even possible?"

"You damn well came close already." Jesse shoved his hands into his pockets, spun to face the sun, cursed at something under his foot and bent at the waist, rapidly drawing air into his lungs. "And you don't seem to remember any of it."

She had nothing. Couldn't think of a word to say. No response and couldn't even say that. Her former best friend was clearly upset...with good reason. She was speechless because he'd said "dead." Meaning, she might have been close to it.

Jesse was a smart man. He'd know if she was breathing or if her heart was beating. She'd never seen him like this. Ever. Through all the scrapes and bruises growing up. Or the awkwardness in junior high. Or even going to the spring dance with her to shut up Garrison's bragging about taking the homecoming queen. This quiet man had never broken down.

If she didn't know him so well, she'd swear he was halfway crying with relief. He pressed the corner of his palms into his eyes—her habit—before standing straight and throwing back his wide shoulders.

Absolutely not. That was impossible. Jesse didn't cry. Nothing affected him that deeply.

"You're obviously tired," she concluded. "But are you ready to get back to Dalhart?"

"No!" He marched to her side and pressed on her shoulders to hold her in place. "We aren't going anywhere. He said to stay put."

"He's talking to you? How? Is he watching? Is that how he knows when you mess with the collar?"

"He knows when *you* mess with it or when *you* try to leave. He's either triggering it or there's a sensor embedded. It starts beeping before you're shocked."

"I can handle a couple of shocks until we can get to a hospital."

"Avery, honey." He rubbed his palms up and down her arms. "You've already tried that. This time you can't remember trying it. We aren't doing it again. We're waiting."

"You can't really expect me to just sit here. Until what? He kills both of us?" She could rest a little longer while she figured this out. She headed back to the picnic table. "What about Garrison? Who's going to warn him?"

"It's already been taken care of."

"Right. And that's the reason you personally came to rescue his little sister." She crossed her arms, not meaning to huff, but sort of huffing all the same. She didn't mean it and regretted the words as soon as they were out, causing a continued tension between them.

Jesse was talking about things they'd experienced a couple of hours ago that she couldn't remember. She wasn't angry at him or his help. She was frightened and didn't know how to admit it.

"Would you put being angry at me on hold? I know I'm the bad guy in your life. I'm willing to accept that responsibility most days. I just think we have a bigger problem at the moment."

Put her anger on hold? That was a ridiculous suggestion and made her want to laugh out loud. But it was also very logical. It was very…Jesse.

"Agreed."

Shoot. Shoot. Shoot. Her heart took a little tumble as she watched his surprised expression and the backward step that he took. His hands drifted from her shoulders to her knees and the outline of her body in between.

Time for her to put distance between them and keep it there. She sat confused on the picnic table. Suddenly cold and warm and severely attracted to him. Even here. She wanted his warmth, his comfort, his concern.

"So how do you know what Snake Eyes wants?" she asked, pulling her knees to her body and weakly wrapping her arms around them. She couldn't dwell on how her body felt. She could stay as strong as Jesse. She could remain strong and logical.

But to think logically, like a law-enforcement officer, she needed the facts, which were all fuzzy. Some danced around in her brain but not as complete sentences. Everything was fragmented like a puzzle.

"Snake Eyes called the sheriff's office when I arrived at the fire—where you were supposed to be. He admitted he had you, asked where Garrison is hiding. Said he'd kill you if I didn't spill the beans."

"Well, you can't tell what you don't know."

Just a flash but she knew he had that answer. The quick

narrowing of his eyes and a slight arch of his eyebrow...
That was his tell. She'd learned it years ago when he tried
to cover for her twin brother.

So he knew where Garrison was staying, but he wasn't
letting anyone else know that he knew. Probably a wise
decision. If Snake Eyes was watching them, it made sense
that he had a listening device somewhere close, too.

"He hasn't made contact since we've been here. I'm
drawing the conclusion that he wants us to stay, since
he shocks you each time you try to leave."

Jesse leaned on the end of the picnic bench, stretching his arms over his head. Avery wanted to reach across
and rub his shoulders. Lord knew, she'd done it often
throughout college. But not now.

Touching him that night... It was what had started the
greatest embarrassment of her life. She laced her fingers
together, holding tighter, pulling her legs closer. She was
still a little chilled and very unwilling to let her compan-
ion know it. She could manage.

"I'm at a loss here, Avery." He shook his head. The
early sunlight reflected off the natural highlights in his
hair. "I honestly don't know what to do except sit tight.
I've combed through this parking lot for a sliver of metal
to pick the lock on that collar. I've got a pair of bloody
kneecaps but nothing else."

"I could try now that it's daylight."

"Too risky if he's watching."

"We just wait? For what?" Fear was pushing its way
to the forefront of her emotions. It was hard to control
it. "I'm attempting to walk this through from the killer's
point of view. We know his purpose is to secure information. How does he plan on doing that? Telepathy?"

Right on cue a phone rang. Faint. Covered by something. They both jumped to follow the sound, searching the brush and tall grass. Not too hard to find when you knew where to look. They found the plastic bag pushed deep in the hollowed part of a tree.

Jesse held it, paused. She had the same thought... What if there were prints inside? What if there was trace evidence? She shrugged, gestured for him to answer. He flipped the phone open and pushed the speaker button.

"Yeah?"

"I'll skip the pleasantries," a voice disguised by a mechanical device said swiftly. "It's been a long night and I'm ready to move on. Are you ready to give me the location?"

"I swear that I—" The collar beeped. "Wait. I can't provide you an address I don't have."

"You have half an hour before the next phase of our game begins."

The screen went blank.

"Is it locked? Make sure you can't dial out. Don't shush me. I know he's probably listening. Just try it." She pointed, wanting to take it into her hands, realizing at that moment just how tingly her hands felt. As if they'd been asleep for a while.

Jesse punched in numbers on the old basic phone. Nothing happened. He flipped it over and tried to remove the back to gain access to the battery. They could see the glue around the edges. Glue around the on and off button.

The screen was locked, just as she'd feared. He stuffed the cheap phone back into the bag, not trying further. He spread his arms wide, ready for her to be comforted, then wrapped her in his hug.

"What the he—"

His hand clamped over her mouth even as his eyes

scanned the horizon like a machine. He held her tight, chest to chest, his lips brushing her ear as his hot breath lifted the tendrils of hair falling free from her ponytail, tickling the sensitive skin.

"Just listen for a second," he barely whispered. "Keep your eyes peeled for movement. I haven't seen a glint of a scope, haven't heard anything to even stop the bugs from chirping. We're casually going to find the way he's hearing us. Don't do anything that will get you shocked. You start beeping, you move back to the table."

"Why can't you leave without me and bring help?" she asked just as softly against his ear.

"Been there. Done that. The second shock knocked you off your feet before I made it to the road."

She pulled back to look into his eyes. Searching for that small squint that happened when he lied. "How many times?"

"Three." His voice cracked. He was telling the truth. "You really don't remember? You don't feel weird or anything? You're good. Not faking it?"

Reading him was so easy for her. Weird because she seemed to have a handle on so few others. "I'm a little sore and my chest hurts, but not half as much as my neck from the weight of this thing."

"I'm surprised you're walking around."

Genuine concern poured from the look he gave her. So much that she opened her mouth to ask him why he'd left her that night. Ironically, even with all the questions floating around in her supercharged brain, that night was clearer than most.

The long kisses, the yearning looks, the feel of his hand hesitantly touching her breast for the first time... It was as if she could feel all of it at that exact moment. Her mind was playing tricks on her. Jesse was only skimming the skin above the monster necklace. She cleared her throat and his hand dropped to his lap. They scooted a little farther apart. Of course, they had more relevant problems—as in how to survive the next few hours.

"Are you sure there's nothing around here to pry this off? This collar weighs a ton."

Searching the back edge of the picnic area with her eyes, there was something lighter in the brush. The sun highlighted a patch that looked a lot like skin.

"Is that a...a body?"

Chapter Twelve

"Can you estimate how long they've been dead?" Avery asked behind him.

When Jesse had searched the picnic area before, he'd missed the two bodies on the edge of the back fence. He carried them closer to the parking lot. Avery was still shaky, but not admitting it to him. Her normally tanned features were pale. He'd heard people talking about turning as white as a sheet. He'd never seen it until today.

"I assume they arrived with us. No animals have been at them. Stripped to their underwear. No ID. No shoes."

His feet were missing shoes, too. Probably a deterrent to running away. He was going to miss those boots.

Scooting off the bench, she stood to take a look at their faces. "I recognize one of them. He's come through Dalhart driving New Mexico plates. But I don't recall his name. The other one, I haven't ever seen."

"They must have set the fires. Snake Eyes doesn't leave witnesses."

"Shoot, Jesse. Snake Eyes doesn't even work with anyone for very long. I can't imagine how many people have been a casualty of his crimes." She sighed.

The shock collar was having more effect on her than she'd admit. "He's left us alive but we're in a public area? It's daylight. People will be driving by. We can ask for help."

"He wants Garrison and Kenderly Tyler, his witness. Without them the state has no case. The remaining evidence would be thrown out."

"We can still ask for help."

"How can we possibly get out of this?"

"Together. I don't suppose there's extra ranger training for this sort of thing?" She tugged at the collar.

"The subject of how to remove a shock collar hasn't come up." Just in case Snake Eyes could listen via the phone, Jesse left it with the dead men, then sat next to her.

The sun was full in the sky, almost topping the trees on the east side of the grove. They could see more clearly and had about ten minutes left before Snake Eyes was supposed to call them.

"What would he do if you gave him a false address?" she whispered.

"Kill anyone there or some other innocent man he asks to check it out. I don't know where they are." He wished he didn't know. Then there'd be no chance in hell he'd share the information.

As it was, he didn't know if Avery would survive a fourth shock. He had no idea how much electricity was flowing through her body. The third time had lasted quite a while and her heart had stopped. She'd come back, but would she the next time?

"Any good ideas? If not, I'm going to the restroom over there. Shock or no shock." She stood and spoke while turning in a circle. "You hear me, Snake Eyes?

I'm going to cross the parking lot and have a private moment."

His mind was a blank. Maybe it was a side effect of the drug he'd been given, but he couldn't think of a single thing to do. Not a damn way to protect her.

"Ah!" she cried out as she opened the door. "It's all right. I'm okay. There are more moths in here than I've ever seen in one spot."

He'd jumped up, ready to do battle as he was, dressed in jeans, a T-shirt and bare feet.

"Ah! More moths. They're creepy."

More creepy than two dead strangers about thirty feet away?

"Oh man, Jesse, can you help me? I'm going to be sick."

He ran across the gravel parking lot, not caring that every step was painful.

"What?" He pushed through the door. Avery had a finger over her lips, instructing him to be quiet.

"I'm all right. I checked every crevice in here. No listening devices or cameras, so I'm testing something," she whispered. "I think you might be able to get the toilet-paper holder off the wall."

"I could have kicked this off easy if I had my boots." He bent to one knee, taking a closer look. "I need something thin enough to work as a screwdriver or a heavy rock. He took everything from my pockets. I've already tried to break my zipper pull. No luck."

"I'm going to pretend to remain sick. Maybe that will give you time to find how he's watching us. Or find something to knock this loose. There has got to be something around here that you can pick a lock with."

They might be in a tight spot—some might call it

hopeless—but Avery wasn't about to go out without swinging. It hadn't crossed her mind to give up. Her color was coming back, so she might be feeling better but wasn't about to let Snake Eyes realize it.

She reached around him to open the door and he saw the solution. "Our answer has been staring me in the face. Literally."

"What are you talking about?"

"Do you still wear an underwire bra?"

She nodded.

"Take it off. I can use that to jam open the lock on that collar."

"Are you sure?"

"It's worth a try. Let me help." He reached under her T-shirt and unhooked the hooks. The collar began beeping.

Without removing her shirt, she slipped the bra off and pushed her arms through the holes.

"I'll get sick again in a few and we'll come back in here to try it." She stumbled out the door, and the red light stopped blinking. Twirling in the parking lot, she spoke to the trees. "There is a lot I want to say to you, Snake Eyes. A lot of words I'd like to call you. I'll wait until we're face-to-face."

Standing half in and half out of the restroom, Jesse held the bra behind his back, working until one of the wire ends ripped through the material. He pulled it out and stowed it under his shirt.

Their situation wasn't good, but he'd never been prouder to watch Avery shake her fist at anyone. They'd both get out of this alive because they'd work together to get the job done.

Avery didn't receive a shock, but the phone rang. She carefully picked up the bag and flipped it open.

"Here are the rules," the altered voice said. "I need an address. You and your ranger stay. I'll let you go once my friend has verified he's there. If someone happens by… It's your choice. I'm glad to kill anyone you invite to the party."

"We know you're going to kill us. Why should we give you my brother, too?"

"There is so much more fun we can have."

Avery dropped the phone, shaking back and forth. If Jesse touched her, he'd be useless.

"How much can you take, Ranger Ryder?"

The shaking stopped and Jesse caught her before she hit the ground.

"Son of a B, that hurts."

"At least this time you're not passing out. Must have been a lighter current."

"Restroom, please." She squeaked out the words as she clung to him.

"I hope you're faking this. At least a little," he whispered and picked her up in his arms. He left the phone on the ground. His only concern was Avery. "You can't take much more of this."

She sat on the closed toilet seat. "Then get me out of this thing."

"I'm with you there, sweetheart." He stuck the underwire into the lock. "This thing looks like a cylinder lock that can sometimes be opened with just a credit card. Worst type of lock there is. So maybe…"

The collar began beeping. A bead of sweat rolled into Jesse's eye.

"Oh God, please hurry, Jesse. I can't—"

"Almost…" He jammed and twisted. "Got it."

The collar fell to the concrete floor, stinging his fingertips as he released it. Avery pressed herself into his body so fast they both fell backward.

"I've never been so thankful something worked before in my life." She kissed his mouth.

Quick with gratitude. It was better than handcuffs for sure.

"You going to be able to run? He's got to have eyes on us. He's going to know you aren't wearing that thing and he has no control any longer."

"There's an empty house on the corner. It's been on the market for months. I don't know what's inside, but it's not in the open like this."

"You said it would be faster to stay on the dirt road and not cut across the field. Yeah, that's where we were heading before the second shock. We've got to blast out of here and not stop. Something happens to me, just keep going. Don't look back."

"There'll be none of your Texas Ranger heroics. This is my county. Remember? We stay together. Don't worry. I can keep up." She held out her hand. "Just as soon as you get me off this filthy floor, because I don't think I can move."

"Elf Face?"

She winked. "Just kidding. I can run a marathon to get out of here. Come on."

JESSE LED THE way from the restroom as the collar beeped and buzzed behind them. The parking-lot gravel hurt. Avery ignored the pain, pushing through the sharp bruising.

"Okay?" Jesse reached back and took her hand.

"Just winded and braless."

They hadn't made it to the road yet. How was she supposed to run a half mile? Blessed relief hit her feet as she stepped onto the soft dirt road. She stayed in the tire tracks, where it was packed down and a little easier to run through.

Jesse ran in sand, imitating an ocean sand dune. If he'd let go, he could take the other tire rut. But he held on tight to Avery.

The wind whooshed by, much different than the stillness of the grove. She barely saw the dirt kick up in front of them. There were definite pops and puffs of sand in the air.

"Snake Eyes is shooting," she panted.

"We can't turn back. Keep going." They both slowed and turned toward the sound of shots. "Down."

He pulled her to the dirt, covering her with his body. Bullets peppered the road. He rolled them closer to the ditch, which was more like an extension of the field.

"What now?"

"I can't tell where the bastard's shooting from." He raised his head even with the wildflowers and some kind of flowy grass. Nothing happened. "Can you run?"

They shifted to where they were looking not only at each other but at the perimeter behind the other.

"I'm slower than normal. But I'm not going back, so it has to be forward."

The dang house looked farther away than before. She could see the roof and more trees. But around them was nothing. No tree or wood fence post or telephone pole... no anything except grass and flowers.

"Make a dash for the house."

She saw the desperation in his eyes. He was about to do something stupid.

"What happens when he shoots you? I can't—" Even now it was hard to admit it out loud. "I can't do this alone, Jesse. Please don't make me."

Weaving her fingers in his, she began to stand. Shots brought them back to their bellies.

"Can you crawl?"

"Watch me." Their arms would be raw from the plants that had dried like tumbleweed.

"This is going to hurt," Jesse said, moving a couple of feet.

"Not as much as being dead."

He sort of snickered as they moved forward. Ten arm pulls along the ground and he tapped her shoulder. "You ready to make another try?"

"Absolutely."

They stayed low to the ground, began running, kicking up dirt behind them. Jesse had a tight grip on her upper arm. She heard the shot. A rifle behind her and on the side of the grove.

"Keep going!" Jesse shouted, instead of falling to the ground again.

The house was closer. Another hundred feet and they'd be on pavement. It was tempting to stop and crawl through the barbed wire, but it might give him time enough to make a shot.

If Snake Eyes was back around the grove, he wouldn't have a shot as they rounded the corner. They kept running past the fence to the driveway. A broken swing set had been left in the yard. They kept running.

The door was locked. Jesse didn't hesitate. He broke the window with something left on the porch. They were inside, leaning against the walls at the base of a stairway, breathing so hard she didn't think she would ever catch her breath. She really needed water and prayed it had been left turned on.

"Now what?"

Chapter Thirteen

The inside of the house was dark with the exception of a morning shaft of light from the broken window next to the door. There was a staircase opposite the front door, a closet under it and two rooms on either side. Jesse couldn't shake the bad feeling.

"I'm going to see if the water's running." Avery dusted off debris from her feet and cautiously moved around corners.

"He has to be following us. Let's stay together."

"Jesse, we've been drugged. I've been shocked to unconsciousness. We just ran a half mile. We're both dehydrated. Water is a necessity for us to be able to think." Avery slid her hand down his arm and laced her fingers through his. "Come into the kitchen."

"We need a plan."

"Dehydration keeps us from thinking clearly. My brain's muddled enough." She turned the handle and cupped her hands to drink. "Your turn. I'll watch. I can see the front door and out back from here."

He'd been staring out one window without a memory of what he'd just seen. She was right. They both needed water, food, sleep…a weapon. Essentials. He splashed his face, scrubbed it to wake up. He began looking through cabinets and drawers.

Avery stood watch at the door. "We can't look for a weapon and keep watch on both sides of the house. He's going to come after us."

"He's probably already here. Maybe already gone through here for a weapon. It's unlikely there's anything to hold him off."

"Okay. We've been quiet. We would have heard him if he came through another window." She had lowered her voice, emphasizing the quiet that surrounded them. "I'll follow your lead on this, Jesse. My mind… Seriously, I'm having problems thinking straight."

"He hasn't gotten what he wanted. His goal is Garrison, not us. We're just a necessary step—even if he enjoys killing." Jesse forced his mind to work.

"You're a smart man. If the positions were reversed, what would you do?"

"Wound us? Drug us so he could start over? He could have shot us on the road, but he didn't. He needs his information. He likes the hunt, wants us to run."

"So we make a stand." She nodded. "With what?"

"A banister rail? Maybe there's something that got left behind." He turned, opened a door. Nothing. "What about the barn? And I noticed a shed."

Avery leaned close to the window, taking in as much of the perimeter as possible. "I haven't seen him come down the road."

"That's it! We've got to find his vehicle. That's how we'll both get out of here alive."

"Together. You promised. Don't go sacrificing yourself for me. You know Garrison would kill me." She smiled.

The thing was…he would sacrifice himself for her. And it had nothing to do with his friendship with her brother.

The strong emotions that rushed through him would have set him on his ear under normal circumstances. Yeah, they already had. Here he had to push them aside until they were safe. Eight months ago he'd pushed them aside and run. He'd be running again, but not away from Avery.

"Let's get out of here before he has us pinned down again."

"We can do this, Jesse."

"We zigzag across the open yard. I don't see a lock on the shed, so we're good. You hear shots, run faster. We're out the door on three." He turned the lock and removed the chain. "One—"

"Wait. Wait."

"Did you see something? What's wrong?"

"I…I can't remember." There was pure panic in her eyes. "Don't laugh, but I can't remember what comes after one."

"Must be the shocks your body has had. Don't worry. It'll come back." He surveyed outside again.

No sun reflected off anything. No one in sight, but Snake Eyes was out there. He was certain of that. Maybe he should leave Avery hidden in the house and take the bastard on by himself. If she couldn't remember how to count, what else would her mind blank on?

It was a fleeting thought. Gone almost as fast as it came. He couldn't leave her alone… She'd never allow it.

"I asked you not to laugh."

"I'm not. I'll wave you forward. Okay?"

She nodded, her eyes big with tears, her heart full of courage. *She must be frightened out of her mind.*

Once again, they held hands and moved as silently as possible across the yard, staying low, darting between the few trees. They made it to the old wooden shed and heard breaking glass inside the house.

"Take cover."

They ducked behind a rusty wheelbarrow with a hole in the bottom. Rapid shots hit the wood, penetrating it and ricocheting off the rusted wheelbarrow.

"I don't think he's trying to take us alive anymore," Avery said, pointing to a rake.

It was equal in rust to the other smaller tools in the shed and not a surprise that it was left behind in the move. The handle looked as if it might break by picking it up. It was the closest thing to a weapon that they had.

"See anything to pry these back planks apart. If we're lucky, Snake Eyes might not see us leave." Another round of fire had them ducking again. Another broadside to the shed, but just a short burst.

Jesse leaned against the bottom support of the wheelbarrow and it moved. Staying low, he worked the screws back and forth until the support popped off. They wedged it and shoved, prying the old planks to where the nails lifted free. A second plank and they were free.

Again.

They squeezed through, dragging the rake and wheelbarrow support along with them. They were behind the barn when another blast of bullets hit the shed.

"How many more times do you think we can escape this guy?" Avery asked.

"None," a voice said.

POINTING A GUN at them, a man dressed entirely in a black rubber skin waved them to the wall. The black material was almost like a wet suit. It wasn't quite like anything Avery had seen. Old-fashioned. He was hooded, wearing thick old rubber gloves duct-taped at his wrists.

Yet with modern reptile contacts. She'd seen them before on kids around Halloween. Yellow with horizontal pupils. A memory of them flashed for a moment. "You were dressed like this when you drugged me."

"Looks like we're repeating the same act," he said, confident he had them. "No one I've ever hunted has gotten away, Deputy. If you won't tell me what I need to know, I'll get the information somewhere else. There's always a backup plan."

"Duck!"

Avery flattened herself on the ground. Snake Eyes realized the rake was coming at him a fraction too late. Jesse made contact with their attacker's side. The man screamed, pulling the trigger, but the handgun was pointed at the sky.

Jesse pulled for another swing, but the handle broke in half, leaving the rusty prongs in their assailant. Snake Eyes screamed again as he tugged himself free. Jesse tried to help Avery up, but she'd seen where the gun had flown.

Snake Eyes stepped on her leg as she scrambled forward. Pain blasted through her calf. She stopped the scream inside her chest. She didn't want to stop her partner.

"Scott, you idiot, get over here," Snake Eyes called out.

Jesse caught the man's arm, spun around and elbowed him in his face. He staggered backward, grabbing his nose.

Snake Eyes had another man with him. Avery crawled toward the only real hope they had...the gun.

Punches flew behind her. She heard fists connecting with flesh. The solid thumps against ribs and jaws. She couldn't take the time to look. Finding the gun was their way out. She got to her knees, searching the overgrown johnsongrass. She'd heard the gun clank against something metal but didn't know exactly where.

Unable to stop herself, she caught glimpses of Jesse's right cross and Snake Eyes responding with two solid body punches. "Where is it?" She smoothed the grass, going through it all, found an old garden tool, then...

"Got it!" Her fingers wrapped around the butt of the gun and she rolled to her back in time to see the second guy round the corner of the barn. "Hold it! Stop!"

The men staggered apart. The young man with the rifle planted his feet and aimed at her. Snake Eyes narrowed his contact slits and backed toward his accomplice.

"Looks like we have a standoff." He got next to the rifle, tapped the guy on the shoulder, and they ran around the corner. "You'll be hearing from me soon."

Avery tried to stand and follow. Her calf was cramping from earlier, her arms could barely point the gun and she was still barefoot. "Are you all right, Jesse?"

"I don't think I can follow, either." They both ran as far as the barn, where they watched the men jump into an old Jeep and drive away.

The younger guy fired his rifle wildly, pinning them at the corner of the barn. He whooped and hollered as Snake Eyes drove south.

"He's getting away," she croaked.

"We're alive," Jesse replied. He took the handgun from her. "Maybe we'll get lucky with this thing. Prints or registration."

"When do we begin walking back?" Avery did not look forward to moving at all. She needed to massage the cramp in her leg and might even need to throw up. "Not before we get some more water."

After a couple of steps, limping back toward the house, Jesse slipped his shoulder under her arm to help.

"I think we can wait five or ten minutes." He panted and pulled her to a stop.

"Good idea. It won't take too long if we double back and cut across a field. If we're lucky, someone heard the gunfire and reported it."

"Yeah. I feel real lucky."

Chapter Fourteen

Scott what's-his-name was increasingly annoying. Snake Eyes should be on his way to find Garrison Travis and the hairdresser witness. Instead, he watched a young man who had shown his face to the enemy. He'd also nearly shot them in that shed.

"You do not take instruction well, Scott."

"Man, I was getting the job done. It's not my fault that collar had a cheap lock." He danced around the hotel room, trying to imitate an American Indian war dance. He wasn't close.

"Stop that at once."

"Hand over my money, and me and my Jeep are out of here, man. You can find your own way back to wherever you crawled from."

The sharp knife sliced deeper through Scott's throat than Snake Eyes had intended. He watched the younger man grab at the wound. Both of them knew there was nothing to do but die.

"This is the reason I don't work with amateurs. Pathetic. What did you expect after you moved the other two bodies to the grove? You actually thought you were better? Perhaps good enough to work with me?"

Scott's blood gurgled to the floor when he dropped.

The life left his eyes. There was no reason to take the kid's eyes. It would just delay his next move having to make another pair. Leaving the body in a hotel room without his signature was against his principles. He gathered his tools.

Still in his suit, he removed the keys from the front pocket of the twitching body. It amazed him how instinct clung to life. He could dispose of Scott's eyes later. Somewhere down the road where animals would use them for nourishment.

From his bag, he removed the eye rocks he'd especially painted for Ranger Ryder. He'd need to find another. Yes, the yellow-faced whip snake's amber around the eye would match well enough. It would be easy and quick to paint in its simplicity.

The black river rocks were a snug fit in the small eye cavity, but looked good. "Oh, to be a fly on the wall when you're found, Scott."

The nosebleed he'd received during the fight would give Avery and Jesse a mental boost. An injury to your opponent would always give hope. As would the blood they were sure to collect from the rake. He wasn't in any of their systems. They'd never discover his identity through DNA, but that wouldn't stop them from searching.

"Finish or die," his father would laugh and joke. He wasn't talking in a literal sense, of course. His father had actually taught him survival skills. He'd been a terrific father.

No regular education or training would have provided the opportunity to become who he was. Or could have taught him to be so independent. Depending upon only himself.

Finish or die.

He would do just that. Finish this job or... There was no *or*. He started. He must finish.

The towels he used on his side were still there as he left the room. No hotel cameras caught him. He'd made certain they didn't work beforehand. He got in the Jeep to drive back to his camper.

A week ago, he'd wanted a greater challenge. Well, now he had one. His prey were wounded. They'd be on guard, wary. They might be protected by others. Yes, this was a challenge.

He'd have to drive into Tucumcari, New Mexico, for additional supplies. Ha. The shortest route was straight through Dalhart. The risk would be... Not any real risk. No one knew him or what he looked like. He'd taken care of the witnesses.

The next phase would be stealth instead of torture. He'd made a huge mistake counting on anyone other than himself to watch the picnic grove. Lesson learned. He sniffed at the blood dripping yet again.

First the information. Then he'd terminate the two people responsible for bloodying his nose. That was a guarantee. He tossed his bag on the seat next to him and put the Jeep in gear.

"Thanks for the ride, Scott."

Chapter Fifteen

Avery should feel safe. Two Texas Rangers were sitting on her porch and another was in her living room. So why couldn't she sleep or even stop her heart from racing with every sound?

A green-slanted-eyed monster haunted every minute she closed her eyes. She was starving, but the thought of eating got her stomach in knots. She kept drinking water, then had to get up every half hour. Both she and Jesse had been seriously dehydrated by the time they got to the hospital.

The Amarillo doctors had wanted them to stay overnight, but Jesse had insisted they'd be safer in Dalhart. She agreed and they were escorted to her house. That was—she looked at the clock—two hours and forty-seven minutes ago.

Almost three hours that she'd been lying on her mattress with the door cracked open—as Jesse insisted. Whatever conversation the rangers had in the other room had been whispered so they wouldn't disturb her sleep.

Avery tossed back the covers and tried to get up. She wanted to act as if everything was normal, but her body caused her to moan. She thought she'd been sore this morning. Every muscle had forgotten how they worked, screaming in agony. The moan couldn't be helped.

And Jesse heard it. His bare feet slapped the hardwood floors as he came through the hall. Head poking through the opening, he was quiet and obviously trying not to wake her. Truth time.

"I can't sleep. I haven't been asleep. I doubt I will be asleep anytime soon."

"Me neither." He extended a hand to help her up but withdrew it. "What do you need? I'll get it for you."

"An ice pack for the back of this leg." The one Snake Eyes had stepped on. "And company. If you help me up, I can sit on the couch."

"I can get the ice pack, but you're staying put. Wyatt and Kayden are chatty and I can hear them through the window." He tapped the door frame and was gone.

"But, Jesse—"

"Let me get the ice."

Avery piled all the pillows in the corner and scooted so she could lean against them. Then alternated pointing her toe away and pulling it back, trying to stretch the pain into submission. Maybe if she asked real nice, Jesse wouldn't mind rubbing the cramping muscle. Maybe.

"Hey, I was thinking." He came through the door empty-handed. "Do you have a heating pad or something? A sore muscle needs to relax, not tighten up from the cold."

"No heating pad."

"I could call one of the deputies—"

"Please don't. Once this is all over, I'd be running errands for them forever. It's bad enough that Dan had to come back from Dallas when we went missing."

"You didn't expect him not to. Did you?" He sat on

the mattress, pulled off his belt and made himself comfortable. "Give me your leg."

Just as if no time or an ill-fated night had transpired between them, he massaged her aching muscle. The rest of her body tingled at the thought it might also get attention. It wasn't fair. She couldn't return the favor.

"Can you count to ten for me?"

"You're joking." She looked at his eyebrow quirked high onto his forehead. "I guess you're not. One, three, five, seven, nine, ten."

"Was that for real? Dammit, Avery. I shouldn't have listened to those guys about moving you. Get dressed. I'm taking you back. You should be kept under observation—"

"Wait. Sorry. I was joking. Whatever it was this morning has passed. Sort of like a concussion. My counting ability returned at the hospital."

"Don't mess with me that way." He'd shoved her legs to the side when he was ready to rush her to the hospital. Now he wrapped his firm grip around them and continued an absentminded rub.

"Yes, sir. Promise. I didn't mean it."

During their captivity he hadn't looked as panicked as right then. He began working the muscles again, but this time a stern look invaded his features. She could see him pretty clearly with the light that came between the window and sill. He clenched his square jaw. His eyebrows were drawn straight and close together.

Since they had been driven back to Dalhart after their fight with Snake Eyes, he hadn't let her out of his sight. That was how she knew that his eyes had lost their usual sparkle.

"Hey. Earth to Jesse. You can stop playing Twister with my leg now."

"Huh? Was I hurting you? I must have drifted."

"I could tell." She didn't pull her legs from on top of his. She was comfortable and the contact felt reassuring. "You know that I've been in some tough scrapes before. We both have. But this… This was…"

"Intense."

"And very personal. Why do I feel…invaded?"

"Snake Eyes did his homework. He messed with us personally. That hasn't happened before."

"Dan said your car had bleach in the radiator. Did he tell you that?" Topics of conversation were limited—at least in her head—to Jesse or the case. She chose to ignore the Jesse topic. "Do you think we'll find that Scott guy dead somewhere soon?"

"Yes. Unfortunately. I couldn't get the plate number to help find him sooner."

"If the Jeep had any at all." She shook his shoulder. "There was nothing you could have done. That teenage hellion almost killed us in that shed."

"Snake Eyes knew more than he should have. Like how I wouldn't leave you. Knew that threatening your life would eventually get the information he wanted."

"I might have told him if I'd known." She rubbed her throat where the collar had been.

Some tech somewhere was analyzing it to see exactly how it worked and all the grim details. The doctors said she'd be feeling the aftereffects of the multiple shocks until she didn't. In other words, they didn't have answers. Especially answers about her returning to work. Or about anything, really.

Those same techs had been here to sweep the house

for electronic devices, had taken their phones, their laptops and had even checked her cable for suspicious whatever. But they'd found nothing. The powers above her pay grade believed Snake Eyes hired someone to gain information to them.

She didn't. The experience was too…

"I advised Major Parker that they should move your brother. When they do, he's going to know something's wrong."

"Are they going to move him? Snake Eyes might find out his location if he's moved." Mixed emotions rushed through her. Was it the thought that her brother might face the insane man who wanted to torture her and kill him? Or a little envy that someone else—maybe him— might catch the bastard before she could?

"That's a risk they're going to take."

"We have to find him. Snake Eyes." It wasn't sibling envy for once. She was scared for her brother. "There's got to be something we've missed." She tried to move past him to get off the bed, but he stopped her. "Come on, Jesse. Neither of us is going to sleep tonight. You know that."

"We're not looking at another crime-scene photo tonight." He cupped her cheeks and gently brought her face even with his. "We're just…not."

Avery wanted to lean in and kiss him. Unusual and stressed circumstances might have brought them back together. Okay, there was the tense part where she threw him in jail. But after that, they'd worked together well. So…

Jesse dropped his hands, leaned back against the wall and crossed his arms over his chest, burying his hands in his armpits. If that didn't speak volumes, she didn't know what did.

Leaning back against her pile of pillows, she wasn't just frustrated. She was on the verge of being angry. More like one step away from already angry. *I'm tired. Exhausted. This isn't the right time. There won't ever be a right time.*

"I want to know why you left me that night. I know I didn't have much experience, but was it that bad?" She bit her lip, anticipating his answer. Preparing for the worst. If he didn't answer at all, that would tell her everything she needed to hear.

She impatiently waited. He didn't move and didn't look lost in thought. He looked worried, sort of ashamed—just like when he confessed he was about to tell Snake Eyes what he wanted to know.

"I'm your brother's best friend."

"Sometimes you seem to forget that I was a third of that trio. I have no doubt that you were closer to Garrison, being guys and all." She popped his biceps with her fist. "We were close, too, you know."

"But I never made a promise to you not to sleep with Garrison."

"Oh, good grief. You slept with Garrison?" She knew what he meant, but couldn't help teasing him. He was so serious all the time. "Are you gay? Bisexual?"

"No! HELL NO! I meant that I…" Jesse squirmed. "You know what I mean. I swore to Garrison that I'd never sleep with *you*."

"Is that all?"

He could tell from her smile that she was ribbing her friend. She knew the answer and had definitely got blood pumping through him again. Life went on. No matter how dire their circumstances, he still enjoyed being with her and wondered if she felt the same.

Then she began laughing. Hard, holding-her-belly kind of laughing. "Oh, Jesse. You're such a goofball. He forced every guy that spoke to me to make that promise. Why do you think I had so little experience?"

Her laughter was infectious and had him going a bit until he asked, "Garrison chased off all your boyfriends?"

"Um...yeah." She laughed some more. "High school was horrible. You were there. What did you think he was saying to them while they waited at the door?"

"I never gave it a thought. You were always hanging around with us. I didn't date that much, so it didn't seem like a big deal."

"Maybe not to you." Avery's elfin-like face lit up. She feathered her bangs to the side. "You had a beautiful date for your prom."

He got the reference, remembering the sexy backless dress that she'd worn. He'd been very aware of how beautiful she'd been. And he could repeat the threats from Garrison about laying a hand on her. "Are you saying I wasn't handsome enough?"

"You wore boots."

"There was nothing wrong with wearing boots with a tux. Men do it all the time."

"Maybe you should have cleaned the hunting mire off them first."

"Hey, I was just a kid. Guarantee it wouldn't happen again. I'm more sensitive to those kinds of things now."

She pulled back, looking at him with a serious question in her eyes. Did she want to slap him because of high school? Wait. He hadn't been sensitive when walking out while she was naked in bed waiting on him to get over his panic attack.

He put his hand over his heart, wanting like a fool to get out of this conversation. "The rest of those guys may not have meant it. But I swore an oath. I don't go back on those."

"So what part of sneaking into corners and kissing on me for three months was keeping your promise?"

"I didn't promise not to kiss you."

"Aha. Manipulating the meaning of words. So you can't sleep with me. I guess you didn't swear not to touch me." Her eyes followed the direction of his hands, both casually dropped across her knees.

He shook his head and caressed the sensitive skin along the inside of her thigh just above her knee and back.

"I don't feel guilty."

Lying through his teeth. He was guilty, just not about touching her. He couldn't tell her the other half of the truth. The real reason he hadn't followed through on making love to her was that he didn't want her to be disgusted after she found out what he'd done.

The truth always had a way of coming to the surface. If he knew anything, he knew that as a fact. Coming clean would make him feel better for the few seconds it took her to utter the words that she never wanted to see him again. If she knew…that was what she'd say.

"Come here." They shifted and he pulled her close, encouraging her to rest her head on his chest and enveloping her in his hug.

It would break her heart to know the truth. He loved her too much to do that. Better to let her think he was a fool. Or a stand-up guy who couldn't lie to his best friend. Not one refusing to lie so she could have fulfilled her lifelong dream of becoming a Texas Ranger.

It was either her or her brother. That was what the choice had been. She'd see it that he chose her brother. And no one could blame her for interpreting the facts that way.

"Let me get you out of here, Avery. Right now before something else happens."

"What about catching this guy in the act? Isn't that why we're here?"

"How do you think that's going?" Jesse's heart might just beat out of his chest. All the feelings and thoughts while she'd been unconscious kept hammering at him. He should have done something sooner to save her.

"Probably about as good as you think it's going. But you have orders to try to catch this murderer alive. The attorneys need him to put away Tenoreno."

"Shoot, Avery. I can't follow orders at the cost of your life."

"And what about yours? Snake Eyes wants you dead as much as he wants me out of the picture. Besides, we're not even certain he'll come back."

Her chest expanded deeply and her warm breath escaped across his arm. It felt comfortable to have her where she was. If circumstances were different… They weren't. Two armed guards were on the other side of the old wooden walls, patrolling the house because they'd both been caught off guard.

Avery was right. Snake Eyes might not come back. What scared Jesse—yeah, he was scared—was that it was the first time anyone had seen the murderer and walked away. That in itself was bothersome. What if the killer didn't return? How long would they be forced to look over their shoulders?

"I'm glad you came in here to check on me. Thanks." She sleepily patted his chest. "Have I mentioned how tired I am? This is exactly what I needed. A friend to help me get rid of the nightmares."

"Or just plain worry." He rubbed her arm. The house seemed secure enough. Then again, they'd had a plan before Snake Eyes drugged them. "Will you consider getting someplace safer?"

"I'm safe right here." She yawned into his chest. "I hope you're okay sitting up the rest of the night, because I'm so...so comfy."

Her last words were barely audible mixed with a long yawn. She relaxed against him completely. She wasn't kidding about getting comfortable.

"I wish you'd let me take you out of here. You could join your mom and aunt." He spoke over her head. His arms held her tight. "Or you could sleep on my chest while I hold you all night...keeping you safe."

She was asleep. That last little bit of resistance was gone as she sank both lower and closer. He helped her roll over onto the pillows without waking. She curled one hand under her face, the other under her chin.

The second he backed away, Avery whimpered. He shifted the unused pillows to under his head, turned on his side and draped his arm across her body. She wiggled a little, getting closer, and continued sleeping.

Did she have any idea what she was doing to him?

Concentrating on his breathing, and not waking Avery as he did, distracted him from the arousal of lying next to her. Every memory of her naked in his arms sneaked between the rapid heartbeats, exciting him all over again.

The sure way to temper the desire was simple. When—not if—Avery found out what him sniffing around her last year had cost…he'd never be allowed back in her life.

It seemed like the way to go. Fast, easy, truthful… But not if he wanted her out of here. Safe. Away from the possibility of Snake Eyes returning to kill them…

"The problem is…" he whispered, spreading his hand across her abdomen when she jerked, already dreaming. "I'm not ready to let you go. So there's gotta be another solution."

Chapter Sixteen

"Did you hear me, Ranger? I said to knock until you wake them up. No, I don't want you to break down the door. Use your common sense."

Sore beyond thought and even more tired, Avery heard Dan's voice on her porch. The tap on the window would have been enough to scare her out of bed. But the heavy arm and light popping noise of the man sleeping soundly against her back had her checking to make certain she was still dressed.

"Thank goodness."

"Is someone knocking on the window?" Jesse asked with a voice full of sleep. He didn't budge.

Avery moved his arm off her midsection. "Dan's outside. He might have news."

Jesse rolled over, falling off the mattress to the floor.

"Avery, darlin'." Dan interrupted her laughter. "Sorry to disturb you, but I need to talk to you a minute. Then you can get back to whatever."

"We're not doing—" She pulled the curtain open, but her boss's back was to the glass. She started to raise her voice. "Oh, forget it. I'll be right there."

It was Jesse's turn to laugh. He pushed himself up from the floor, extending a hand once on his feet. Let him laugh. She'd straighten Dan out on the circumstances. Of course, it wasn't anybody's business, so she didn't have to bother.

She moved slowly to the couch. Much slower than Jesse, who had opened the door, let Dan inside and already headed to make coffee.

"I'm sorry to wake you up or..." Dan winked.

"Nothing was going on, even if it is my personal life." She felt her lips flatten, then tried to relax her face to look normal. "Is there news?"

"Want some coffee, Sheriff?" Jesse asked from the kitchen.

"Had my limit hours ago."

"Holy smokes, is it really four?" No wonder she was stiff. They'd been asleep for thirteen hours and had barely moved. That hadn't happened...well, ever.

"We figured you were both just sleeping, but I told everybody involved that I'd come by personally and check when you didn't answer the door."

Jesse joined her on the small couch after moving the folded linens. Dan raised an eyebrow and she shook her head. Jesse just grinned like an idiot and then frowned. "They must have found the kid who was shooting at us. Right?"

"Ten this morning. A motel over in Clayton, New Mexico. The maid found the body. No Jeep in the parking lot. And all the towels were missing."

"Knife?" she asked.

"Sliced him all the way to his spine." Dan shook his head. "People in Clayton didn't recognize him. They think he might have been part of the harvest crew. Same as the other two at Thompson Grove."

"I imagine they're canvassing the other motels," Jesse said.

Dan nodded.

"I'd like to see the crime scene. Who's got jurisdiction? Who's collecting evidence? Do I have time for a shower?"

"Hold on, Deputy. They're practically done. I've been there and back."

Jesse shrugged when she looked at him for backup.

"Mainly here to see how you're both doing. And to tell you that Bo will go get anything you need. Including a cot." Dan gave a fatherly glance in Jesse's direction.

"I'm good."

Dan awkwardly cleared his throat. "I bet you are. Think I'll have him bring by a cot anyway."

Avery was sufficiently embarrassed admitting to herself that the possibility of sharing a bed hadn't left her mind. "House arrest, then, huh?"

"Protective custody," Jesse corrected her. "I'm getting coffee."

"Before you step out…" Dan paused. "Here are some new phones, courtesy of the state of Texas. There's a couple of people expecting some calls from you both. Your personal phones and laptops will come back after they're checked out for tracers or hackers or traces of a hack. You know more about that stuff than I do."

"Working on the case will be harder without a laptop."

"Guess you'll have to do your detecting the old-fashioned way with pen and paper and tape."

"Maybe a whiteboard," Jesse said before she could.

"No one comes in or knocks on the door. That's the way this works. Just making certain you understand that those two rangers, Bo and me…that's it. If anyone else comes or calls—"

"Something's wrong," she finished for him.

"Is it better if we leave, Sheriff? I suggested it last night, but we didn't really have a chance to talk about it yet."

"The powers that be agreed for you to come back here. Here's good." Dan was matter-of-fact most days, but this wasn't one of them. "This is important, Avery."

"I know, sir. I wouldn't put anyone else at risk. Everyone at the office knows what's going on? They'll be careful? Work in twos?"

"We got it covered. We brought in extra help from Amarillo. I better be on my way so you can get on with your…um…breakfast." He looked toward Jesse. "Make a list. Bo will pick it up."

"Sounds good. And you'll copy the Clayton crime scene?" she asked.

"Got my word and the word of your Major Parker." He nodded at Jesse. "Nice fella."

"Yes, sir." Jesse politely excused himself with a motion for coffee.

"Just say the word and I'll put him up at the jail." Dan winked.

"Who told? Julie, I bet."

"Well now, you can't blame her for being forthcoming with information. This has all been on the exciting side of our lives." Dan leaned forward and took her hands in his. "You're very fortunate to be alive. You know that?"

"Yes, sir." She wouldn't let herself cry because Dan or the others in the office cared. It was natural, and she needed to do her job.

"You need these days to recover."

"You could say the same thing for Snake Eyes. They should check all the hospitals and clinics—don't forget veterinarian offices, but I don't know if they carry tetanus, which he'd probably want a dose of. That rake was pretty rusty and he might be worried."

"Make a list, Avery. You aren't shut out from the case. Speak with Major Parker. He's waiting on you to feel up to a debriefing." Dan stood. "I better be going for real this time." He got to the door and nodded at the shotgun. "That thing loaded?"

"Always."

"I'll add that to *my* list. You'll need a couple of weapons. Glock okay?"

"Sure. Please stay safe out there, Dan."

He left, and once the door was locked, he said, "Boys, you take care of my girl in there."

"Throw me in jail again?" Jesse handed her the coffee with a wicked grin. "If I go, so do you."

"No privacy, remember?" She sipped. "Are you ready to get started?"

"Not really. We've missed breakfast and lunch. I want to begin with those. Where's the food?" He'd leaned toward the door and spoke louder. "Isn't the state supposed to provide food?"

"Under house arrest two minutes and already complaining," one of the rangers said. "Whoever you send, choose something for us, please?"

Jesse affirmed.

"Thin walls," he mouthed at her.

"I'll have to remember to keep my voice down."

Jesse grinned like a man with a secret. "Coffee good?" he asked instead of stating the off-color remark she was certain had passed through his male brain.

"I'm going to shower. Alone," she said, loud enough for the ranger at the door. "But I'm starving. There's frozen hash browns and eggs."

"Guess that's my cue."

In spite of the headache, she managed to move quickly through a shower. She imagined all sorts of scenes in a sordid little motel in Clayton. With the spray adjusted to beat on her shoulders, she thought of hundreds of ways to collect evidence and crossed her fingers that it would be done correctly.

Normally, she wasn't good with anyone doing her work for her. If they were shut out of the case, she would probably go cabin crazy in a matter of hours. Her list of potential items grew. She'd have to give Bo her debit card to pay for everything.

She was reminded that she was really recuperating when she stepped from the shower and landed on the side of the tub. No thuds or screams or even an "oops." Jesse didn't rush to the door, so she didn't have to be embarrassed. But her hands were shaking until she weaved her fingers together and took a couple of trembling breaths.

No warning. Her legs just seemed to stop holding her for a moment. It seemed the shocks her body had tolerated had left her with a physical problem after all. She got dressed carefully and could only manage fingercombing her hair.

The smell of eggs and pepper hit her nose, and a migraine headache seemed to arrive without any warning. Her legs started shaking again, so she curled up on the couch and pulled Jesse's blanket over her.

"Still hungry?" Jesse asked, smoothing back her damp hair.

"Not really. Can I have that notebook and pen?"

He'd used it a couple of times, so she didn't have to use more words to be specific about where or what.

"You could rest instead of making a list." He handed her the writing tools anyway.

"I'm okay. I want to get a list written while it's fresh in my mind."

"I'll hold off scrambling your eggs, then."

She propped up the notebook and held the pen, but couldn't make it move on the page. The letters were there. She could see them. One at a time they danced around just like the numbers from the day before. She shoved the notebook to the floor and tossed the pen.

Of course Jesse looked at her from the small dining table in the corner. If their roles had been reversed, she'd be searching him critically, too. She'd have sympathy for him and the challenges he'd be facing.

"You're right. I'm too tired and think I need some aspirin." She pushed at the covers, but he jumped up and lifted a hand, indicating to wait. Water, aspirin, no pity and no "I told you so."

Jesse Ryder was a good man.

WYATT MCDONALD AND Kayden Cross were rotating shifts. One catnapped in the truck in the driveway, since they hadn't got a room yet. Jesse was very aware how often they changed out positions. He'd walked onto the porch only to be confronted and politely—yet firmly—asked to return inside.

Avery had been asleep about four hours. His first call had been to the doctor to see if that was normal. This was a woman who rarely slept six hours a night, so yeah, he was concerned. The doc had said he'd be more concerned if she wasn't.

The second phone call was to Major Parker. He'd gone to the back corner of the kitchen to place it. As far away from Avery as he could get. You could hear everything in this house. Small and compact. He hadn't meant to listen to Avery and the sheriff, but it had been impossible not to.

Dan didn't have anything to worry about. Jesse wasn't going to sleep with Avery when she was in this shape. But he also wouldn't sleep with her having a lie between them.

"Sir, I think you should reconsider adding me to the guard detail outside." He tried one more time to do something useful.

"If there's something wrong with your detail…"

"No, sir, nothing like that. It would just be easier with four-hour shifts split three ways."

"I'll reconsider it next week. Right now your rest is as critical as Miss Travis's. I have the doctor reports. Severe dehydration. Possible concussion. If you were here you'd be on leave at least a week. I doubt you'll have that long. Did you get the laptop?"

"They delivered it a half hour ago."

"I'll be back in touch in the morning with decisions on how we'll proceed."

"Yes, sir."

"Rest up. This isn't over yet."

Jesse wanted to throw the phone across the room. He didn't normally throw a tantrum. He wasn't the person in the room raising a ruckus or who questioned authority. Garrison had always been around to ask the questions and Avery had been close by to voice objections.

He missed their three-ring circus.

"Finally off the phone?" Avery asked from the table.

"I think I could eat those eggs now if you don't mind. Or we could ask Bo to pick something up from the diner if you need to sit awhile."

"I think I can handle scrambling eggs. I ate all the hash browns, though. Want this teakettle thing going?"

She leaned against the counter. "Eggs, tea and toast would be great."

"When did you start drinking hot tea?" He set to work. He could scramble eggs in his sleep and it was a good thing. Most of his attention was on observing Avery. She didn't look as pale as she had before she'd fallen asleep. She was resting her head in her left hand and not using her right nearly as much.

"Julie introduced me to it. Got me hooked, actually. She was concerned with the amount of coffee I consumed."

"I remember your mom voicing that a couple of times. I gave a list to Bo. He said he doesn't mind making another trip in the morning if I forgot something. I, um… had him pick up a puzzle and a card table."

"Since when do you work puzzles? You hate puzzles. We both do."

"I noticed…" Did he have to say it? She looked away. "The doc said a puzzle might help."

"Don't you think we have a big Snake Eyes puzzle to solve?"

He removed the eggs and scooped them onto a plate, handing them to her. She leaned back and let him set it on the table. "I'm just trying to help."

"Each time you call the doctor, he's probably telling Dan I need more time to sit here."

"If he doesn't I will. You can't go back on the job like this."

"What do you know? I'm fine, just tired." She took a bite and glared at him.

"Then use your right hand."

"I'm good."

He couldn't strong-arm her. She'd keep pushing until they were angry. He didn't want that. "Avery, please use your right hand."

She shook her head. "It feels like it's asleep and sort of disconnected. I…I just want it to be over."

"You need some time. Eat and try not to think about the case while I clean up." He pushed bread into the toaster. "I forgot your tea."

The knock in front saved him from making a complete fool of himself. It was on the tip of his tongue to tell her not to worry about anything. She could come home; he'd take care of her. *Those words would have been grounds to throw me out on my ear.*

"That must be Bo." He tossed the hand towel to the counter.

"I can see that."

"Right," he mumbled, opening the door. "Looks like he has everything on the list and then some."

"Hey. I got you two whiteboards. The bed frame was harder to locate. That's what took me a bit longer. It's about time she bought one." Bo, laden with paper and plastic sacks, pushed past him. His demeanor brightened when he faced Avery. "How you feeling?"

"Pretty good, Bo. We appreciate you doing all this."

"Beats waiting for speeders out on Highway 57. I better get the rest of the sacks."

"Let me help," Jesse offered, glaring at Avery when she got up and headed to the door.

"I got this. You aren't supposed to be out of the house. More than one person told me to keep you both indoors."

Jesse held the door and noticed Avery eating left-handed but stopping when Bo entered the house. Kayden stood on the corner of the porch obviously watching for movement—other than Bo coming in and out.

Bo brought in the bed frame and whipped out a multi-tool to put it together. Avery just rolled her eyes. She couldn't like rolling out of bed every morning instead of sitting on the side.

"I'm paying for it," he blurted.

"Oh, I know. And you can take it with you when you leave because you aren't using it while you're here."

"The thought didn't enter my mind."

"I bet it didn't." She took her plate to the kitchen. "Did you see the puzzle Bo got?"

"Popcorn. Colored popcorn. Sort of made me hungry. Maybe I'll add that to my list."

"All done," Bo said, wiping his hands. "I'll stop by around lunch tomorrow if you want me to pick you up anything from the Dairy Barn."

"Thanks," they answered together. He might have been a little oversensitive, but he got the impression Bo was only asking if Avery wanted her standing order for lunch.

It was totally dark by the time he finished putting everything away. The card table was stuck against the wall by the television after they'd moved the couch closer to the door. Cards, dice and a puzzle sat on top. But the main, clear focus for Avery was the crime-scene photos getting taped to the hall wall. First up were the photos from Clayton, then the picnic grove.

"You ready to look at all this?"

"I need to catch this sicko, Jesse. Are you?"

Chapter Seventeen

Five days, four nights sounded absolutely perfect for a vacation. All winter Avery had dreamed about five days on a sunny beach, baking to a crisp golden brown. The cold Panhandle wind had cut through her until she learned to buy pants a size bigger and wear long underwear.

Five days going on five nights stuck in the same sixteen hundred square feet was absolute torture.

Not that Jesse wasn't a perfect gentleman. He was. A perfect gentleman all the way. Considerate to the point of ridiculous. He let her use all the hot water for her shower. Always put the toilet seat down. He cleaned up after himself. And he slept on the cot.

After the first night when he'd held her close to him and she'd slept so soundly…nothing. Not so much as an accidental touch. Which was hard to do in a one-bedroom, no-dining-area, overcrowded cracker box.

Oh yeah, she was good and ready to be sent to the funny farm.

The window unit in the front room was working overtime. She'd kicked off most of the covers and the bedroom door was open wide. Spring had taken a turn toward summer today. She needed to install ceiling fans or buy a box fan. She'd lived here during only the winter, so she had no idea how hot the place got when it heated up outside.

"Avery?" her forced roommate called.

"Yes?"

"You're not asleep?" He was just outside the door and could have checked for himself.

"Too hot."

"Want to trade?"

"Quit being so damned nice!" she shouted. She was ready for a rousing discussion, excitement, a break in the case, some sighting of Snake Eyes or even a good old-fashioned fight with Jesse.

No workouts. She couldn't handle it if Jesse discovered just how dizzy she was all the time. She never knew when her hand or her leg might give way and she'd fall flat on her face… Everything had taken its toll on her. She needed a change.

"What was that for?" He stood in her doorway as pretty as you please with only his boxers. He had been standing in the hall.

"Do you remember that discussion about me *not* being your sister?"

"Yes." He crossed his arms, covering his muscles.

"Then why don't you have clothes on?"

"You got me, Avery. Why do people tend to not sleep in their clothes. Sorry. I'm tired of sleeping on that cramped cot. However I'm dressed doesn't matter." He did an about-face and left. "I didn't exactly bring pajamas with me."

"Sorry."

"Can't hear you," he bleated.

"All right, you can have the bed tonight and I'll take the AC." She gathered her pillows and turned right smack into his chest. She still wasn't 100 percent stable on her feet. His arms caught her before she wobbled.

Their eyes met. She hoped hers weren't shouting as loudly as Jesse's. His told her just how much he wanted her, like nothing else mattered but her. All in one close-up.

He swallowed hard.

She swallowed hard. "I'm good."

"I'm not."

This wasn't how she pictured their first real kiss after everything—that horrible night or Thompson Grove. She dropped the pillows as soon as his lips touched hers. Her arms circled his back, getting their fill of his bare skin. Tough-guy skin stretched tight across his muscles, yet smooth.

Jesse didn't wait to get reacquainted slowly. His tongue darted into her mouth, teasing her, making her want more of him. His hands circled under her backside and drew her closer to his...boxers. She wanted him, but he couldn't hide how much he wanted her.

His lips moved to her shoulder. He tugged the over-size T-shirt down and nipped at her skin. She tried to take a step back to the bed, but he trapped her closer. He kissed her faster, completely in control. Taking and not asking permission.

Man, did she love it. Her mind kept repeating "it's about time, it's about time." Her heart felt...everything. The firmness of his lips smashed the softness of hers and she didn't care. His hands kept a firm grip at her hips, but she longed for him to explore, to pull off her shirt and tease her breasts.

She backed up again, trying to let him know she was

ready for the next step. They could finally discover what they were like together. If he'd only...

She broke off his kisses. She hated to bring it up, but she also didn't want a repeat of their night in Austin. "I thought we were past the whole promise thing to Garrison."

"We are."

"Then if I want to be with you and you want to be with me... What's wrong with the bed?" She smiled as best she could, but something was wrong. "This feels like your party night all over again. But this time you're completely sober and unable to run away. Darn my overprotective brother. I could wring Garrison's neck, in a loving sisterly fashion, of course."

"It was never about Garrison."

"But you said..."

"Yeah. I thought I could do this. I wanted to have at least one night. Make love to you one time. You know, then I'd have memories."

"Are you dying? Even living as far apart as we do, we could still—" She inhaled so fast she choked on air but still managed to yelp out, "You're... You...you...you found someone?"

"No. Of course not. I would never do that to you. Do you really think I'd fool around if I had a girlfriend?"

"You aren't fooling around, Jesse."

She pulled the sheet off the bed and wrapped it around her. She felt vulnerable standing there braless, in PJ shorts, about to cry. Tears were in her very near future. He'd never seen that. Or at least not since ninth grade when her mother had forced her to stop trying out for football.

"Get out." Her voice was surprisingly somber, considering she wanted to scream.

"I need to tell you why I can't do this."

"I don't want to hear it." She kept her back to him as the first tear slid down her cheek. She tried to wipe it inconspicuously with a knuckle.

"I don't want to tell you, but that doesn't matter." He cupped her shoulders in his hands.

Hot skin to hot skin just made her burn for him more. She dipped a shoulder, attempting to free herself. He wouldn't let her go.

"It's nothing to do with your body or mind or anything like that. I want you till I ache, Avery," he whispered near her ear. "So bad it hurts. Every night on that cot has been hell, knowing you were here craving the same thing. I didn't want to do this to you. Or hurt you."

"What could be worse than humiliating me like this a second time?"

"I swore to myself I wouldn't put you into this position. If I just kept my distance, I'd never hurt you."

"I got news for you, Jesse. *This* hurts."

JESSE SWALLOWED HARD, needing water to wet his suddenly dry mouth. "It was me. Okay? I'm the reason you aren't a Texas Ranger. It had nothing to do with the fact that you're a woman. I mean, it did. That's the whole reason for me, but not *their* reason. It was my reason."

Avery turned to face him. He could see the wet paths her tears had made. She tucked the sheet under her arm and put her palms into her eyes. She slapped her thighs and sat on the mattress.

"I'm not quite following. You're trying to take the blame for me not being selected as a ranger. My being passed over wasn't because I was a woman, but it was wholly because I was a woman." She clapped her hands together and shrugged. "I can't possibly be mad at you, Jesse. At least not yet. I can't understand anything you've said."

"It made more sense inside my head when I planned it out. I think you're going to get mad. I just hope you can forgive me one day."

"Then I'll reserve the right for both."

"Let's sit in the living room, where it's cooler." Jesse took her hand and led her from the room. She slipped her feet under the swishing sheet wrapped around her. Then leaned on the arm of the couch, waiting for his explanation.

"Oh gosh, it's better in here. Now, what's this all about? Why am I going to be angry?"

"You see, the higher-ups at the highway patrol thought you and I were having an affair. Someone must have reported seeing us together, kissing. You know they have a strict no-fraternization rule."

"No one mentioned an affair to me."

"They didn't mention it to me, at least not first thing. But it's what instigated the situation they presented to me."

"Please stop trying to word everything perfectly, Jesse. Just tell me."

Explaining to her was difficult. Or maybe explaining by trying to make himself *not* look as guilty as he felt. Which wasn't the truth. She needed the truth before they could move forward in a relationship.

"All right. They pulled me into the office one day, reminded me of the rule, then said there were three candidates for two ranger positions. I had one. The next on the list was you. If I could swear there was nothing between us and wouldn't be in the future, then they'd send us to Waco."

"And your conscience wouldn't allow you to do that. I see."

"It was an impossible position to be put into. Garrison wasn't just my best friend. He was my partner."

"So you chose him."

"But I didn't choose. I didn't know Garrison was one of the three. Don't you see?"

"I see perfectly."

Could she? He couldn't swear that they weren't involved because he wanted to become completely involved with her. Did she understand? Why couldn't he just say what was in his head?

"I see that you couldn't lie to your boss, but you could lie to me." She stood, straightening the sheet, tucking it under her arm tightly like a wall of protection. "We were sneaking behind Garrison's back and hiding from everyone. As I recall, you kissed me. You started the whole thing. But what you really did was set me up. I should be wearing that badge. Not you. You never even wanted to be a ranger. Garrison pulled you kicking and screaming to the Texas DPS and...you went along for the ride."

"That's not—"

"Please don't. I'll finish this assignment with you. I'd be stupid to turn away your experience. You might be telling the truth about it being an innocent mistake. But you're right. I don't see how there can be anything between us if you felt like you had to lie."

Whether she was calm or not, she put on a good front

as she walked to her bedroom. "You've had to choose between me and Garrison for the last time."

She cried herself to sleep and he heard every tear.

JESSE HAD TO hand it to Avery. She was a professional in every sense of the word. Until she closed the bedroom door. For two nights, under the hum of the air conditioner in his ear, he could still hear the echoes of her crying.

He'd predicted her reaction and it was killing him that he'd been right. It might be killing him a bit more because he wanted to hold and comfort her. He hated being the bad guy. Never liked it when he was the robber to Garrison's cop. And he didn't like breaking the rules.

Yeah, he'd cleared his conscience, but he'd lost his best friend. *Professional* was the word of the day. Polite. Shared the coffee. Fix your own dinner—or get Deputy Bo to bring it to you. Then sit and laugh over a burger.

I am not going to be jealous of that kid.

Aw, hell, he was very jealous of the man who had just left after a painstakingly boring conversation. It had taken nearly an hour to update Avery on everyone in their county. Long enough to set Jesse's teeth to grinding.

"Dammit." It wasn't the conversation. It was her laughter. She wasn't smiling or laughing around him any longer. He caused her to cry.

Avery joined him in the hall. "I guess lunch is over. Where were we?"

"The DNA familial tie led us back to this guy." He tapped the latest picture on her bedroom door. "Father, grandfather or brother—we were trying to decide before Mr. Smiley Face showed up."

His dig didn't receive even an arched eyebrow from

her. She took the rushed DNA report from his hand and was reading it for the third or fourth time. He'd been staring at the thing for the past hour and hadn't made any headway.

Most likely because he'd been listening to how Julie chased Miss Wags through the yard with bubbles all over the little dog. Avery had laughed. Bo had laughed. Jesse had read the same paragraph six times.

"Ted Hopkins, aka T-Bone Hop, was covert ops in the '80s. So, yes, he could be any of those connections. But we'll never know. He's off the grid and has been for over a decade." Avery closed the file and stared at the photo. "Since Snake Eyes wore the hood hiding his face, there's no way to even compare bone structure for a possible match."

"Do you think it's a dead end? Maybe we get someone from headquarters to keep searching?"

She tapped her finger against the wall, thinking. "I believe our resources and energy are better used to analyze what he'll do. Even if we know who he is…our personal experience with him tells us more."

"Still no reports of anyone with abdominal rake wounds at hospitals in two hundred miles. They widened the search—"

"I don't think he'd use a hospital. He was obviously trained by someone. Maybe T-Bone Hop?" Excitement—real excitement—had returned to her eyes. "He was military and disappeared. What if he taught Snake Eyes his survival secrets?"

"So we're looking for a ghost."

"A ghost who got sloppy and left us alive." She turned her attention to thumbing through the file they'd printed.

"What if it wasn't sloppy work?" Jesse wondered.

"This man has been excellent working alone. No trace. Hell, no one really put together how many murders he's committed. He could have taken us anywhere, Avery. Why leave me untied? I can't stop going back to the very public place he left us. Why there? What good did it do *him*?"

"You mean why out in the open with a house a quarter of a mile away? Why involve a kid who could and seemingly did mess up his plan?"

"It's almost been a week and he hasn't resurfaced. Not even an attempt to finish us off."

"This man is a hunter. Remember, he called us his prey. He's patient. He lies in wait until the perfect opportunity." Avery dropped the file to the floor and put her palms over her eyes, concentrating.

"I don't think so. Yes, that he's a hunter, but he didn't wait for us to be alone before drugging us. He created a perfectly planned and executed trap."

She looked at him, excited. "So Thompson Grove was just a cog in the wheel he's turning to get to his real prey…my brother. But what did he expect to happen?"

"I need to talk with Major Parker." He pushed past her, taking a couple of the pictures down with him. "We recommended they move the witnesses."

Pure and simple panic ramped up his adrenaline. He grabbed his phone. Dialed. "Come on. Come on."

"If something had happened, we would have been notified. Right?"

Even during this moment of fear for Garrison and the men protecting him, he wanted to comfort Avery. His hand reached out to pat her shoulder. "Snake Eyes wouldn't do anything rash. He'd have a plan. He'd take his time to plan it. But he's had six days."

She pulled away from his touch. "You think he's going to act soon."

"Yeah. They should— Dammit, there's no answer. They should take extra precautions."

He wanted to smooth away the worry line on her brow. He wanted to swoosh back those crazy long bangs so he could see her eyes more clearly. But he'd lost the right to touch her. She wasn't his and wouldn't be.

"Jesse, he said he had a plan B. If he can't get the information from us, he thinks he can obtain it from somewhere else. But where? From who?"

"I know how to catch this bastard."

"What do you want to do?" She watched him dial the phone.

If the powers above him went for this crazy, half-baked plan, Snake Eyes wouldn't be a threat to anyone else. "We're leaving. Whether they know it or not, they're going to need us to finish this thing."

Chapter Eighteen

Snake Eyes to his enemies. Buster Hopkins to his family, but that was a long time ago. Of course, none of his family were left, so no one really knew him by that name any longer. Back when his dad was alive, they'd got several IDs from different states.

Although Snake Eyes fit him better than Buster, Carl, Sanchez or Nigel, he couldn't walk around in a thirty-year-old diving suit while in town. So for the moment Nigel Washington was checked into a five-star hotel in Austin. He couldn't imagine anyone visiting him in the camper owned by Carl.

After stitching his wounds and resting a day, he was living it up until his plans came to fruition. He knew how to play a role and that looks made all the difference. He'd exceeded his father's ability to blend in or hunt.

Today was the part of a potential campaign donor who was hard on crime. Yes, Nigel was a do-gooder, but he required a little proof in exchange for his monetary contributions. Dinner tonight would be interesting, eye-opening, in fact.

No, he laughed at his faux pas, this woman would keep her eyes. Information only. No one would realize who he really was or why he wanted to know details about Texas Mafia families. Nigel's looks were different than the killer Snake Eyes. They still wouldn't be traced back to him. The real him.

The computer system he'd breached prior to Rosco's death had been secured since his attack on Avery. Nigel's approach—money, love and blackmail—that normally found a vulnerable spot with anyone. The good Avery had made certain her mother and aunt were hidden away, so finding his prey required imagination now.

Dinner drinks would be quite amusing. There were so many ways to compel information from actual people. He stopped thinking about the steps needed for his venture this evening when Avery's pale face replaced the glass elevator zooming to his level. She seemed to push her way more and more into his thoughts.

Returning for the deputy and her ranger had consumed him the first two days after leaving them. He wanted completion. Needed their deaths. Desired another confrontation.

No one had attacked him like that before. It wasn't revenge, just more of a need. Finishing the job should come first. His reputation…that was all that should matter. When his last job was finalized, it could possibly be five-star hotels around the world.

What he should do and what his plan was…two very different things. Avery Travis fascinated him. She'd survived the collar and still fought back. She had a will to live that would be amazing to watch die. How much would it take to break her? His curious nature couldn't stop wondering what satisfaction would be gained from discovering that answer.

Yes, it would be a mistake to get sidetracked, but it was also a mistake to continue with the Tenoreno job that he wouldn't walk away from. He didn't need the money. He only needed to finish. Avery was only a part of the need to conclude his business.

Mistakes had delayed shutting the file on the Tenoreno family. His father would have been upset to find out how careless—or maybe arrogant—he'd been with his work. Which led to thinking about his father. That was probably because of the DNA they'd be processing.

Someone would discover who T-Bone Hop was and they might find out how he was related to Buster. But not to Snake Eyes. T-Bone had drilled it into Buster's childhood that he could be tracked through DNA. His father had left the navy a decorated hero, but his DNA was in the system. That was before he met the love of his life and before he killed her. Before he'd raised Buster to be a competent huntsman. Before Buster had surpassed his father's ability.

There would be no love of a lifetime for Snake Eyes or Buster. Love was for weaklings, for people who had nothing else to do other than conform to an everyday existence. He was above everyday anything.

He took a deep breath, jerked and remembered that he wasn't above making a bad decision. Scott. That cocky kid had been a mistake who caused Nigel's chest to hurt and brought Buster's father into the picture.

Finish the Tenoreno job and Snake Eyes would be gone forever. Perhaps Carl or Sanchez would take on a new lifestyle. He could try big-game hunting. He'd always wanted to hunt a tiger. That might be fun.

Leaving any of his identities behind would be strange. He'd been moving between them so easily for two decades. He liked living as them all. Snake Eyes was special. By being completely cloaked in black, he was able to tap into the hidden depths of his darkest curiosity.

The new prey arrived. They had a drink and conversation. But he changed his mind about dinner. He tossed down the three pictures he'd printed in his room. Three photos of a child playing at school.

"Where did you get pictures of my son?" the young woman asked.

"Anybody can park across the street from a school and click a few pictures. What's the world coming to?"

"What do you really want, Mr. Washington?"

"I need the location where a witness is being held. That's all."

"I might not have access," she said, her voice already filled with fright and cooperation.

"Sweet woman, I wouldn't be wasting my time with you if you didn't."

She shivered and began to cry.

Whatever he decided about Avery and her Texas Ranger, it wouldn't involve hiring another person for quite some time. He patted the stitches Jesse Ryder had caused. He needed to make certain that man was alive and suffering for days. He'd be his final kill. The one that he'd remember for his lifetime.

Chapter Nineteen

Avery had her bag packed sitting by the door with her daddy's shotgun on top. The files were stacked on the table. The cot Jesse had been sleeping on was upended on the wall by the puzzle table. Jesse had walked Dan through their conclusions. Then they'd both answered questions on a conference call with the State's Attorney's Office.

But they were still sitting here. Not being allowed to leave. Two Texas Rangers blocked the door and had taken their keys.

"I was right the first time. House arrest."

"Still protective custody," Jesse said pensively. "They haven't agreed that we're necessary for our plan. Even though we know this bastard."

"Can't a citizen refuse protective custody? Is there something I can sign?" She'd been reduced to walking her floor in as large a square as possible to make sure she moved.

"That means going against what they're all advising. If we leave, we won't know where Garrison's being kept. Won't know if Snake Eyes is following them."

She circled her arms and stretched them above her head. The button-down shirt wasn't ideal for optimum movement. She didn't care. She was dressed to leave as soon as someone came to their senses. "We'll know if he's following us."

"True. But if we're right and he's already in place, then we won't be allowed to help. Won't be a part of the solution. They could jail us to keep us out of their way."

"They they they they they." She pointed a different direction with each word to emphasize her frustration. "If you only knew how sick I was of hearing that pronoun. They this. They that."

Jesse ducked his head. She could tell he knew he was part of her frustration.

"Sixteen hundred square feet. Feels more like six hundred. Every day we're stuck in here feels like we lose footage." She stretched her arms over her head, wondering if there was anything else she could do. "I need to go for a run. Oh, wait, give me a punching bag. I need a serious workout."

She threw some air punches, feeling the tension in her shoulders. Not feeling any of the tingly leftover insecurity of being shocked. She was back. She turned to tell Jesse, then remembered that she was keeping it professional.

The only time she allowed herself to think about his confession was late at night...alone in her bedroom. It saddened her to be second best to her twin brother. Always. That was natural. Or at least she hoped it was natural and that she wasn't just being an insecure child.

The reason she cried? She missed her friend. Sure, she wanted more. But truth be told, if nothing else had developed between them, she'd never imagined her life without Jesse in it. Even during the past eight months while she'd been upset with him...he was there.

Idiot. He's still there. Sitting right there. What would you have done? Lied?

"During the conference call, didn't someone ask why you were still here in Dalhart?"

He shrugged. "Maybe."

"You're in a mood. I just wanted to say that you don't have to stay here and babysit me. I already have two rangers outside the door." She raised her voice and Wyatt didn't move from leaning on the porch post. "You could take all that work to Company F. Let them validate, analyze or whatever you guys do. The state's attorney might believe us then and do something about the threat."

"And you'd stay here doing what?"

"I have a popcorn puzzle. I'm good for three days." Okay, she'd offered an olive branch and he had to recognize it wasn't poison oak. He had a look.

Oh my goodness.

He had a look, all right. It simmered and made her bubble to a boil. She was standing in front of the air conditioner. She knew it was working but could swear she was heating up like a kettle. No hot jasmine-blossom tea for her. "Want some iced tea? I think I need a glass to cool down. Something chilly."

"Sure."

She escaped to the kitchen. Standing at the sink, she stared mindlessly out the window until the tea steeped. The pitcher was ready with a tray of ice and a cup of sugar. Two glasses poured. Her hands were around them and she couldn't move.

"I've been thinking."

She jumped so hard the tea seemed to hop from the top of the glasses.

"I didn't mean to scare you." His deep rich voice comforted.

She grabbed a dish towel, dabbed at the counter, then lifted the glasses. "I was just thinking. My fault."

"So was I. And you're right. I should go back to Waco. My job's been done here. I've been off my mandatory week. I should get back to work." He took his glass, steadying her fingers, keeping them wrapped gently within his.

The man's eyes were just incredible. He had a quiet strength. A mixture of confidence and concern that set her up for instant attraction. And when he smiled, he changed his chiseled features into a movie-star grin.

"There's not a reason to stay if you're mad or if I'm just going to continue to upset you." He wasn't smiling and still had a magnetism she didn't understand. No other man made her feel this way.

"I…um… I… Dammit, Jesse. I stopped being angry ten minutes ago. I don't want to lose your friendship."

Jesse pulled her to him, his fingers across her lips stopping her words. The tea she held spilled between their bodies. "I'm not just your friend, Avery. And I most definitely do not think of you as my sister."

The smoldering look he gave from her eyes to her lips devoured her before really kissing her. His fingertips were smooth across her lips while his thumb tipped her chin. He lowered his mouth and that was all she could see as she watched his lips take possession of her.

Soft, long luxuriating kisses. Then his thumb trailed down her throat. Shocks ran through her body, pleasant palpitations that had her pulse racing harder than any workout she remembered. His mouth followed the nails he scraped along her collarbone. He nipped, skimmed, then licked. She could only watch and…feel.

One arm encircled her back, bending her slightly so he could have more access. His free hand unbuttoned her shirt, one excruciatingly slow button at a time. Her knees weakened when his lips skimmed the top of her breast.

Sometime along the way, Jesse's skilled hands had untucked her shirt. Unbuttoned, he pushed it back to her elbows. His thumbs slipped higher under the edge of her bra, brushing skin, slowly advancing until the fastener released, giving him carte blanche.

Had time stood still or was Jesse memorizing every freckle she had? Her world went from slow motion to fast-forward. Jesse pushed her shirt off and tugged her arms free from the bra. When his lips and tongue circled her nipple, she stumbled backward with the sparks of delight.

Glass cracked under their boots, taking them both by surprise. "The tea glasses. I should clean— Oh…maybe… not…"

Jesse took advantage of the small space between them and sucked, alternating between her breasts until both were puckered and more alive than ever before. He worked his way back up her neck, then kissed her mouth, consuming any doubts she had.

"Might get dangerous if we stay in here." He lifted her in his arms, walking across wet glass and her favorite lacy bra. Her arms went around his neck and tugged his face back to hers.

She hoped that the curtains were still closed or the ranger on the porch was going to get an eyeful.

JESSE CAUGHT AVERY'S chest to his as they left the kitchen. He protected her from the window, locked lips, then realized he'd frozen that way while walking around the corner and into her bedroom.

They broke apart and laughed when he set her on the bed. He tilted his head to the porch. "You're going to have to keep the wildness down. Remember, there's someone listening for trouble."

Avery was wide-eyed innocent. He had no idea how much that "little experience" that she'd referred to actually meant.

"You know, I'm usually good with words, but around you it's like there's no connection to my brain." He unbuttoned his shirt as she tugged the sheet loose from under the pillows. He had no intention of letting her cover up the perfection he was gazing upon. But he was also so dang nervous he didn't know how to prevent it.

His mind was blank of ideas. He got to the last button and dropped his hands to his sides, totally in awe. That was what he should tell her.

"You are the most beautiful person I've ever known, Elf Face. Completely beautiful all the way through." He leaned on the bed and feathered her hair away from her jade eyes.

He stretched out next to her, kissing every inch of skin he could reach. Gently pulling the sheet to the side, he lightly drew circles and skimmed her breasts with his fingertips.

"Jesse?" She tugged his shirt off. "Why in the world do you call me Elf Face?"

There was no rush as their hands explored the other. "Remember when you got your hair cut?" he whispered. "Your mom was having fits, but my mom said it fit your elfin-shaped face. I thought it was cool...at least at the time. I might have been into a couple of movies that had elves. I know the nickname irritates you."

"No it doesn't. I could never let you know, but I sort of liked it."

His circles continued across her flat stomach to the top of her jeans. They were loose on her hips, enough that he could get the button through the hole one-handed.

"You sure about this?" He paused with his hand on the zipper pull.

"I swear, Jesse. If you stop…you won't walk out of this room alive."

Sexual frustration was something he was familiar with. He didn't question what they were doing any longer. This was right for them both. He unzipped her jeans and she unzipped his, hesitating only a second with what was hiding behind the cloth.

He brushed his hands up her thighs to her hips.

Skin to skin. Finally. He'd been dreaming about this since they'd crept into the dorm after a late-night party. There had been something about that night. Something different in the way she'd looked at him all bright-eyed and ready.

The same way she was looking at him…right now.

"Well?" she whispered.

"I can't stop looking."

"But you've seen it before." Her fingers searched for the edge of the sheet.

"No, ma'am." He shoved the cover away from her. "I want to remember this. Broad daylight. No alcohol involved. And no regrets for either of us."

"I can go with that." She skimmed a fingernail on the outside of his thigh, mimicking in her own way.

Jesse stretched out next to her, loving that she matched

him inch for inch. No one ever had. She was the only woman he'd ever looked at eye to eye when he was standing. The only woman he wanted.

Kissing her was something he should have been doing all his life. He shouldn't have avoided their attraction. He shouldn't have listened to Garrison all those years.

Part of the hesitation came because Avery was important to him. No second-guessing now. They had an instinct when they worked together. They meshed even when they were angry at each other.

The slow burn of kissing soon built into a wildfire of sampling every part of her. Touching her brought her to life. He loved seeing how skimming her skin sent shivers throughout her. Kissing her skin and tasting her made his blood run hot.

Intimacy with her was taking him to a new level of sensuality. He didn't want to rush, but waiting was infinitely painful.

"I swear, Jesse, I'm as flammable as I was days ago. Dammit, do something." Her nails dug into his arms.

He reached for the nightstand. The first night he was here, he'd seen the condoms. A small discreet unopened box shoved in the back.

"What are you grinning at?" she asked when he paused.

"The box is open."

"Would you do whatever you need to do and get this over with?"

"Believe me, Elf Face, this isn't going to be over for a long while. No matter how much *I* want it to be. I'm going to make certain of that."

Powerful and concentrated. That was how he would describe the way Avery watched him. But before he could move to join her, she took him in her hands.

He could die right there in her bed. Maybe he did a little. He shuddered with her gentle caress and almost made a fool of himself. He'd had no idea that her feeling the weight of him would be his undoing. If he was going to make good on...

He slid the condom into place with shaking hands. Caught himself breathing deeply in an effort to slow his blood. This was Avery. His Avery. She might think that she wanted quick until he showed her slow. Their lips met for a second or two and then he kissed her jawline, up to her ear and then down the column of her neck. She was trying to tug him on top of her, using those long legs to lock her ankles behind his back.

Jesse found Avery's wrists and, in one motion, pinned them to the bed above her head. "There's no rush, babe. We've got nowhere to go."

Avery bucked underneath him. "Please, Jesse, no more waiting."

His lips skated to the pulse beating at the base of her throat and continued down her rib cage. It was difficult to stay focused when Avery was hell-bent on fast and furious. Her hips thrust upward, trying to make contact with his.

He wanted to touch her breasts but couldn't trust her to keep her hands to herself. "Jess—ee." She said his name on a groan as his lips grazed her nipple.

He loved hearing the catch in her voice. Loved knowing that she wanted him as much as he wanted her. He licked one nipple before gliding his tongue across her chest to taste the other one. Her legs loosened from around his waist.

"I need to touch you," she said. "Not fair."

He nearly laughed, but knew it would break his concentration. If he thought too much about how he could have taken her, could have satisfied both their needs in less than two minutes, he'd already be inside her.

But this wasn't just sex. This was his chance to explore every inch of her body knowing she wanted him just as badly. Her chest arched against his lips and he released her hands. Wanted to feel her touch against his skin.

Wanted her. Now. "Avery." Her name felt like a prayer and he wasn't sure if he was saying it out loud or only in his head. He found her lips, kissed her as her hands gripped his arms.

He entered slowly and made her completely his. They quickened their pace with even strokes. None of their past would get in their way. Her hands gripped his arms as their bodies became one. Their bodies burned, climbed and met thrust for thrust. She wrapped her legs around his, opening to him, keeping him meshed with her.

With a few frenzied moments, they both cried out in fulfillment. Shuddering for real, he made a connection he'd never had. One that Avery might not understand.

The woman, the girl, the best friend, the partner-in-crime… She was his lifeblood. His for keeps. He loved her with his heart, body and soul.

Convincing her, on the other hand, was going to take careful planning. Or maybe for once he shouldn't censor himself, because it never seemed to work with her anyway.

Chapter Twenty

Avery flung her arms wide, one falling on Jesse's chest, patting him with the back of her hand. Totally, 100 percent exhaustingly satisfied...that was her.

"Oh. Wow." She had never experienced anything so complete. "That was better than amazing."

Who cared if she inflated his big ego? It didn't really matter. The truth was the truth. "I think I'm going to regret every minute we spent *not* doing this while we were stuck inside this house. Wow."

Avery finally caught her breath and propped herself up on one elbow. Jesse remained flat on his back, his chest still visibly rising and falling. She drew circles in a perfect amount of chest hair and fell silent. She'd been the only one talking. He hadn't mentioned anything about it being the best sex he'd had.

Or how good she was.

Looking at him, at the sheer power she'd felt with each thrust of his hips, she wanted him all over again. Then the awkward "after" moment began. She rolled to her back, reaching for the sheet to cover her nakedness. And maybe his if she could manage it.

His arm crossed over her body, stopping her from moving.

"You taste like sweet tea," he finally said.

"That's because you spilled it all over us with the first kiss in the kitchen." *That* was all he could say?

Here she was, sharing from her heart about how wonderful he was as a lover, and he wanted to talk about the tea on her skin? He laced his fingers through hers, then pulled their hands to his chest.

"I love you."

"Is that normal pillow talk? It's really not necessary if you want to do this again." Did he think she needed to hear that to feel better about herself or them together? She didn't.

If the words had been true, he would have picked a better time to let her know. Or even looked at her when he told her.

"I thought—"

"Stop thinking." She moved her lips to his chest. "You taste a bit like tea, too."

She'd ignore this lie. It was probably just the heat of the moment. Something he thought she needed to hear. Jesse was just like every other guy. So what? They were still stuck here together and should enjoy the time.

"Avery, I—"

This time she raised a finger to stop his words. She was a grown woman and didn't need them. "Shh. There's only one thing I need to know. How soon can we do this again?"

THE FLOOR WAS clean from the tea and broken glass. So was her skin after a long shower. Jesse seemed sort of quiet, though…even for him. They'd made love again. She'd imagined feeling this way.

Life had a strange way of making things happen. She

and Jesse had been so close all these years. She'd been head over heels for him on so many occasions that she'd let other guys and opportunities pass her by.

Now this.

She was putting the mop away and heard banging on the door. Before she could run to the front, Jesse answered wrapped in a towel from his shower.

"What now?"

Kayden handed him a phone. "Major Parker's been trying to reach you."

The phone was up to his ear. He stood in the open door for all her neighbors to see his bare-chested glory. Not to mention the look on Kayden's face that said he was slightly embarrassed.

Thin walls.

"I got it. We'll leave immediately." Jesse returned the phone, acknowledged Kayden with a nod and shut the door. "Ready to get out of this town?"

"They're going with our plan?"

"Sounds like it. There's a plane waiting to take us to Fort Worth as soon as possible." He didn't look at her.

In fact, he frowned, covered his eyes with his free hand—the hand that wasn't wrapped in the edge of the towel, keeping it in place. Was he worried about her seeing something? Hadn't they—

"Avery, about what I said earlier."

"Don't think a thing about it. I didn't take you seriously, so we're good. Really. Don't waste any more time on it."

Jesse shook his head. "I need to get dressed."

Had she said something wrong? What was bothering him? She'd forgiven that he'd spoken honestly about their relationship before he became a ranger. She'd forgiven that he'd misspoken in the heat of passion.

She wanted to play it cool. She didn't expect anything from him.

"Are you upset because you broke your word to Garrison? I promise I'm not ever going to tell him." She raised her voice a little so she could be heard through the door.

His reply was several curse words at himself. Not her...definitely himself.

"I have no idea what to do." She wasn't certain he'd heard her or not. She walked away to sit on the arm of the couch. Her bag was packed. Things were put away.

The little house was perfect for her. Her life in Dalhart was good. Without Jesse living here with her, it would feel big here again. *And lonely.* But she'd manage.

Jesse was dressed this time and clean shaven. There was a nick on his chin where he'd cut himself. Probably the source of his four-letter-word vocabulary. He grabbed his bag and the files, pausing at the door.

"You really bringing your dad's shotgun?"

"You can transport it on the plane. Right? I'd really like it there." If the State's Attorney's Office had approved the plan to try to trap Snake Eyes, she was a much better shot with her daddy by her side.

"That's not a problem." Another simple nod to Wyatt and Kayden and they were on both sides escorting her to the car. Then they were the armed escorts on the drive to Amarillo.

After their afternoon, Avery was full of energy— exhausted, good energy. Why was it so different for Jesse? He put his hat over his eyes and pretended to sleep for the hour to Amarillo.

There was no way he'd stay asleep without relaxing

a little. She'd witnessed it over and over during the past week. Nap-time features were totally different than the closed-off, tightly wound man next to her.

The newly topped road was smooth and steady. She made notes of things that could go wrong. Possible scenarios. The one thing that would help would be to know the location of the safe house. Then variables would be limited and she could present a finalized plan.

They arrived at a private hangar. Jesse even yawned a couple of times for show. *Smile. Please.* She wanted him to confess what was wrong. If he withdrew like this every time after seeing her naked, she was going to end up with a complex.

Calling on the fact that they were lifelong friends, she decided to speak to him before they boarded. "Stick out your tongue."

"What?" He looked at her almost as strangely as after getting the call from Parker.

"Just do it."

He hesitatingly obeyed.

"Dab your finger and wipe the dried blood from your shaving nick."

He obeyed. "Why didn't you just say that to begin with?"

"You're welcome. Now are you going to tell me what's wrong?"

"Nothing's wrong." They leaned on the car, waiting for the crew to tell them to board. "Drop it, Avery. You want to talk about Dalhart, your job, the long drive to nowhere… I can accommodate those subjects. But right now everything else is off-limits. Do you understand?"

"Of course. I understand English. I also understand that we're not supposed to talk about particular plans in a public venue or even on this private plane. I get it. What I don't understand is how you went from a very cool friend with benefits to a complete a—"

"Good evening and thanks for flying with us."

The flight attendant had interrupted her at an appropriate time. They sat. They belted up. They took off and landed in silence.

JESSE'S THOUGHTS SHOULD be occupied with their plan. Details, how to act, potential pitfalls. But no. He was staring at the woman across the table from him. In a room with some of the best law enforcement in the state—he could hardly hear them.

One hand mindlessly spun a ballpoint pen on the oak table. The other propped up his head, sort of like being exhausted from a long stakeout. Neither was true.

Maybe the answer was a very exasperating woman.

"Have we had any luck tracking down a mailing address for the contacts?"

"We have our people looking, but it's a long shot. Some of the companies are overseas. The field is so wide. We can't even narrow it down to one state," Avery said.

They had been invited to participate in a planning session. A secret meeting in Fort Worth in some law offices he'd never heard of—a friend of one of the men barking out orders. Jesse half listened, slumped enough in his chair that he looked like an uncaring slouch.

He knew this was a time he should be impressive with knowledge and skill. If he hadn't known it when they walked into this conference room, the darting glares from Avery were stressing that he appeared like a kid who didn't want to be in church.

The chatter at the front of the room became more and

more about the traditional way to fend off an attack on witnesses. Escorts. Routes. Secrecy. Limited resources.

"The hell with this." The pen bounced across the wide table right into Avery's breakfast roll.

"Do you have something to say, Ryder?" the lead prosecuting attorney asked.

"It might get me kicked out of this room, but this isn't the plan I was told we'd be executing. You're asking Avery—Deputy Travis—to put her life at risk again for—"

"Hold on, Jesse. You don't speak for me." She spoke on top of him, even after his own glare at her to keep quiet.

"—for nothing. We've already been toe-to-toe with this bastard. Don't you think we know a thing or two? You had a profiler look at some pictures. I gave Snake Eyes a bloody nose and stabbed him with a rake." He pushed the rolling chair a little too hard when clearing the table to stand.

"We get the picture, Jesse," Parker said from behind him.

"I don't think they understand this killer at all, sir. He's nothing like what we've encountered—"

"Enough." The major said the word softly and laid a hand on Jesse's shoulder.

It took the steam from his actions and put his brain back in control. Avery sat straighter in her chair, fingers over her lips. When she caught his eyes, she silently shushed him.

He shook his head. "I won't be quiet. This guy is everything your profiler says but more. He's calm in a fight. Things went wrong and he didn't panic. He didn't yell. Didn't run. He's a planner, not a reactor. It was like he had a contingency for everything."

"This procedure has been proven to draw out threats," one of the men said. "Especially assassins."

"And that's exactly why it won't work with Snake Eyes," Avery spoke out. "I—we—respect how you're drawing your conclusions. But this man isn't just an assassin. He's more like a serial killer who's learned how to make money at what he loves."

"Good description, b—Deputy." He'd just come very close to ruining their credibility by calling her "babe." "He's got a plan."

"And we believe we figured it out," she added.

"What do you think, Major Parker?" the lead guy asked.

"I think they're right. We have a possible way to catch this guy. The information these two have given us over the past week has connected at least eleven murders from different states. And those are just the victims we discovered." Parker relaxed against the wall, totally at ease, arms crossed. "You should hear them out."

Jesse took note of the major's relaxed, authoritative posture while the men argued at the front of the room. Jesse was normally the laid-back guy, but these men hadn't stared into the eyes of a soulless reptile. It was more than that. The bastard had held a gun on the woman Jesse loved. He'd electrocuted her until her heart had stopped.

Looking at her now, no one would know that she'd died for a few seconds a week ago. She was a confident, strong Amazon. If she wasn't carrying a badge and gun, they might have taken her for a model. But there was a badge. More than one gun.

God, I love her. How can I make her see that?

"Major, we need to keep our witnesses alive. Understanding that the outcome rests completely on your shoulders, what plan do you want us to hear?"

"Go ahead, Ranger." Parker nodded.

"Right. We know Snake Eyes had a backup plan to discover the location of the witnesses being held in protective custody," he began.

"We also know that your state office computers were breached three weeks ago," Parker said, taking a seat at the table.

"No one told us about this," the attorney blustered.

"We didn't know until the attack on Travis and Ryder." Parker nodded to Bryce Johnson to distribute material. "Their abduction prompted a check of the system."

"That might have been his original plan B that he mentioned. Security was tightened and he's punting." Jesse caught the pen that skidded across the table from Avery. He also noted the tilt of the corner of her mouth.

"This is all just a theory." Came from the front of the room.

"Supported by the fact that Snake Eyes hasn't been seen or taken any action since our confrontation." Avery was a professional who knew her facts. She could handle the lead attorney. "So we asked ourselves, what did the man want? To kill? He'd just killed four people in two days. So no. It was pride."

"Ego. Serial killers can be caught through their egos," said one of the analysts who worked for the state.

The attorney's palms were flat on the table. Then he began tapping his fingers. Was he waiting for a pause in their explanation to respond or a flaw in their reasoning?

It didn't matter. If the state wanted to draw Snake Eyes out with their worthless plan, he'd throw Avery over his shoulder and resign. They'd contact Garrison and protect themselves the old-fashioned way. But they could catch this madman. He knew it. They just had to convince the six people sitting at this table.

He imitated his boss with relaxed self-confidence. "Snake Eyes threatened Avery to get the information he needed. When I showed up, I made it easier for him because of our long-standing friendship. When it didn't work, there was only one modification to the plan that he needed to make. Find another target."

He finished, flattening his palms on the table, too. A symbolic gesture that all his cards had been played. He didn't look at the attorney making the decisions. He looked at the woman who had stolen his heart and wondered how he was going to keep her alive while they trapped a serial assassin.

Chapter Twenty-One

Waiting was the hardest part. It was day two at the address leaked to nonessentials. The house was perfect for a trap. The plan was to lure Snake Eyes inside the house. Unless he attempted murder, they might not get more than trespassing. They needed a DNA sample and needed a crime to compel one.

Limited access in or out at the end of a cul-de-sac. There was an empty house across the circle where backup could stay and keep watch. It felt like a fishbowl, and yet she was so nervous she had trouble thinking straight.

Pacing the house wearing a blond wig and bulletproof vest, she passed in front of windows exposing herself to sniper fire. As long as he didn't take a head shot, she might only get the breath knocked out of her.

"I thought for certain they were going to kick you out of that meeting the other day." Avery had been full of excitement as they walked into the hotel. They'd won. They were setting a trap for Snake Eyes.

But could she face him? This wasn't the first time she'd had a moment of doubt creep inside her that she wouldn't be able to do it. Then again, if she didn't have that fear, she'd be more worried.

"You convinced them a little too well." Jesse had the

shotgun on his hip, leaning against the inside wall by the television.

"What do you mean?"

"There are other cops or rangers who could pose for Kenderly Tyler. It doesn't have to be you." He shook his head. "We could still bring someone on board to take your place."

"This is my case." She fingered a see-through curtain panel, pulling it slightly to the side to view the street. Nothing. Not even a street lamp in this new housing division.

"You've been through a lot."

"Haven't you?" She didn't blame him for doubting her. It did sort of hurt, though. She wouldn't want to work with anyone else. "Are you worried I'll fall apart or something?"

"Of course not."

"You're lying, Jesse Ryder."

"Of course I'm worried about you. But not that you can't do your job." Jesse cupped her shoulders.

Should she? Should she kiss him or even go to bed with him right now? Wow, that answer was a definite *of course not*. They were on the job and the idea shouldn't have even popped into her brain. But it had. And she would.

Her hands lifted to his cheeks and she drew his lips to hers. A gentle touch, firm, a little rough around the edges because he hadn't shaved that morning. His hands skimmed her shoulders, then her neck and into her hair.

She was next to him but wanted his body closer. She broke her mouth free. "We don't have time."

"We do if we hurry." He swooped in for another assault on her senses.

"Would you be thinking about making love to *me*? I have a lot of mixed images in my mind. I'm not really sure I can concentrate." The photos of murders popped into her head. She shivered and started pacing again.

"Who said timing was everything?" Jesse was dressed like her brother. He'd even ridden a motorcycle from Fort Worth and parked it in the garage. "I'm sure Garrison will appreciate what you're doing for Kenderly."

"I'm not doing this for Garrison. Or his girlfriend."

"Fiancée," Jesse corrected her. "He told us on the phone that he'd asked her. This isn't up for debate."

"He's marrying a woman we haven't even met after knowing her a couple of weeks. Don't you find that odd? I also find it very hard to believe that he'd settle down after so many." She stopped, and Jesse motioned her to keep moving. She did. "It's completely unrealistic that the witness would be moving in front of the window *all* the time." She went to the drapes and pulled them closer together. Anyone watching could see her silhouette because the light was on behind her.

"We agreed that we'd stop at eight thirty-five. So you have five more minutes."

She twisted her hands, flipped the long hair of the wig off her sweaty neck. "This thing is so hot. I don't miss long hair at all. It weighs a ton."

"Yep."

He agreed with her, just as he had the other twenty times she'd complained about it. She needed to stop but was afraid he'd want to really talk.

Laughing off that he'd said the *L* word... She still didn't know if that was good or bad. She hadn't determined if he wasn't talking to her because they'd simply been too busy getting this sting operation organized. Or because he didn't have anything left to say. Or it was a slim possibility—yet highly unlikely—that he'd actually meant it.

She wished it was the highly unlikely scenario. Loving him was second nature to her. But after their conversation about Garrison and the promise, she didn't want Jesse to feel obligated to say he loved her.

"Time."

Jesse turned the lights off. Turned the TV on. They both sat close on the couch as if they were Garrison and his girl, Kenderly—the second witness for the Tenoreno case.

"You have your second Glock on your ankle?"

"Do you?"

"Don't hesitate, Avery. You pull the trigger and don't think about taking this guy alive." He pointed his finger toward the kitchen doorway, then imitated pulling a trigger.

"We need him alive. You know we do. Everyone has emphasized—"

"I don't care. We both know what he's capable of. If he's gotten past the security outside, it means we don't have any backup close enough to help." Jesse squeezed her hand. "No matter what you want to think or hope, no one will get here in time if he gets near you."

"You are so full of optimistic enthusiasm. That was sarcasm, in case you didn't recognize it." She searched his expressive eyes. He meant what he'd said. "Jesse, I'm not sure about just pulling the trigger. I mean, we're law officers. Deadly force is a last resort. Promise me."

He watched the game and didn't answer. He'd said before that he kept his promises. By not giving his word about this…he was sort of promising he would shoot first.

It didn't matter. After everything they'd been through, she knew he'd do the right thing.

The TV could barely be heard. The house they'd chosen had basic cable and they were watching a previously broadcast Major League Baseball game. The organ played. The crowd yelled, "Charge."

And nothing happened.

"We can't do this much longer. Two days is sort of my limit to be stuck inside again. Are we sure that he obtained this address?"

"Relax, Avery," Jesse whispered. But when he dropped his hand on her thigh, she bolted off the couch.

"I need a shower."

"Not unless you want me in there with you." It was obvious that he meant it. "I don't think the vest is that waterproof."

She returned to her assigned seating, tugging on the protection she wore that he'd refused. "Don't read anything into that. I'm not afraid of you, just jumpy."

"Right."

"Do you think this will work?"

"Last chance."

Leaping out of her skin hadn't stimulated the conversation. To prove she wasn't afraid of his touch, she rested her head on his shoulder. Her eyes got heavy. She had dozed several times, hearing different high points of the game. Then it was two different teams playing.

This time when her eyes opened, more than her head was hot. Jesse had his hand over her mouth. She lifted his fingers away when she realized he wasn't looking at her. His focus was on the rear window.

A shadow.

This is it.

They had elected not to use outside electronic surveillance just in case Snake Eyes was watching the area. No panel van or utility vehicle was anywhere near the place. The team was just down the street, a phone call away from saving the day. With the hacking ability their target had shown or hired, she'd talked them out of video cameras in the corner of every room.

Jesse texted a message to Major Parker. The phone vibrated with a message that the shadow they'd seen was not one of the rangers stationed on the perimeter. Everyone outside was ready.

The stakeout team listened to them through their phones. Undercover units did this all the time. Let the screen go black and no one could tell it was on. Both their phones were activated, recording.

The clock was ticking.

"I'm tired. Are you ready for bed?" She opened her eyes wide as she delivered her preassigned dialogue.

His response would be… "I think I'll shower and work this kink out of my neck."

"Meet you in bed, then," she answered.

The television went off and everything was eerily silent. Jesse stood and stretched out his hand, pulling her into his arms. "Shoot him. As much as you'd like to take my head off…just make sure it's him you're aiming at," he whispered, then kissed her forehead.

Snake Eyes wouldn't take them by surprise. They could do this. They were prepared. Avery went to the bedroom and heard the shower turn on. She set the dummies under the covers and took her place in the dark corner. Phone in her pocket, she wanted to talk to the men who had her back. It was better if she let them concentrate on their jobs.

The plan was to have the men guarding the perimeter meet, and instead of immediately turning around, they would carry on a conversation for a few minutes. It would give Snake Eyes an opportunity to breach the house without killing the men.

Shoving off the hot wig, she let it fall to the floor and pulled her Glock, wishing it was a "make my day" .44 Magnum that she held instead. The recoil would have been murder, but if Snake Eyes got that near to her...

Could she kill him as Jesse had instructed?

Could the man she cared for more than any other really want her to? She heard the shower start up.

The Glock rested between her knees from her cut-off corner of the house. She'd set her phone on the nightstand. Over there she had less chance of accidentally disconnecting if she was in a fight.

She sort of wished for the comfort of it in her jeans pocket. *No, stay put and concentrate.* There was no one to protect except herself. At least for the moment. She rested her shoulders propped against the corner, but she wouldn't last long in this position.

Someone *oofed* as they ran into the coffee table in the television room. Their target must have hired another accomplice. She couldn't imagine the professional killer they had set a trap for bumping into a table.

The next sound was a curse word in a familiar voice. She slid up the wall, keeping her weapon in a ready position, but she was pretty sure the body coming through her bedroom door would be...

The lights flipped on.

Garrison.

"What the hell do you two think you're doing?" he shouted.

Her brother looked good. Fit. Rested. The normal

twinkle in his eye contradicted his words. So did his arms that were spread wide waiting for her to enter them. She stayed put.

"I could have shot you." Jesse's voice came from directly behind her twin.

"I should shoot you," Garrison retorted. "What are you thinking dragging my sister into this mess?"

"Me? Drag? You need to get your facts straight."

"Guys." She tried to interrupt.

"I know what I'm talking about. I've been fully briefed in spite of your efforts to prevent it." Garrison's fingers rested through his belt loops. He looked at ease, not worried about a thing—at least at first glance. All of his body language had changed as soon as he laid eyes on Jesse.

"Guys," she tried again. It reminded her of the summer she'd been invisible. No matter what she did, she couldn't get the attention of either of the boys. She'd even pretended to drown in the swimming pool. They'd both gone on with their horsing around while the lifeguard rescued her.

"If you knew your sister, you'd have figured out a long time ago that no one drags her anywhere. You've been practically on vacation for the last month."

"Vacation? I was on assignment, nearly getting my head blown—"

It might have been easier to go around them, but she shoved through, successfully separating them. She placed her weapon on top of the dresser. Jesse's was at least holstered.

She elbowed her way through again to get to the nightstand, where she'd left her phone, switching it off and cutting one of the connections. Those on the other end of the line must be laughing or seriously cursing. But they would stay where they were, hoping to salvage this mess.

Both men stared at her. "What?" she asked. "Hello, Garrison. What are you doing here? And, Jesse, you should probably have the team stand down."

She led the way out of the bedroom, pausing to turn the water off in the shower then sitting in one of the armchairs. She pressed her palms to her eyes, unable to envision anything but chaos for the next several minutes.

The attempt to block the men's arguing voices from her mind battled with the images of Snake Eyes laughing at their entire sting operation. If he was watching the house, he'd just seen her brother enter. And if he wasn't watching…well, then it had completely failed.

"Oh, would you both just hug it out or something? I need to think." She'd raised her voice. They were both looking at her strangely. "I can tell that you aren't used to me being in charge. Well, guys, I hate to break it to you, but if we're voting…mine's the only one that counts."

"Who asked for a vote?"

"What are we voting on?"

They both spoke at the same time and each poked the other in the chest as if they were teens. "Enough. Seriously. We are all adults and we have a rather difficult problem to solve."

"There's no discussion. You're heading to the house where they're guarding Kenderly." Garrison sat closest to her on the couch. "I'm here to take care of this problem."

"You aren't in charge, pal." Jesse propped the shotgun along the wall and took a seat. He reached for her hand.

What was that supposed to be? A statement of comfort between them or a statement that Garrison didn't have any say over her but Jesse did? *Unreal*.

"Both of you need to shut up and listen."

Surprisingly, they both relaxed against the cushions, waiting. It took a couple of seconds for her to decide where to start. It was with her twin and his tendency to sweep in and come to her rescue.

"I outgrew you bossing me around about ten years ago. You missed it. I let you because I enjoyed hanging around the two of you. I followed after you like a bad habit I refused to kick."

"You don't have to do this tonight, Avery." Jesse had a cautious look that she understood, but ignored.

"Garrison, you haven't explained why you stuck your nose in here during the middle of the night. You probably blew our sting." She popped out of the armchair, adrenaline pumping hard through her veins. "I'm sure you convinced yourself that leaving your protective detail was necessary in order to protect me, but you're wrong."

Exploding like this felt a little freeing. She was ready to bang some heads together, but kept her cool.

"You're overreacting, Avery."

Her brother didn't get it. Until that very minute she hadn't completely understood what living apart from the important people in her life had taught her. Somewhere between the boring, mundane speeding tickets and flat tires she had become an adult. She was capable of making decisions and living on her own.

"I don't need your help, Garrison. Do. Not. Need. Your. Help. Brand it across your forehead or simply repeat after me… 'Avery does *not* need my help.' Can you hear me this time? You've made a very big mistake coming here."

"You might be right about that," her brother mumbled.

"Oh, I know I am. Why would you put this operation at risk? Not to mention that one of your ranger friends could have mistakenly killed you."

"I thought you could use some help, but I needed to eliminate any threat against Kenderly, too." Garrison folded his hands together in his lap, tilting his eyes to the floor.

"Aw...the fiancée we've heard nothing about. If Snake Eyes is watching, he saw you. The whole thing's a bust. Your entire hero routine is for nothing."

Garrison popped his head up to stare at her. She shoved his shoulders back to the couch when he tried to stand. He could stay put; she was the one who needed to move around.

"You know there's more to why I'm here." Garrison's knuckles turned white gripping a throw pillow. "I got you into this mess. It's my responsibility. I'm not going to let you face it alone."

"I'm not. Jesse's here. An entire team of Texas Rangers is across the street. Someday you're going to have to have faith that I'm capable of doing my job."

"Faith has nothing to do with it. I know you're capable, but this wasn't—or shouldn't be—your fight. I didn't jeopardize the operation. Nobody saw me come in here. Nobody. Which in itself is a problem."

"It's part of the trap. Oh, I give up." She turned away, staring out the window.

"Man, you haven't faced this son of a bitch. He's a ghost with connections. We didn't make it a secret we were here waiting on him." Jesse acted relaxed, but his jaw muscles flexed continuously. "That was the plan."

"I guess I sort of messed things up," Garrison admitted.

"I bet that hurt to admit." Jesse snickered behind her. "You knew I was here taking care of things. You could have at least trusted me."

Had he forgotten his role in this debacle? Or that he'd lied to her all those months? She'd barely been angry with him, but suddenly the whole situation seemed to irritate her again.

"You aren't innocent in all this, Jesse Thomas Ryder. Your decisions changed my life last year. Just because we've slept together, that doesn't give you the right to make decisions for me. Or try to talk me out of doing my duty as a cop. This is who I am as much as you. Especially after the week we spent together." She blurted the words, then cringed, realizing that Garrison was still in the room. Well, it didn't matter. She turned to address both of the men in her life. "I am perfectly capable of making my own decisions. You two need to...to just... grow up."

Before her brother or Jesse could react, she bolted from the room. She couldn't referee their arguments or face what they might say about her love life. And she couldn't hang around any longer just waiting for something to happen.

Leave the investigation and manhunt to the competent Texas Rangers. She'd left her own department short-handed long enough. It was time to go home. She returned to the bedroom, locked the door and dialed Major Parker.

Chapter Twenty-Two

Jesse watched Avery retreat to the bedroom. He wanted to go after her, but she was already upset with him sticking his opinion into her life. He didn't know he'd stood until Garrison's blow knocked him to the couch.

"You slept with my sister!"

Jesse rubbed his jaw. "I probably deserved that from her brother. And because I did, I'm not getting up to pound your face."

"You swore to me," the man who was like his brother whispered. "When? Last year? Is that what she meant about changing her life? Have you been lying to me for a year?"

"You have to calm down, Garrison. We have bigger catfish to fry."

"Dammit, Jesse. I came as soon as I heard what was going on. They should have told me sooner." He crashed back to the couch looking very defeated and speaking softly. "How could you do this to her? Now she'll never come home from the Panhandle."

"Don't let her hear you say that. You haven't spoken to her about her job or her life since she left. So don't blame me for what's going on between you guys." He'd accept the blame. He just wouldn't admit that to anyone but Avery. That was between him and her.

"You slept with her, man."

"It's not what you think."

Jesse's lifelong friend jumped up and paced the inside wall, obviously shaken by Avery's revelation. "I don't see how it could be much different unless you tell me it didn't happen."

"I can't do that. It happened, and if I have my way, it'll happen again." Jesse slumped in his chair, matching Garrison's dismayed attitude look for look. "I know I broke my promise to you. But like I said. It's not what you think. I'm trying to keep a promise to myself. And if she'll have me, one to Avery. I told her I loved her."

"You mean that? So you two are getting married." His best friend looked surprised.

Why? Was it so hard to believe that someone would fall in love with his sister? Or was it that Jesse Ryder had fallen for her?

"She accused me of kidding around." Resulting in the longest three days of his life.

"But you meant it? You weren't joking? You're really in love with Avery?" He glared down from above his chair. "So why didn't you just set her straight?"

"You seriously don't know your sister." Jesse shook his head, wondering how long he had to put up with the Garrison grilling. And when the roller coaster of up-and-down emotions would end. "She never gave me a chance to say it was for real. We haven't had much of a chance to talk since then. Well, we've been a little busy."

"I see."

Jesse looked at his friend, who shouldn't have a clue. The charmer who could talk his way out of every situation had nothing more to say? Maybe he did understand. They hadn't spoken more than a couple of sentences in the time that he claimed to have fallen in love.

Jesse looked around the dark room, wondering not only what to say but what would go wrong next. "Dammit, the phone. The team is still listening to this."

He leaped to where he'd left the cell a few feet away. The conversation was one way, but he knew they were there. The guys who would use his confession to razz him for the rest of his career. They'd never let him live this down.

As soon as he disconnected, it vibrated.

"I stuck my neck out for you," Parker said. "Can you explain why one Travis is there instead of at a safe house under protective custody? And the other Travis just notified me she's returning to Dalhart?"

"The first Travis can answer for himself. I'll find out what's up with Avery." He handed the phone over to Garrison and in two shakes was knocking on the bedroom door.

"Avery, we need to talk." He couldn't hear anything on the other side of the door. Had she already slipped by him to leave through the back? She was too smart to leave on her own and had already requested an escort from Parker. "Avery? Open the door."

Training kicked in. He didn't think, just trusted his instincts that something was wrong. Gun in hand, his boot was on the door handle busting through. He felt Garrison behind him, hand on his shoulder, tapping him forward.

They'd practiced the entry hundreds of times over the years. This time meant everything. And there was nothing there.

No Avery. No weapon. No bag on top of the dresser.

And no cell.

"Call Parker. Snake Eyes is out there."

"You don't know that, man." Garrison argued, but holstered his SIG and swiped numbers on the phone.

"She's gone and the bastard has her because Parker doesn't."

"The patrol may not have— No, you're right. He has to have her."

Jesse had to think fast. Snake Eyes would. He'd leave the talking and explanations to Garrison. Forensics would be too late and they wouldn't find anything. So he left through the yard.

The guards were out cold, drugged but alive. It was doubtful they'd seen anything. And if they had, it would be too late by the time they woke up.

"Why take her? Why not just kill her here? He doesn't need her. He should have known that Garrison was in the next room." Jesse weighed one side then the other. He and Avery had made more progress when they approached from the view of Snake Eyes, but he couldn't find a logical reason for the man's actions.

Their adversary had taken an unpredictable road. That was the rub. They thought Snake Eyes was obsessed with completing this job. So why was Garrison still alive?

It was no longer about the Tenoreno contract. Now it was about the woman he loved.

"Avery!" he shouted, his voice carrying into the dark. "Avery!"

Chapter Twenty-Three

Avery had walked straight into his arms, seeking a protective escort. Straight from the men she loved most in life to the animal who scared the life from her.

"Avery!" Jesse's voice called in the distance. "Avery!"

"Keep walking, Deputy Travis."

It was one of the oldest tricks in the book. "You took out one of the guards and dressed in his shirt. I practically tripped over you coming out of the house."

As the ranger posted on the west side of the house, he'd grunted, had a hand on her weapon and turned to stare at her with those reptile contacts. Then he'd dropped her phone. Never appearing in a hurry or as if he was worried about a thing. Especially a bunch of Texas Rangers following his trail.

Hooded, he pointed for her to lead the way between houses with no fences. Old neighborhoods that didn't fear the people who lived next door. Three streets behind her, she'd left the new edition of unfinished rooms where they'd set their trap.

But it was the middle of the night and everyone was asleep. She'd been warned first thing that if she cried out for help, whoever answered that plea would be shot with her gun.

"You're fascinating, Avery. And smart. Probably smart enough to know that you don't have long to live." Snake Eyes found an entrance gate from the utility-access path between the homes. "Your problem isn't that you aren't good enough to bring me down. It's that all the people surrounding you aren't as good. The best defense is usually the best offense. Don't you agree?"

"If we'd known where to take the fight, you're right—we would have taken it to you."

"I'm very glad to learn you've suffered no ill effects from the shocking experience in Thompson Grove."

"I turn on lightbulbs when I hold them now, but everybody thinks it's a good party trick."

"Aw, a sense of humor about your misadventure. As charming as your brother."

Avery felt sick to her stomach. The question of why he hadn't just burst into the house and killed them all as they were arguing still loomed as bright as that bulb she nervously joked about. Then he used the words *fascinating* and *glad* and *charming*. Yeah, she was getting sick at the thought he liked her.

For a man who'd never left behind a trace of himself, it bothered her that he was pushing through gates and lifting latches as if no one would be following them.

It bothered her a lot. Even after hearing Jesse shout her name into the night, Snake Eyes hadn't run or even walked faster. *He doesn't think anyone can catch him.*

The road they were on had no street lamps. The houses were farther apart. He shoved her into the side of a luxury car. *I can't get inside that car.*

The thought that it was all over if she did was all she could focus on. The thought repeated over and over in her mind. He had a gun and the knife he'd placed to her throat before. But she turned from the car, hands in a single fist, and hit him in the side where Jesse had stabbed the rake. He hissed in pain.

She prepared for his backhanded slap, rolling with the sting but losing a lot of the force behind it. She spun away from Snake Eyes, dropping to the ground, searching for a stick or rock. Hoping for a piece of glass. Nothing but dirt.

The reptile contacts glowed brighter with him surrounded by the dark.

Dirt. She dug her nails into the earth, coming up with a fistful when he lifted her to her feet.

"I would expect nothing less from you, Avery. If you didn't give me your best, I wouldn't be compelled to try my worst. But I've brought you an incentive to behave."

"There's nothing that's going to make me get in that car easily. I'm surprised you haven't used your knockout drug."

He opened the door to where a young woman sat. Her eyes were wide with fright, makeup smeared from crying a long time. She was gagged and both her hands and feet were bound.

"You see, Avery? Incentive."

"This doesn't involve her."

The woman tried to scream as he shut the door and clicked a lock. She was hysterical, thinking that Snake Eyes intended to kill her. Avery knew, too. It was a one-way ticket if she got in that car.

"Well, she has kept her part of the bargain. She did give me the address where you were staying. I could let her go if you promised to cooperate." Snake Eyes gestured for her to get into the car.

Avery shook her head. "Not…not until you let her

out. Leave her on the street just like she is…but she's left here. Then I'll go with you."

"Deal, Deputy." He pointed her weapon at her again. "Now give me your word."

"Why do you need me to promise?"

"I trust you, Avery." He cocked his head to the side, waiting for her answer.

Avery shoved her hand with the dirt into her pocket. If she gave him a face full of dirt now, the car was locked and she wouldn't get the keys before he reacted. She could wait until the door was open, but the woman was so hysterical she might think they were taking her into the trees to kill her.

Unfortunately, the best scenario was to get the woman out and wait for a chance to get away.

"I promise, on my father's grave…" *…that I will take you down tonight or die trying.*

"Good. Good." He opened the door again, grabbed the woman's ropes and yanked her from the car. He pulled her across the grass, gun pointed first at the woman, then at Avery.

To her credit, the woman didn't make it easy. She tried to be difficult, bucking with muffled screaming. Avery got halfway into the car, waiting to see if the gun fell away from her direction so she could run.

Snake Eyes didn't drop her from his aim. He moved the girl behind some bushes and left her there, then came back to Avery. He took plastic cuffs from his pocket and tightened them around her wrists. She sat and he placed another pair around her ankles after removing her boots.

Then he laughed, throwing back his head. As he did, she finagled a boot to slip to the ground. The door shut and she prayed that her father was keeping an eye on her tonight.

Jesse would find it. He'd find her. They'd get out of this mess. There had to be a way out.

It HAD BEEN almost ten minutes when Jesse pulled onto the third street. The surveillance team agreed that Snake Eyes had to be on foot. Garrison had taken the north streets and Jesse headed south. Back and forth along the streets, one extra block either direction. The team was out beyond the first three blocks.

One more turn and he'd have to admit defeat. How had Snake Eyes got her cooperation? It didn't make—

A boot was next to the curb. He cut the engine of the motorcycle to pick it up, taking a close look at the darkened homes along the unlit sidewalk.

"Help!"

It was a muffled "help," but still a cry for help. He came off the bike so fast it toppled to its side. He hurdled a shrub, nearly landing on a woman. He knelt, removing the gag.

"Please help me. He's crazy. I think...I think he's going to kill her."

Jesse didn't have to ask who. Avery's boot on the side of the road told him she had got inside the car. He dialed Parker, giving him the address. Then Garrison.

"He's got her, buddy. Meet me three blocks my direction. Can't miss me."

"I'm Texas Ranger Jesse Ryder, ma'am. What's your name?"

"Um... Cindy Crouch. He had pictures of my little boy and said if I didn't find the address for him that he'd… He said horrible things. I brought it to him and then he drugged me."

"You're very lucky to be alive." Those were the wrong words. She'd been coherent before. Now she was just hysterically crying. "It'll be okay. Help's on its way."

"You. You might…catch them," she managed to say between gulps of air. "I'm okay. Go."

"Can you describe the vehicle?" He propped her up against a tree.

"Black Lexus, tinted windows, Texas tags KWX198."

"You're sure about that?"

"I took a good look when he moved me over here. I… She only got in that car to save me." Cindy began crying again.

"Give them the car's description first. You can save her." Jesse started the bike as cars rushed up behind him. He didn't stay for a plan to be developed.

His only hope was that Snake Eyes would be driving the speed limit so as not to draw attention to himself. There was one way out of the subdivision. Two directions from there.

"Garrison, I'm hitting the main road and taking it west. You've got east. Black Lexus, dark windows, KWX189. We have to find her."

"Taking it east and we will, man. We will."

He put the phone away and sped up. He had a fifty-fifty chance Snake Eyes was heading west. The open fields seemed to fit what they knew about him when he killed. He took the hill, searching for taillights.

Nothing.

Remember that this bastard is smart. He might have turned off the lights. If he did…he'd be going slower.

There wasn't a moon, no way to naturally light up the two-lane road.

Jesse would find him. There was no way Snake Eyes would be terrorizing anyone else.

THEY WERE OUT of the subdivision. Snake Eyes was humming under his hood. It wasn't a song that Avery recognized. Why did it matter? It didn't. Another distraction. Good for her because he was less likely to hear her popping the plastic cuffs against the seat next to her.

For the past eight months, nights off meant cable television or studying on the internet. She'd decided to test the plastic handcuffs normally used with riots. If you hit them hard enough, they'd break. Just like the instruction video had suggested.

The humming wouldn't cover the noise. She had to wait or he'd have the gun back in her face.

"Why me? I thought Tenoreno hired you to take care of the witnesses to his wife's murder." Avery wanted to see his face, wanted to rip the contacts out of his eyes and make him normal.

"I have special plans for you, Avery. I think you and Snake Eyes are going to have hours of fun together."

That was *not* normal. Her imagination didn't need a lot of help figuring out what this awful man meant. "Wait. Aren't *you* Snake Eyes?"

"There is a little bit of him in all of us, I suppose."

"All of you? If you aren't him, then who are you?" This was freakier than anything she'd had to deal with throughout her career. This was the same man she and Jesse had faced in Dalhart. He had the wounds proving it.

"I wouldn't be a good associate if I gave my name to you so easily."

"Then maybe you can explain why Snake Eyes wants me? Why is he fascinated with me?" She could see around the front headrest and noticed that the lights were off. There was no one around for miles.

"I see you inching toward the middle of the car. Please move toward the door."

Avery replayed the man's voice in her head. It had the slightest British accent. A different cadence in the phrasing. If she didn't know that the same man who put her in the car was still driving it, she might have thought a second had been waiting to drive them away.

There was just one man. Snake Eyes, the murderer.

"We never got to finish phase two of my project with you and Jesse. I'm afraid you took me by surprise by escaping the collar. And I'm afraid that Scott was just too useless. The other two young men, well… They were fine with setting the fires for the right amount of money. But when it came to abducting a deputy sheriff and a Texas Ranger… Let's just say I won the argument."

That sounded just like the man behind the hood.

"Phase two?"

"That's right. I never got to explain it." He slapped his thigh and hummed his tune. He wasn't going to give her any extra time to think her way out of his plan by giving her a warning.

Avery heard the motorcycle. Seconds later, Snake Eyes turned off the road. She wasn't certain he knew where he was, but she could tell it was unplanned by the way he looked around the field. It was easy enough to decipher that even if it wasn't Jesse, he didn't want the car he was driving spotted.

It was her last chance at getting help.

She twisted her body and grabbed the dirt in her pockets, then hit the cuffs against the seat. Then hit them again.

Snake Eyes swerved enough that the tires fell off the smoother ruts of the dirt road. She hit the seat and pulled, breaking the cuffs from her wrists. Her captor stepped on the gas, throwing her to the side. Her feet were behind him, so she kicked while he swerved.

When he turned to see what she was doing, she threw the dirt in his face.

He stomped on the brakes and threw the car in Park. The gun must have slid away from him, because he began searching around his legs. While his body was bent, she climbed on top of him and honked the horn.

Short. Short. Short. Long. Long. Long. Short. Short. Short.

Short. Short.

Snake Eyes stuck the gun against her jawbone. "Valiant effort, Avery. Too bad no one can hear you."

She raised her hands and sat on the smooth leather seat.

"Out of the car. Do it. Now." He popped the trunk.

Her first thought was that he was going to put her inside. She could break a taillight, get someone's attention. Then she saw the wire, the duct tape, the vials of drugs. And just as a chef unrolled his knives before he began cooking, Snake Eyes displayed his instruments of death.

Chapter Twenty-Four

The horn had been faint at seventy miles an hour on a motorcycle. Jesse almost ignored it. Then he came to a skidding stop and knew the SOS was Avery and did a U-turn.

Leaving the bike on the side of the road, he used Avery's shotgun to hold the barbwire fence away from his face as she went through. On the other side, he sent a text to Garrison and Parker, then switched his cell to silent mode before stuffing it in his jeans pocket. He watched the dirt road, listened without hearing anything—even bugs.

On the next rise he got low to the ground and shoved his way behind a pile of dry brush and dead branches. He could see the black car's silhouette, along with Avery.

Snake Eyes had her on her knees and was wrapping something around her neck. She wasn't attempting to get away or struggling. He bent and yanked her head backward, then connected whatever was around her neck to her hands. She cried out in surprised pain.

Whatever the madman had planned to do with Avery when he casually left the subdivision, it was clear that things had changed. Snake Eyes paced the length of the car, hitting his forehead, clearly shaken by whatever had given Avery the opportunity to sound the horn.

He walked to the trunk. The light reflected off a slew of knives neatly laid out in rows. Jesse had to get to Avery fast. Her captor had changed. He was no longer cool and collected, and his hands shook with such force Jesse could see them.

Snake Eyes fingered several knives before dropping the largest and walking away. Jesse began breathing a little easier, but then his target hurried to the trunk and placed the knives in order, talking to himself.

"He's nuts," Jesse mumbled.

No time to lose, Jesse backed out of the brush to approach from the front of the car. It was darker there and should give him an advantage. The closer he got, the more he heard Snake Eyes mumbling.

"Kill her now and forget your fun." He pivoted.

"But you left her new eyes at home," he answered in a different voice.

"Forget your signature—everyone will know it's you. Kill her!" He twisted his head as if listening for Jesse. Then kept up his argument.

Totally nuts.

Closer, Jesse crawled on his belly. If Snake Eyes came to this side of Avery, one blast from the shotgun and he'd be stunned for a few minutes. As luck would have it, he continued his debate with himself at the trunk. He'd lift a knife, walk in front of Avery, point it, shake his head, then return it to his stash.

Avery was in the light from the car door. Jesse could see that she was wrapped in wire. Loops around her feet stretching to her hands, multiple wraps around her hands connecting tightly to strands around her neck.

If she moved her hands or feet, she'd pull the wire into her neck. Hell, if she fell forward she might slice her neck open.

He couldn't get her free from that mess without wire cutters. He'd have to unwrap the wire by hand. And he had no time. There wouldn't be any distractions, then swooping in to pull her out.

His only choice was to remove the threat. And he had to get closer if he intended to use this shotgun to do it. At her Dalhart house, having buckshot wasn't a terrible decision. It gave Avery enough range and power inside.

Here was a different story. He might hit his target from twenty yards, but he was at least thirty or thirty-five from Avery. To his right, the car blocked everything. To his left, the only cover was well over seventy-five yards away.

Snake Eyes was sure to hear him moving through the grass and twigs before he got close enough. Opposite was the road. Pretty much flat and bare about ten yards on either side. This was his only route.

Getting to Avery would be tricky, and once there, he couldn't get her free, couldn't knock her over. She was close enough to Snake Eyes for him to slice her open or just shoot and kill her. Jesse didn't like his odds. He could save Avery by simply eliminating the target.

This was one time in his life that he wished he could just damn the consequences and head in guns blazing without thinking about it. No thinking. Avery needed him to save her. But he had to think. It was who he was.

Who he was... A planner who thought about everything too much.

Weapons... He'd take the shotgun and keep his handgun ready. Safer. Better coverage. But he'd still have to aim. If Snake Eyes kept up his monologue with the knives, Jesse would be aiming at a moving target for eight or nine more passes. He'd be hard to hit.

Position... He moved to his left for a better line of sight.

Rescue... Then what?

No choice... Take out the target so the hostage would no longer be threatened.

Execution... He inched his way through the field. He had a decent shot. He aimed. He tried to pull the trigger.

All he heard was Avery's voice telling him she wouldn't use deadly force as long as there was a chance. She would shoot to defend herself. This was why they practiced and trained...so they wouldn't think; they'd just do.

Delay... She was right. He loved her with everything and he still couldn't just shoot a man in cold blood. No matter what kind of man the target was.

With his hesitation, he'd lost opportunity.

Snake Eyes had something in his hand and quickly got behind Avery. *I can't be off six inches or I'll hit her.* "Raise your hand, you son of a—"

His body was braced. He was ready with a follow-through shot and began squeezing. But he immediately stopped when Snake Eyes snipped the wire connecting to Avery's feet.

What was the perp going to do now?

"You are quite a subject, Avery Travis," Snake Eyes said. "I haven't had many who could balance without their panic forcing me to intervene."

She continued to be perfectly still. Jesse didn't know how she was doing it. He kept his finger ready. He'd shoot before she could be hurt.

Snake Eyes forced her to her feet. She turned, refusing to get inside the car.

"You can do whatever you want. Do you understand me?" She'd raised her voice.

The words were for him. She knew—or hoped—he was there. She stepped away from her captor. One small step, then another long one before Snake Eyes realized why.

Jesse pulled the trigger, sending buckshot into the man's side.

Avery ran. Arms twisted high behind her, she ran.

Snake Eyes dropped to the ground, then half crawled, half dragged himself into the backseat.

"Jesse!"

"Over here!" They met a little off the road. "This is the fastest way to the bike."

"He's got the car. Can you…?" She stretched her neck and turned for him to help untie her. "Two guns that I know of."

Headlights bathed them in light as Snake Eyes bore down on them. If she fell, the thin wire could slice her windpipe, but they ran anyway. Jesse couldn't stop to untwist the wire yet. Up and over the slight rise. The car followed, bouncing through the uneven field, heading to cut them off.

"This way. Do you see them? He can't follow through the stacked hay bales," Avery said, sliding to her knee. She needed her hands. It was too dangerous for her to keep going like this. "We can still get to the motorcycle, can't we?"

"If he stays on the road, he'll cut us off or be waiting on us. Stop behind the hay bale for a sec. You need to be free." The shotgun dropped to his feet as he used both hands to untwist. "This thing is worse than a bread tie."

NO DEBATE. JUST ACTION and keeping herself from inappropriately laughing at his analogy. Avery lifted her hands behind her as high as possible. It was a bit painful as Jesse twisted and then twisted some more. It was frightening to think of what might have happened if she'd moved before her feet had been snipped free.

Don't go there. Think about now. They were being surrounded in more light from the car. One wrist could now move.

"You have to hurry, Jesse."

"Just a couple more and we're…there. That's it."

She started to face him, but he held her in place. She felt him gathering the wire and shoving it down the back of her shirt.

"Done. Now you won't get caught. Let's go."

The wire still around her neck reminded her of the shock collar. The helplessness knowing that a sadistic monster had control of her fate. As they took the first steps, the car drew closer to them and Snake Eyes fired.

Jesse dropped to the ground, pulling her with him. He swung the shotgun around and fired the second barrel into the side of the car. Snake Eyes drove past and circled. They had seconds before he'd be able to fire at them again.

"You're going to listen to me for once, Avery. No questions."

"I'm not leaving you." She couldn't save herself while he stayed behind.

"I didn't think you would. But one of us has to get to the road and let the team know where we are." He gave her the shotgun and the phone. "Empty. But you can swing it, okay? First, climb the hay, babe. Up and over. Can you do that? Get clear on the other side and call Garrison. He's on his way. He just isn't in the right place yet."

She nodded. He was right. To a point. Snake Eyes wouldn't be looking above Jesse's head. She could take him by surprise. "Don't do anything stupid."

"Count on it. Now get out of here so I can stall him."

Jesse cupped his hands and gave her a boost high onto the bales. They were packed firmly and close together. She lay on her belly, getting ready to swing when Snake Eyes got close.

And he would get close. Even though he had the guns, he was fascinated and fixated on his knives. He was a sicko who would want to end Jesse with a blade.

"Here he comes," Jesse said below her. "Get ready to move. Please do this, Avery. For me."

Avery backed away from the edge so the headlights wouldn't shine on her. It was so dark out here that when you were out of the beam, you couldn't be seen. Snake Eyes pulled around wide.

The back of the car fishtailed across the pasture. He was going to ram Jesse and the stack of hay. The engine revved. The headlights blinded. She screamed Jesse's name, but he was already on his toes like someone playing chicken with a two-ton vehicle.

Snake Eyes didn't flinch. He shot forward. Jesse jumped out of the way at the last second. The car struck the bales, shaking her to one side. She clawed her way back to the top.

Jesse was already pulling the stunned Snake Eyes from the car. He quickly jerked away from a knife arcing toward his abdomen. Jesse continued backing away but took off his shirt and wrapped it around his forearm. It stopped the blade from slicing his skin to the bone and allowed him to get closer.

The headlights were buried in hay, creating an eerie effect. Avery jumped to the hood of the car, waiting for Snake Eyes to get closer. She had the stock of the shotgun raised and ready to hit the back of his hooded head.

Then the fight changed.

Snake Eyes locked his arms around Jesse's midsection and started moving the knife closer to his throat. He absorbed Jesse's elbow that repeatedly hit him in the side. The murderer ignored the pain he must have felt because of the shotgun blast. With his other hand, Jesse kept the knife inches away, holding it at bay.

The madman's grip around Jesse's middle had him pinned. Jesse threw his head backward, connecting with the man's nose. Then Snake Eyes spun him and shoved him into the car trunk, backing away. He pulled his mask off his head, sniffing at the blood coming from his nose.

"Avery, Avery, Avery," Snake Eyes chanted. "Here I am. Can you see me?"

She could barely make out the outline of his face. She didn't have to see his features to know the man had experienced a psychotic break. He spun around like a child watching snowflakes fall.

Jesse roared like a lion, shoving away from the car and throwing his shoulder into Snake Eyes's belly. He tackled him to the ground like a linebacker sacking a quarterback. Snake Eyes just wouldn't stay down. He fought like a crazy person who needed a straitjacket.

The glowing contacts made spotting Snake Eyes eas-

ier. A punch caught Jesse in the chin, momentarily shooting him backward, but he returned with three quick jabs.

Get the guns! Avery jumped from the hood, determined to find them inside the car. She could end this
with a loaded weapon in her hand. Snake Eyes would be
forced to stop. But when her feet hit the dirt, she caught
the attention of their attacker.

He raised the knife with a maniacal cry and sliced
into Jesse's uncovered arm. Jesse staggered. Snake Eyes
was on her so fast she couldn't react. He shoved her back
against the car, holding the knife to her throat.

"I wanted to play with you, Avery. We all did."

His rancid breath choked her after the sweet-smelling
hay. The edge of the sharp blade held her where she was.
She could see the dust floating in the buried lights. She
would have been as crazy as Snake Eyes if she hadn't
been frightened.

But she wasn't crazy. She had reason for hope. Jesse
was slowly approaching.

"See the special eyes I have for you?" Snake Eyes
took two rocks from his pocket and pushed her face to
the hood. They were cool against her cheek where he
set them.

As the blade moved from her neck to the corner of
her eye, she asked, "What…what color did…did you
choose for me?"

He seemed excited that she was curious. She didn't
really want to know. Ever. She was trying to stall to give
Jesse time. Still holding the shotgun, she wanted to club
Snake Eyes with it but couldn't.

If she moved, the knife point might take out her eye.
Jesse was close. She shoved the knife away from her
face and kicked the shotgun to him. Snake Eyes turned

to face Jesse. She rammed the crazy man in the back, causing him to stumble forward, away from her.

Jesse brought the butt of the gun straight up, hitting Snake Eyes's chin. The man lost his balance when his head snapped back. Jesse hit him again in the gut. The knife fell to the ground and Avery kicked it under the car.

Snake Eyes fell near the hay and stayed there. He didn't get up. Finally. She could no longer see the contacts that haunted her dreams.

"You didn't leave," Jesse panted between inhaling deep breaths. He shut off the car.

The world was strangely silent.

"You've got my back. I've got yours. That's the way it works." They walked toward each other.

"Next time—"

"There isn't going to be a next time."

"Point taken. But if we're ever in a…situation…try to remember I can handle the bad guy on my own." He tugged her close into the circle of his arms and kissed her quick, hard and possessive. "Your gun?"

"Should still be in the front seat."

"If he moves…"

She had the shotgun poised and ready to knock him for a loop again. "Got it covered."

Jesse found her Glock, picked up the cell from the ground and handed it to her. "Can you make sure those guys haven't missed the turn? Garrison should have been right behind me."

"Sure." With one hand she called Major Parker, who said they estimated that they were two minutes out. With the other she kept the crazy man they'd fought at gunpoint. Injured or not, she wasn't allowing him any freedom.

The Snake Eyes Killer's side was soaked red from the

buckshot, and the wound on his head had left a streak across his uncovered face. Jesse used the shirt he'd fended off the knives with to slow the man's bleeding.

She was proud of Jesse for being such a good man. She wasn't certain she would have helped the monster who had nearly killed them.

"There's more wire and tape in the trunk. Get it. We can't let him hurt anyone else."

Instead of going to the back of the car, Jesse pried the shotgun from her fingers. "Go sit down. I'll watch him."

"He deserves to be tied to where he can't move. We shouldn't have to think about him ever again." She wanted to secure him just as he'd tied her, but that wouldn't happen. Wire around his wrists should be enough. She'd make certain two rangers escorted him to the hospital and kept him handcuffed.

"He's not going to hurt anyone again. It'll be okay, Avery."

Even unconscious he was dangerous. Everyone needed to know that. "He's crazy treacherous. They need to be warned."

"Yeah, babe. We know. He's not going anywhere while I'm watching him. I promise, he's still out cold. Let me get this off of you." He twisted the knots of wire from her neck and dropped it on the ground. Then tipped his head toward the road.

Multiple vehicles were turning, and leading them all was a lone motorcycle. She had a few seconds at most. There was no telling how long it would be before they were alone again. There'd be statements and debriefings and whatever else the state needed for their case.

"Jesse, I just want to say that— Well, you know I'm

grateful. Thanks for finding me. I couldn't have gotten out of this one."

"Sure you would have, Avery. You were always smarter than him." He tucked her into the fold of his arm and kissed her forehead.

This man was everything she'd ever wanted. When was he going to realize they needed each other? More and more of the team arrived, shining headlights and flashlights on them and the scene. They suggested they sit in a car, offered them first aid and asked them to move away from Snake Eyes. But they didn't.

They stood with their arms around each other, sort of in a daze. She didn't know about Jesse, but she didn't really hear what they were saying. She took a bottle of water, and Garrison pried her free when the second ambulance arrived.

The guys said it was shock. The logical side of her agreed they were right. The emotional side of her watched Jesse from the gurney. There was no going back to the way things were before. They'd reached a turning point.

It was over. Everything was over.

Chapter Twenty-Five

The last time Avery had sat at a picnic table, both she and Jesse were barefoot. She'd had a shock collar around her neck. And she was wondering if they'd really get away from Thompson Grove alive.

No one had found her boots. Just an everyday pair she didn't mind replacing. Jesse's had been found on the feet of Scott Sutter. He didn't take them from the young dead man. Horrible to think no one took responsibility for him. They hadn't found any family yet.

"Enough about that." She checked her watch one more time. "He is late. So late."

She saw the white hat before anything else. Her heart literally skipped a beat in anticipation. But it wasn't Jesse. Her brother had been in the building and now was heading toward her.

"Clearly you don't need me coming to your rescue any longer. Looks like you can take care of yourself," Garrison admitted.

"Took you long enough to realize that *and* to find us in that field."

"I was sent for the cavalry. That takes time." He compressed his lips as if he wanted to say something.

"Where have they been hiding you?"

"I can't say, for obvious reasons. And they'll move Kenderly soon anyway. But it wasn't far from where they set up your sting. That's how I got there before they really knew I was gone."

"Makes sense."

Garrison pulled her close, squeezing her in a bear hug. "Avery," he whispered. "I'll always come to help whether you can fend for yourself or you find someone to help with that job. You're my sister. You'll always be my sister. I just came because I love you and would never forgive myself if something happened to you."

"I love you, too. And that's exactly how I felt when you were in trouble." She let him go and he stood protectively with his arm around her for a few seconds, gave her another squeeze and moved.

More men—rangers in white hats—walked to a car in the lot. "I've got to go."

"Sure."

"He's a good man." Garrison walked backward, pointing at her. "You need to give him a chance."

"What are you talking about?" But she knew. Jesse must have said something to him.

Blurting out that they'd slept together had put Jesse in an awkward position. And regarding her sex life, her brother treated her like an old-fashioned overprotective father would. Of course, he wanted them to get together.

Well, he'd get over it.

Now that she knew she was good enough to be a Texas Ranger—that she'd almost been one—it was a little awkward sitting in the park behind the headquarters for Company F. But she was over it. Dalhart might be on the edge of Texas—almost New Mexico, almost Oklahoma—but it was where she belonged.

Her home and friends were there. All but one of them...

Jesse walked up with a picnic basket. Officially in his white hat, his white shirt, jeans, new boots and his badge hanging over his heart.

"Thanks for having lunch with me before you head home to Dallam County."

"The least I could do for the man who saved my life. How's your arm?"

"Good. Stitches. They said there would be a scar."

He'd always have a reminder from that crazy night and crazy man.

"So I guess I'll see you again when it's time for Buster 'Snake Eyes' Hopkins to go on trial. It might be a long time. It seems he's gone pretty crazy." She tucked her bangs under a Stetson her mom had given her.

"Nice hat." He unpacked sandwiches in plastic bags, homemade potato salad.

Recognizing his mother's handiwork, her mouth watered a little for the picnic dessert... Yes, there they were—two individual servings. "It's been ages since I had your mom's banana pudding."

"She made a batch this morning. One of the reasons I'm late."

Avery helped him with the rest of his mother's basket supplies. An official picnic with cutlery, plates, wineglasses...and food.

"The hat was Dad's. It's a little big."

"Doesn't look like you'll have trouble fitting it. I think he'd be real proud of you, Deputy Travis."

"And of you, Ranger Ryder." She took a bite of the pimento-cheese sandwich...also her favorite. Then waited while he poured the fruity wine she liked. In fact, everything on the table was her favorite. "What's going on, Jesse?"

"Just trying to be nice."

"Are you forming words in your head? Looking for the right way to say something?"

"No. Why don't you go ahead and eat. You'll have plenty of time to get to the airport."

The situation made her a little tense. They could have stopped anywhere and grabbed a burger. He'd gone to a lot of trouble to make sure she had a pleasant picnic that included her favorite plain ruffled potato chips.

"I was about to say that I think my father would have been proud of you and Garrison."

"Are you still upset that you don't work here?" he asked.

"Not anymore."

"Still upset with me or am I forgiven?"

"We're friends for life, Jesse. I was mad for that long." She held her finger and thumb about an inch apart. "I was never going to stay that way. Eat. I'll need to get on the road soon."

His eyebrows rose, ready to ask her something. She responded with all her attention while raising a wineglass to her lips.

"Did you consider taking a later flight? I know your mom would like you to hang around awhile."

"Sorry, I have to get going. The guys have been covering for me long enough. I got a text from Bo that he needs a night out."

"Yeah. That makes sense. You need to work."

"Jesse, what is the matter with you?"

"I just thought we might have a stress-free evening together."

"No can do, my friend." She was really hoping that she'd pulled off the whole friendship thing. No matter what happened between them, she wanted to stay on good-enough terms to talk to each other.

After Garrison told her that he'd met *the one*, it looked as though she and Jesse would be standing up for them. Garrison said they'd be getting married as soon as the trial was over.

The first trial date for Tenoreno to face a jury was in September. So that meant she had to remain all friendly smiles and shoulder punches with Jesse through at least October or November.

The truth was, she didn't want to say goodbye to Jesse. Leaving before had been completely different… They weren't speaking. This time, would he call or text or message her? What would it be like to be his friend after sleeping with him?

Food finished, she put the last chip in her mouth and crunched to get Jesse's attention. He was staring off toward the football stadium. Working up his courage?

Talking himself out of something was more likely. She could see the cogs turning one by one.

"Avery, I wanted to ask… I mean, we never got a chance to hang out and catch up."

Brilliant man, but would he ever learn to just say what he was feeling? *Probably not.*

Hypocrite.

"There's no catching up necessary. Hey, that looks like my ride." She moved to his side of the table and awkwardly hugged him.

"I thought I was taking you."

"Sorry again. Mom and Aunt Brenda asked and I couldn't say no. Like you said, they hardly got to see me."

"But you didn't finish. What about your pudding?" He grabbed the bowl.

"Thanks. Tell your mom I'll return the container next trip home." She took hold of the container and he pulled her hand, forcing her to stumble a little toward him.

Jesse met her halfway, wrapping her in his arms, smashing his lips to hers. Their kiss sent shivers throughout her body to all the right exciting places. And the second, then the third did the same.

If he kept kissing her like this, he didn't have to say anything at all.

"I've got to go."

"I wish you wouldn't."

"It can't be helped." She backed away, tripping on an oak root but catching herself before landing a face-plant in the dirt. He tipped his hat, acknowledging that she was leaving. She couldn't stand the sadness that crept into her heart. So she ran to her mom's car.

"My goodness, Avery. My, my, my," her aunt said.

"How long has that been going on? I thought you were upset with Jesse before this little episode," her mom lectured a bit.

How her mother could categorize two attempted murders on her daughter as a *little episode* was probably how she dealt with both her children serving in law enforcement. Someday it would be a bump of excitement that happened way back when. When the trial was over, she might tell her mother everything that had happened.

"I was a little," she mumbled as the car pulled away and Jesse picked up their lunch. "And I wasn't upset very long."

"Why in the world did he kiss you like that?" the sisters said sort of together.

"Because I...I'm pretty sure he was about to ask me to marry him."

Chapter Twenty-Six

Three weeks later

The ring in Jesse's pocket had been on the tip of his finger so many times, it would have stretched if that had been physically possible. He fingered it constantly. Every time he'd spoken with Avery on the phone, he pulled it out to look at it.

Proposing had been on his mind for a long time. Now it seemed possible.

This was it. He pulled up in front of the tiny house, heart and hat in hand. Either a final chapter or the start of the rest of his life.

"Hey there." Avery sat on the porch. Cutoff jean shorts, black spaghetti straps across her shoulders, black hat on the crown of her head and a shotgun next to her hip. "You're late."

"Hit some construction north of Fort Worth."

"Everybody good at home?" she asked, extending him a beer.

He took it, nodded yes to her question and tapped the bottle neck against hers. "Nice shotgun."

"Saved my life once."

She'd taken him off guard again. All he could think

about were the long legs wrapped around him instead of resting on the top of those steps. And the top she had on had one of those built-in bra things, so it wasn't much of a challenge.

They'd been talking. For hours. They'd known each other their entire lives but still found something else to say. Standing here in front of her, with the most important question clearly ready to be asked, he couldn't figure out how.

"Bo called. Said you were speeding at the edge of town."

"That the reason you have the shotgun ready?"

"Just a reminder. I bring it out with me most days I'm here." Avery traced the initials they'd carved. "I feel Dad's comfort when it's by my side. And I can't help remembering the last time it was used."

Their years of history, their shared experiences— awkward, good, bad or frightening—were something he never wanted to give up. The first and last images of when he'd held the gun flashed in front of his eyes. "I've only been frightened like that one other time in my life. When you pretty much died in my arms."

"You haven't really talked about that or given me details."

Jesse pulled her to her feet. "Promise you won't do that again, Avery."

"I can't. If you're around I hope to die a little in your arms every night."

"That, I think I can live with." He caught a glimpse of the shotgun.

It was sort of like getting permission from Avery's dad. He pulled the ring from his pocket, keeping it in his fist. No box. No flowers. No bended knee. No prepared, memorized words. No special dinner at the closed diner that evening that he'd arranged.

They weren't anywhere special as their parents had advised.

"Avery, I love you. You're a smart woman and I'm sure you've figured that out by now. What you might not know is that there's never been anyone else for me. Life is just better with you in it. Might not have seemed that way when I came here before, but we're better as a team. Always have been."

"I—"

"Hold on. Before you tell me it's a logistical nightmare to have a relationship. I got a transfer to a special unit, so that won't be as much of a problem. I've told you this plenty of times in the last three weeks, but I wouldn't think of asking you to leave the sheriff's department. You're good at your job. They deserve you. No, I'm serious. As long as you like it here, you should stay."

"Jesse—"

"You gotta let me get this out, babe. Would you marry me and put me out of my misery?" He unfolded his fingers, producing the ring.

"If you'd stop talking long enough for me to say yes."

Hands shaking like a dog after a dip in a swimming hole, he slid the ring into place, staring at the smile in her eyes.

Kissing Avery was just about everything to him. Someday he might need more, like a kid or two, but he was whole with her. "You did say yes. Right?"

"I did."

His hands were still shaking. She took them into hers, steadying him. "I have this thing all planned for tonight.

You'll have to act surprised or something. Otherwise, you're going to disappoint the diner folks or your friends."

"I can do that. For such a smart man, it sure took you long enough to figure out I've been in love with you my whole life." She admired the simple ring. "Is this…? It can't be the same one. You went back and found the ring I saw at that antique shop in Austin?"

"I…um…I didn't have to go back."

"But that was— Jesse, that was two years ago."

"Close to it."

He could kiss on her all day. Right there on the porch, learning every possible way to hold her. But there were also more private holds he was ready to discover. He skimmed his hands up her arms, surrounding her delicate yet capable fingers with his, then moved a step toward the door.

Avery stopped him. "That was a beautiful speech. Did it take you the entire drive up here to think it all out?"

"Straight from the heart, babe. I saw your daddy's shotgun and forgot every word in my head."

"That's all I've ever wanted…words from your heart."

"I probably need to cancel the marching band, then."

She laughed, dabbing at her eyes. Then she glanced at his face, which must have let her know he wasn't joking. "You're not serious."

"Yeah, but I can call Julie. She'll cancel."

She flung herself into his arms, knocking their hats to the porch. "Oh no you don't. Words and a ring are great—don't get me wrong. But a marching band? All for me? I'll take it." She kissed him, smiling so bright he was certain she was happy. "I'll also take you."

* * * * *

Angi Morgan's TEXAS RANGERS: ELITE TROOP *miniseries continues this fall. Look for it wherever Harlequin Intrigue books and ebooks are sold!*

WHAT HAPPENS ON THE RANCH

USA TODAY Bestselling Author
DELORES FOSSEN

Chapter One

Anna McCord figured she had committed a couple of sins, maybe even broken a few laws, just by looking at the guy in the bed. He was naked, so it was hard not to have dirty thoughts about him.

Drool, too.

Mercy, he was hot.

Thick blond hair all tousled and bedroomy. Lean and muscled. At least what she could see of him was muscled anyway. He was sprawled out on his stomach, his face cocooned in the fluffy feather pillows of the guest bed. He reminded her of a Viking just back from a good pillaging, minus the bed and feather pillows, of course.

But who was he?

Even though she should have bolted out of there the moment she opened the guest room door and saw a partially exposed butt cheek, Anna stayed put. Someone had obviously glued her feet to the floor. Glued her eyeballs to the hot guy, too.

She glanced around the room and spotted a clue as to who he was. There was a military uniform draped over the back of a chair and a duffel bag on the floor near the bed.

Anna didn't actually need more clues to know he was

an Air Force officer and likely a friend that her brother Riley had brought home. But she also saw the dog tags. The ball chain holding them was still around the hot guy's neck, but the tags themselves were lying askew on the bed like smashed nickels.

Maybe he sensed she was there, because he opened an eye, and the seconds trickled by before it must have registered in his mind that he had a woman ogling him.

He made a grunting sound mixed with some profanity and rolled over, no doubt because that was the fastest way he could reach the sheet to cover himself. However, the rolling over gave her a view of his front side.

Definitely more dirty thoughts.

"Sorry, I didn't know anyone was in here," Anna said, as if that explained the gawking. The drool. The long, heated look that she was giving him.

But both the heated stuff and the drool came to a quick halt when Anna got a better look at his face. "Heath?"

He blinked. "Anna?"

Good gravy. It was Heath Moore, all right. Well, a grown-up Heath anyway. The last time she'd seen him had been nine and a half years ago when he was barely eighteen, but he had filled out a lot since then.

Oh, the memories she had of him came flooding back.

He'd been naked then, too—for part of those memories anyway, since she'd lost her virginity to him. Though she certainly hadn't seen as much of him during that encounter in the hayloft as she'd just witnessed. He had filled out *everywhere*.

He sat up, dragging the sheet over his filled-out parts, and still blinking, he yawned and scrubbed his hand over his face. More memories came. Of his memorable mouth. The equally memorable way he'd kissed her.

She fanned herself like a menopausal woman with hot flashes.

"Why are you here?" she asked at the same moment that Heath asked, "Why are you here?"

Anna figured he was going to have a lot better explanation than she did. "I thought I might have left a book in here," she told him.

A total lie. She had been in search of a book that the housekeeper, Della, had said she'd left in her room on the nightstand. But when Anna had seen the guest room door slightly ajar, she'd opened it and had a look.

She made a show of glancing around for a book that had zero chance of being there since it was all the way at the end of the hall.

"This is your room now?" Heath asked.

"No. But I come in here sometimes. For the view." Anna motioned to the massive bay window. She wouldn't mention that every bedroom on the second floor had similar windows, similar views. As did her own room on the first floor.

Heath glanced in the direction of the bay window as if he might get up to sample that view, but his next glance was at his body. Considering he was naked under the sheet, he probably didn't want to get up until she'd left, and that was her cue to leave. First though, she wanted an answer to her question.

"Why are you here?" she repeated.

"Riley. He saw me at the base in San Antonio and said I needed some…R & R before I left on assignment. He was headed back here to the ranch to finish out his leave, and he asked me to come."

All of that made sense because Riley, too, was an Air Force officer and had indeed been at the base the day before. Yes, it made sense except for Heath's hesitation before R & R.

"You weren't here last night when I went to bed." She would have noticed Heath, that's for sure.

"We stopped for a bite to eat, then to visit some mutual friends, and we didn't get in until late. We didn't want to wake anyone up so Riley just sent me here to the guest room." Heath paused. "Riley's my boss."

Uh-oh. That wouldn't play well with Riley if he found out about her lustful thoughts over his subordinate. It wouldn't play well with Heath, either, since he probably didn't want to do or think anything—or have *her* do or think anything—that would cause his boss to hit him upside the head with a shovel.

A threat that Riley had first rattled off nine and a half years ago when he thought a romance was brewing between Heath and her.

If Riley had known what had gone on in the hayloft, he might not have actually carried through on the shovel threat, but Anna would have never heard the end of it.

And there was that whole underage-sex thing.

When Heath had first started working at the ranch, he'd been eighteen. But she'd been only seventeen. Riley and her other brothers had made a big deal about the attraction they'd sensed going on between Heath and her.

The term *jail bait* had been thrown around.

Since Heath had been making a big deal of his own about going into the military, it was an issue. Heath wanted to go into special ops, which would have required a lengthy background check for a top-secret clearance, and Riley had brought up her age for the sole purpose of scaring Heath into keeping his jeans zipped.

It had worked. Until the day Anna turned eighteen, that is. After that, she'd made the trip to the hayloft with Heath, and she had the memories of the orgasm to prove it.

Heath smiled at her, but it felt as if he'd had to rummage it up just to be polite. Again, the nudity was probably driving that. But the nudity didn't stop him from looking at her with those sizzling blue eyes. Also bedroomy like his hair. He slid his gaze from her head to her toes, lingering in the middle. Lingering especially on her breasts. Perhaps because she was wearing a T-shirt and no bra.

"Riley didn't mention you'd be here at the ranch," Heath said.

"Oh? Well, usually I leave the day after Thanksgiving, but I decided to stay a little longer." Since it was already two days after Thanksgiving, she probably hadn't needed to add that last part. "I'm in law school at University of Texas, but I finished my courses early this semester. I'm also planning a transfer. I need a change of scenery…or something."

And a life.

And perhaps sex, but she'd only gotten that idea when she'd seen Heath naked.

"Yeah, a change of scenery," he repeated, as if he were aware of what she meant by the *or something.*

"So, how long will you be here?" Anna tried to keep her eyes directed just at his face, but her gaze kept drifting a bit to that incredibly toned chest. Either he'd gotten very good with contouring body paints or the man had a six-pack.

"Until the cows come home," he said.

That's when she realized both her eyes and her mind had seriously drifted off, and she didn't have a clue what he'd been talking about before that.

The corner of his mouth lifted. A dreamy smile, and he hadn't had to rummage up this one. It was the real deal.

"I'll be here about two weeks," he said. Probably repeated information. "How about you?"

"Two weeks. More or less. I was going to stay until the final exams were over and the campus was less busy. Then, the plan was to talk to my advisor about the transfer."

"For that change of scenery or something?" Heath made it sound like a question.

Anna pretended not to hear it. No need to get into all that. Instead, she glanced at his left hand, the one part of his body she'd failed to look at during her gawking. No ring.

"I'm not married," Heath volunteered. "Never have been." He looked at her left hand, too, where she was still wearing the opal ring her Granny Ethel had left her.

Anna shook her head. "No I-do's for me, either." Close, though, but best not to get into that after her change-of-scenery slip. "So, catch me up on what you've been doing."

"Maybe I can do that after I've put on some clothes? Or we can talk like this?" Another smile.

He was flirting with her, a ploy she knew all too well since she'd been on the receiving end of his flirting that summer. Well, she could flirt, too.

"I guess I can restrain myself for a quick catch-up," she joked. "A *quick catch-up*," she emphasized. "What are you doing these days? I mean, other than sleeping naked, that is. How's the job going?"

The smile faded, and she was sorry she'd taken the conversation in that direction. Of course, it was something a normal nondrooling woman would have asked the man who had been her first.

Even though it was a dumb-as-dirt thing to do, she went closer. Much closer. And she sat down on the bed. Not right next to him, though, because she didn't want to move into the dumber-than-dirt category, but it was still too near him. Six miles would have been too near.

"Sorry," she added. "Didn't mean to hit a nerve. And I should have known better because Riley doesn't like to talk about his assignments, either. I think he believes it'll worry me, but whether he talks about it or not, I still worry."

"You shouldn't. Riley's been on plenty of deployments and hasn't gotten a scratch. Some guys are just bulletproof, and Riley's one of them."

Maybe. But Anna had a bad feeling about this deployment coming up. A bad feeling she definitely didn't want to discuss with Heath. Or Riley. If she didn't mention it aloud, maybe the feeling would go away. Maybe the danger would as well, and her brother would come back with his bulletproof label intact.

"You okay?" Heath asked.

That was a reminder to push aside her fears and get on with this catch-up conversation. "Riley always says if he tells me about his job, he'll have to hit me with a shovel afterwards. Riley really likes that shovel threat."

"I remember." Heath took a deep breath, causing the muscles in his chest and that six-pack to respond. "Well, shovels aside, I can tell you that I just finished up a deployment in a classified location where there was a lot of sand, followed by eight months in Germany where there was a lot of paperwork. That's where Riley became my boss. Small world, huh?"

Yes. Too small, maybe. "Riley and you are in the same career field?"

"For now." The short answer came out so fast. As did his hand. He brushed his fingers over the ends of her hair. Even though he didn't actually touch skin or anything, it was enough of a distraction. "Your hair is longer," he said.

"Yours is shorter." And yes, she achieved dumber-than-dirt status by touching his hair, as well. Since it was on the short side, she also touched some skin.

She felt everything go still, and even though Anna was pulling back her hand, it seemed to be in slow motion. The only thing that was in the revving-up mode was this flamethrower attraction that had always been between Heath and her.

"Yeah," he drawled. No other words were necessary. They were on the same proverbial page along with being on the same actual bed. The flamethrower had had a go at him, too.

"I, uh…" Anna stuttered around with a few more words and syllables before she managed to say something coherent. "This could be trouble."

"Already is." He drawled that, too. Hitched up another smile.

The past nine and a half years just vanished. Suddenly, Anna was eighteen again and was thinking about kissing him. Of course, she hadn't needed vanishing years for that to happen, but it was as if they were back in that hayloft. On all that warm, soft hay. Heath had taken things so slow. Long kisses. His hand skimming over various parts of her body.

Then, into her jeans.

That had been the best part, and it'd all started with a heated look like the one he was giving her now.

Even though they didn't move, the foreplay was in full swing. His gaze lingered on her mouth. She picked up the rhythm of his breathing—which was too fast. Ditto for her heartbeat. Everything was moving in sync.

"Anna, we're playing with fire," he whispered. It was a drawl, too.

She was near enough to him now that his breath hit against her mouth like a kiss. "Yes," she admitted, but she was in the "fire pretty" mindset right now, and she inched closer, her drifting gaze sliding from his mouth to his abs.

"Is it real?" she asked, but was in the wrong mindset to wait for an answer. She touched that six-pack.

Oh, yes. Definitely real.

It probably would have been a good time to snatch back her hand and be outraged that she'd done something so bold, but she kept it there a moment and saw and heard Heath's reaction. He cursed under his breath, and beneath the sheet his filled-out part reacted, as well.

He cursed some more, but it was all aimed at himself. "I really do need you to leave now so I can get dressed. Once I can walk, that is. Maybe you can shut the door behind you, too."

That caused the past nine and a half years to unvanish. Heath was putting a stop to this. As he should.

Anna was about to help with that stopping by getting to her feet and doing something that Heath clearly would have trouble doing right now—walking. But before she could budge an inch, she saw the movement in the doorway.

And saw the source of that movement.

Riley.

His eyes were so narrowed that it looked as if his eyelashes were stuck together.

"What the hell's going on here?" Riley growled. He opened his eyes enough to look at her. Then at Heath. Then at the other *thing* that was going on. "And what are you doing with my sister?"

No way was Heath going to be able to explain with the bulge of his filled-out part beneath the sheet. And neither could Anna.

Chapter Two

Well, hell in a big-assed handbasket. This visit was off to a good start.

Heath had known it wasn't a smart idea to come to the McCord Ranch, and he was getting a full reminder of why it'd been bad, what with Riley glaring at him.

"Get dressed," Riley ordered, and yeah, it was an order all right. "And we'll talk." Then he turned that ordering glare on his sister.

But Anna obviously wasn't as affected by it as Heath was, even though Riley was in uniform and looked thirty steps past the intimidation stage. Still, Anna matched Riley's glare with a scowl and waltzed out.

Thankfully, Riley did some waltzing as well and left, shutting the door behind him. Though it was more of a slam than a shut. Still, he was gone, and that gave Heath some time to take a very uncomfortable walk to the adjoining bathroom for a shower. Cold. Just the way he hated his showers. And if he stayed on the ranch, there'd be more of them in his near future.

It was time for a change of plans.

Not that he actually had plans other than passing time and moping. Yeah, moping was a definite possibility. At least it had been until Anna had shown up in the doorway. Difficult to mope in his current state.

Regardless, Anna was off-limits, of course.

He repeated that while the cold shower cooled down his body. Repeated it some more while he dressed. Kept repeating it when he went down the stairs to apologize to Riley and tell him that he'd remembered some place he needed to be. Riley would see right through the lie, but after what he had witnessed in the guest room, he'd be glad to get Heath off the ranch.

Heath made his way downstairs, meandering through the sprawling house. Since he was hoping for some coffee to go along with the butt-chewing he would get from Riley, he headed toward the kitchen.

He heard women's voices but not Anna's. He was pretty sure they belonged to Della and Stella, sisters and the McCords' longtime housekeeper and cook. Yep. And Heath got a glimpse of them and the coffeepot, too, before Riley stepped into the archway, blocking his path.

"I know," Heath volunteered. "You want to hit me on the head with a shovel."

"Hit who with a shovel?" Della asked, and when she spotted Heath, she flung the dish towel she was holding. Actually, she popped Riley on the butt with it and went to Heath to gather him into her arms for a hug. "It's good to see you, boy."

Heath hadn't even been sure the woman would remember him after all this time, but clearly she did. Or else she thought he was someone else.

"Nobody's gonna get hit with a shovel in this house," Della warned Riley, and then she added to Heath, "Have you seen Anna yet?"

"Earlier," Heath settled for saying.

"Well, I hope you'll be seeing a lot more of her while you're here. Never could understand why you two didn't just sneak up to the hayloft or somewhere."

Heath choked on his own breath. Not a very manly reaction, but neither was the way Riley screwed up his face. Della didn't seem to notice or she might have used the dish towel on him again.

"Have a seat at the table, and I'll fix you some breakfast," Della offered.

"Heath and I have to talk first," Riley insisted.

"Pshaw. A man's gotta have at least some coffee before he carries on a conversation. Where are your manners, Riley?"

"I think I left them upstairs."

Della laughed as if it were a joke and, God bless her, she poured Heath a cup of coffee. He had a couple of long sips, figuring he was going to need them.

"Thanks. I'll be right back," Heath said to Della, and he followed Riley out of the kitchen and into the sunroom.

No shovels in sight, but Riley had gone back to glaring again, and he got right in Heath's face. "Keep your hands off Anna, or I'll make your life a living hell."

Heath had no doubts about that. He didn't mind the living hell for himself so much, but he didn't want any more of Riley's anger aimed at Anna. "I'll get my things together and head out."

Riley's glare turned to a snarl. "And then Anna, Della and Stella will think I've run you off."

Heath had some more coffee, cocked his head to the side in an "if the shoe fits" kind of way. Because in a manner of speaking, Riley was indeed running him off. Except that Heath had already decided it was a good idea, too. Still, he didn't acknowledge that. He was getting some perverse pleasure out of watching Riley squirm a little.

"I'm guessing Anna, Della and Stella will make your life a living hell if they think you've run me off?" Heath asked. And he said it with a straight face.

Riley opened his mouth. Closed it. Then he did a wash, rinse, repeat of that a couple more times before he finally cursed. "Stay. For now. And we'll discuss it later. I've got to do some more paperwork at the base. Just keep your hands off Anna while I'm gone. Afterwards, too."

His hands were the least of Riley's worries, but Heath kept that to himself. Besides, Riley didn't give him a chance to say anything else. He lit out of there while growling out another "Stay" order.

Heath would stay. For the morning anyway. But it was best if he put some distance between Anna and all those parts of him that could get him in trouble.

He went back into the kitchen, got a hug and warm greeting from Stella this time, and the woman practically put him in one of the chairs at the table.

"How do you like your eggs?" Della asked.

"Any way you fix them." Heath added a wink because he figured it would make her smile. It did.

"Tell us what you've been doing with yourself for the past nine years or so," Della said as she got to work at the stove. "I seem to recall when you left here that summer you were headed to boot camp."

Heath nodded, took a bite of the toast that Stella set in front of him. "I enlisted in the Air Force, became a pararescuer and took college classes online. When I finished my degree, I got my commission and became a combat rescue officer."

"Like Riley," Stella said.

"Yeah, but he outranks me."

"How is that? Didn't you go in the Air Force before Riley did?"

Heath nodded again. "Only a couple months earlier, though. We've been in the service about the same amount of time, but for most of that I was enlisted. I've only been an officer for three and a half years now. And Riley's my boss. Well, until the rest of my paperwork has cleared. That should be about the time Riley leaves for his assignment in two weeks."

Della stopped scrambling the eggs to look at him. "You won't be going with him?"

There it was. That twist to the gut. Heath tried to ease it with some more toast and coffee, but that was asking a lot of mere food products. And Della and Stella noticed all right. He'd gotten their full attention.

"No, I won't be going with Riley this time," Heath said.

He still had their attention, and judging from their stares, the women wanted more. Heath gave them the sanitized version. "The Air Force feels it's time for me to have a stateside assignment. It's standard procedure. A way of making sure I don't burn out."

His mouth was still moving and words were coming out, but Heath could no longer hear what he was saying. That's because Anna walked in. Or maybe it was just a Mack Truck that looked like Anna because he suddenly felt as if someone had knocked him senseless.

She'd changed out of her sweats and T-shirt. Had put on a bra, too. And was now wearing jeans and a red sweater. Heath tried not to notice the way the clothes hugged her body. Tried not to notice her curves. Her face.

Hell, he gave up and noticed.

Not that he could have done otherwise. Especially when Anna poured herself a cup of coffee, sat down next to him and glanced at his crotch.

"Back to normal?" she whispered. Then she gave him a smile that could have dissolved multiple layers of rust on old patio furniture. Dissolved a few of his brain cells, too. "So, did Riley try to give you your marching orders?"

Since Della and Stella got very, very quiet, Heath figured they were hanging on every word, so he chose his own words carefully and spoke loud enough for the women to hear. "Something came up—"

Anna glanced at his crotch again and laughed. Obviously, a reaction she hadn't planned because she clamped her teeth onto her bottom lip after adding "I'm sorry." Too late, though. Because Della and Stella weren't just hanging on every word but every ill-timed giggle, too.

"Well, I'm sure whatever came up—" Della paused "—you can work it out so you can stay here for at least a couple of days. That way, Anna and you have time to visit."

"Especially since Anna needs some cheering up," Stella added.

Anna certainly didn't laugh that time. She got a deer-about-to-be-smashed-by-a-car look. "I'm fine, really," Anna mumbled.

Which only confirmed to Heath that she did indeed need some cheering up. Maybe this had to do with the "change of scenery or something" she'd mentioned up-stairs.

Well, hell.

There went his fast exit, and no, that wasn't the wrong part of his body talking, either. If Anna was down, he wanted to help lift her up.

Stella dished up two plates of eggs for Anna and him, and she smiled at them when she set them on the table. "You two were as thick as thieves back in the day." She snapped her fingers as if recalling something. "Anna, Heath even gave you that heart necklace you used to wear all the time. It had your and his pictures in it."

Hard to forget that. Heath referred to it as the great engraved debacle. He'd spent all his money buying Anna that silver heart locket as a going-away gift. Something to remember him by after he left Spring Hill and the McCord Ranch. It was supposed to be engraved with the words *Be Mine*.

The engraver had screwed up and had put *Be My* instead.

Since Heath hadn't had the time to get it fixed, he'd given it to Anna anyway, but he hadn't figured she would actually wear it. Not with that confusing, incomplete *sentiment*.

"Where is that necklace?" Della asked.

"I'm not sure," Anna answered, and she got serious about eating her breakfast. Fast. Like someone who'd just entered a breakfast-eating contest with a reprieve from a death sentence waiting for the winner.

Della made a sound that could have meant anything, but it had a sneaky edge to it. "I think Heath needs some cheering up, too," Della went on. "And not because Riley was going on about that shovel. That boy needs to get a new threat, by the way," she added to her sister before looking at Anna again. "I get the feeling Heath could use somebody to talk to."

Heath suddenly got very serious about eating his breakfast, as well. Either Della had ESP, or Heath sucked at covering up what was going on in his head.

Anna finished gulping down her breakfast just a bite ahead of him, gulped down some coffee, too, and she probably would have headed out if Stella hadn't taken her empty breakfast plate and given her a plate of cookies instead.

"I need you to take these cookies over to Claire Davidson at her grandmother's house."

"Claire's back in town?" Anna asked, sounding concerned.

Heath knew Claire. She'd been around a lot that summer he'd worked at the McCord Ranch, and if he wasn't mistaken Claire had a thing for Riley. And vice versa.

"Her grandmother's sickly again. Thought they could use some cheering up, too." Della shifted her attention to Heath. "And you can go with Anna. Then maybe she could show you around town."

"Spring Hill hasn't changed in nine and a half years," Anna quickly pointed out.

"Pshaw. That's not true. The bakery closed for one thing. And Logan bought that building and turned it into a fancy-schmancy office. It has a fancy-schmancy sign that says McCord Cattle Brokers. You can't miss it."

Logan—one of Anna's other brothers who ran the family business and probably also owned a shovel. Ditto for Logan's twin, Lucky. At least the two of them didn't stay at the ranch very often, so Heath might not even run into them. Well, he wouldn't as long as he avoided the fancy-schmancy office and any of the local rodeos since Lucky was a bull rider.

"I thought I'd go out and see if the ranch hands needed any help," Heath suggested.

That earned him a blank stare from the women. "You don't have to work for your keep while you're here," Stella said. "You're a guest."

"I know, but I like working with my hands. I miss it." He did. Not as much as he'd miss other things—like having the job he really wanted—but grading on a curve here, ranch work was missable.

"All right, then," Della finally conceded. "At least walk Anna to the truck. There might be some ice on the steps. We had a cold spell move in."

"Now, go," Stella said, shooing them out. "Della and I need to clean up, and we can't do that with y'all in here."

This wasn't about cleaning. This was about matchmaking. Still, Heath grabbed his coat so he could make sure Anna didn't slip on any ice. He only hoped Anna didn't ask why he needed cheering up, and he would return the favor and not ask her the same thing.

"So, why do you need cheering up?" Anna asked the moment they were outside.

He groaned, not just at the question but also because it was at least fifty degrees with zero chance of ice.

"Is it personal or business?" she added.

"Is yours personal or business?" he countered.

She stayed quiet a moment and instead of heading toward one of the trucks parked on the side of the house, she sat down in the porch swing. "Both. You?"

"Both," he repeated. But then he stopped and thought about her answer. "Yours is personal, as in guy troubles?"

For some reason that made him feel as if he'd been hit by the Anna-truck again. Which was stupid. Because of course she had men in her life. Heath just wasn't sure he wanted to hear about them.

She nodded to verify that it was indeed guy trouble.

No, he didn't want to hear this, so he blurted out the first thing that popped into his head. He probably should have waited for the second or third thing, though.

"I had a girl break up with me once because I kept calling her your name," he said.

"*My* name?" She didn't seem to know how to react to that.

"Uh, no. I kept saying *your name* because I couldn't remember her name." And he added a wink that usually charmed women.

But, of course, it'd been Anna's name. The way stuff about her often popped into his head, her name had a way of just popping out of his mouth.

"Any other confessions you want to get off your chest and/or six-pack?" she asked. And she winked at him.

Man, that's what he'd always liked about Anna. She gave as good as she got. "Let me see. I don't wear boxers or briefs. I like mayo and pepper on my French fries. And my mother's in jail again."

All right, so that last one just sort of fell from his brain into his mouth.

Anna didn't question the *again* part. Maybe because she remembered the reason he'd ended up at the McCord Ranch all those years ago was that his mother had been in jail then, as well.

In jail only after she'd stolen and spent every penny of the money that Heath had scrimped and saved for college. She'd also burned down their rental house with all his clothes and stuff still in it.

Heath had snapped up Riley's offer of a job and a place to stay—since at the time Heath had had neither. His father hadn't been in his life since he was in kindergarten, and what with him being broke and homeless, he'd had few places to turn.

If it hadn't been for his jailbird mom, he would have never met Anna. So, in a way he owed her.

In a very roundabout way.

"Want to talk about why your mom's in jail?" Anna asked.

Well, since he'd opened this box, Heath emptied the contents for her. "Shoplifting Victoria's Secret panties. She'd stuffed about fifty pairs in her purse—guess they don't take up much room—and when the security guard tried to stop her, she kicked him where it hurts. Then she did the same to the manager of the store next door. Then to the off-duty cop who tried to stop her. My mom can be a real butt-kicker when it comes to high-end underwear."

Anna smiled, a quiet kind of smile. "I do that, too, sometimes."

"What?" And Heath hoped this wasn't about butt-kicking or stealing panties.

"Diffuse the pain with humor. I'm not very good at it, either. Pain sucks."

Yeah, it did, and he thought he knew exactly what she was talking about. "You lost your parents when you were a teenager."

"Yes, they were killed in a car accident before you and I met. I was fourteen, and I thought my world was over. That was still the worst of the *world's over* moments, but I've had others since."

"Is that why you need cheering up?" he asked.

She didn't answer. Anna stood. "I should deliver these cookies before the ice gets to them."

Heath put his hands in his pockets so he wouldn't touch her as she walked away. Not that he would have had a chance to do any touching. Because someone pulled up in a truck. Not a work truck, either. This was a silver one that Della would have labeled as fancy schmancy. It went well with the cowboy who stepped from it.

Logan McCord.

The top dog at the McCord Ranch and the CEO of McCord Cattle Brokers. He made a beeline for the porch, passing Anna along the way. She said something to him, something Heath couldn't hear, but it put a deep scowl on Logan's face.

"Smart-ass," he grumbled. "She threatened to hit me with Riley's shovel if I didn't make you feel welcome. So—welcome."

Warm and fuzzy it wasn't, but at least it wasn't a threat. Not yet anyway.

"Riley called," Logan continued. "He said I was to come over here and convince you to stay."

"Because of Anna, Della and Stella."

Logan certainly didn't deny that, and his gaze drifted to Anna as she drove away before his attention turned back to Heath. "You're only going to be here two weeks at most, and then you'll leave, right?"

Since that pretty much summed it up, Heath nodded.

"Well, the last time you did that, it took Anna a long time to get over you. *Months*," Logan emphasized. "We all had to watch her cry her eyes out."

Hell. Crying? Months? This was the first Heath was

hearing about this, but then he hadn't been around to see those tears. He'd been off at basic training at Lackland Air Force Base. He'd written her, of course. In the beginning at least. She'd written back to him, too, but she damn sure hadn't mentioned tears.

Logan took a step closer, got in his face. So close that Heath was able to determine that he used mint mouthwash and flossed regularly. "You won't hurt my kid sister like that again."

"The shovel threat?" Heath asked, aiming to make this sound as light as a confrontation with Logan could be. Heath wasn't sure friendly bones in a person's body actually existed, but if they did, Logan didn't have any.

"Worse. I'll tell Della and Stella what you've done and let them have a go at you. If you piss them off, the shovel will be the least of your worries."

Heath didn't doubt that. In fact, the whole McCord clan would come after him if he left Anna crying again. And that meant Anna was way off-limits.

He'd survived months in hostile territory. But Heath thought that might be a picnic compared to the next two weeks with Anna and the McCord brothers.

Chapter Three

Heath had been avoiding her for the past three days. Anna was certain of it. And she was fed up with it, partly because if Heath avoided her, it was like letting her knot-headed brothers win.

The other *partly* was that she couldn't get him off her mind, and she didn't know what riled her more—her brothers' winning or her own body whining and begging for something it shouldn't get.

Shouldn't.

Because another fling with Heath would only complicate her life and possibly get her heart stomped on again. That was the logical, big-girl panties argument, but the illogical, no-underwear girl wanted Heath in the hayloft again.

And the hayloft was exactly where she spotted him.

He was standing in the loft, tossing down bales of hay onto a flatbed truck that was parked just beneath. He was all cowboy today: jeans, a blue work shirt, Stetson, boots. Oh, and he was sweaty despite the chillier temps.

She wasn't sure why the sweat appealed to her, but then she didn't see a single thing about him that didn't fall into the appeal category.

Anna stood there ogling him, as she'd done in the

bedroom, and she kept on doing it until his attention landed on her. Since she should at least make an attempt at not throwing herself at him, she went to the nearby corral and looked at the horses that'd been delivered earlier. It wasn't exactly the right day for horse ogling, though, because the wind had a bite to it.

An eternity later, which was possibly only a couple of minutes, the ranch hands drove off with the hay, and Heath made his way down the loft ladder. Then he made his way toward her.

"You've been avoiding me," she said. All right, she should have rehearsed this or something. For a soon-to-be lawyer, she was seriously lacking in verbal finesse when it came to Heath.

"Yeah," he admitted in that hot drawl of his. And he admitted the reason, too. "Your brothers are right. I'm not here for long, and they said you cried a lot the last time I left."

Her mouth dropped open, and the outrage didn't allow her to snap out a comeback. But her brothers were dead meat. Dead. Meat.

"They told you that?" She didn't wait for an answer. "I didn't cry. That much," Anna added.

Heath lifted his eyebrow, went to her side and put his forearms on the corral fence. "The fact that you cried at all tells me that I should keep avoiding you."

"Should?" she challenged.

He cursed, looked away from her. "You know I'm attracted to you. You saw proof of that in the bedroom."

She had, indeed. "And you know I'm attracted to you."

There, she'd thrown down the sexual gauntlet. But it caused him to curse again.

"I don't want to hurt you," he said.

"And I don't want to get hurt—"

A commotion in the corral nipped off the rest of what she was about to say. And it wasn't a very timely commotion.

Sex.

Specifically horse sex.

It went on a lot at the ranch. So often in fact that Anna rarely noticed, but because Heath was right next to her, she noticed it now. And he noticed that she noticed.

With all that noticing going on, it was amazing that she remembered how to turn around, but she finally managed it. She took hold of Heath's arm and got him moving away from the corral and toward the pasture.

Where she immediately saw cow-and-bull sex.

Dang it. Was everything going at it today?

Heath chuckled. "The Angus bull was getting restless, trying to break fence, so the hands brought in some company for him."

The ranch's version of Match.com. And the icy wind definitely didn't put a damper on things. Not for the bull anyway, but it did for Anna. She shivered and wished she'd opted for a warmer coat instead of the one that she thought looked better on her. It was hard to look your best with chattering teeth and a red nose.

"In here," Heath said. He put his hand on her back and maneuvered her into the barn.

"The scene of the crime," Anna mumbled. She'd fantasized about getting Heath back in here, but not like this. Not when she needed a tissue.

He glanced up at the hayloft, his attention lingering there a moment before coming back to her. The lingering lasted more than a moment though, and he took out a handkerchief and handed it to her.

"I should probably take you back to the house so you can warm up," he offered.

She considered it just so she could blow her nose. It was tempting, but Riley was inside. Della and Stella, too. So Anna touched the handkerchief to her nose and hoped that did the trick. In case it didn't, she went for what Riley would have called a tactical diversion.

"I'm surprised you're not off somewhere enjoying some *company* like that bull before you leave for your deployment," she said.

Anna figured that would get Heath to smile. It didn't. And she saw it again—the look on his face to remind her that he needed to be cheered up about something. Apparently, it had something to do with his assignment.

"Unless a miracle happens, I won't be deploying," he finally answered. The strewn hay on the floor was suddenly riveting because he stared at it. "The Air Force wants me to take an instructor job in Florida."

With the hay-staring and the gloomy look, Anna had braced herself for something a lot worse. "You make it sound as if you're being banished to Pluto."

"In a way, it is like that for me. I trained to be a combat rescue officer, like Riley. I didn't go through all of that to work behind a desk."

Anna wasn't sure how far she should push this so she just waited him out. Waited out the profanity he muttered under his breath. Waited out more hay-staring.

"I feel washed up," he added.

Ah, she got it then. "But the instructor job is temporary, right? You'll go back to being a combat rescue officer?"

"In three years."

She got that, too. It was an eternity for someone like Heath or Riley.

Anna touched his arm, rubbed gently. "The three years will fly by. Look how fast the past nine and a half years went."

The hay finally lost its allure for him, and he looked at her. "Yeah." Not so much of a sexy drawl this time. The hurt was still there. Time to pull out the big guns and do a little soul-baring.

"Remember when I told you I needed a change of scenery? Well, what I really need is to get away from my ex-boyfriend," Anna confessed. "We had a bad breakup."

Evidently, Heath didn't like this soul-baring so much because he frowned. "Are you telling me this is rebound flirting you've been doing with me?"

"No. The breakup happened two years ago, but he's getting married to one of my classmates. And they're having a baby. Twins, actually. The classmate is a former Miss Texas beauty pageant winner."

He nodded, made an "I got it" sound. "You're still in love with him."

"No!" And she couldn't say that fast or loud enough. "He's a lying, cheating weasel. My need for a change of scenery isn't because I still care for him but because I'm sick and tired of everybody walking on eggshells around me."

Her voice had gotten louder with each word, and she couldn't stop the confessions now that the floodgates were open.

"Poor pitiful Anna McCord got dumped for the beauty queen," she blathered on. "It reminds me of the stuff my brothers pull on me, and I'm tired of it. Tired of being treated like someone who needs to be handled with kid gloves."

She probably would have just kept on blathering, too, if Heath hadn't slid his hand around the back of her neck, hauled her to him and kissed her.

All in all, it was the perfect way to shut her up, and Anna didn't object one bit. In fact, she would have cheered, but her mouth was otherwise occupied, and besides, cheering would have put an end to this kiss.

She didn't want it to end.

Apparently, neither did Heath, because he put that clever mouth to good use and made the kiss French. And deep. And long.

All the makings of a good kiss even if Anna's lungs started to ache for air.

Heath broke the kiss just long enough for them to take in some much needed oxygen, and he went in for another assault. Anna was no longer shivering, could no longer feel her nose, but the rest of her was hyperaware of what was happening. The heat zoomed from her mouth to her toes, but it especially fired up in her orgasm-zone.

Soon, very soon, the kiss just wasn't enough, and they started to grapple for position. Trying to get closer and closer to each other. Heath was a lot better at grappling than she was because he dropped his hands to her butt and gave her a push against the front of his jeans.

Anna saw stars. Maybe the moon, too. And she darn near had an orgasm right then, right there while they were fully clothed.

Her heart was pounding now. Her breath, thin. She was melting. And there was a roaring sound in her head. That roaring sound was probably the reason she hadn't heard the other sounds until it was too late. Not horse or bull sex this time.

Footsteps.

"Interrupting anything?" someone asked.

Not Riley or Logan. Her brother Lucky.

And he was standing in the barn doorway with a shovel gripped in his hand.

ONCE AGAIN HEATH was facing a McCord brother when he was aroused. Hardly the right bargaining tool for dealing with Anna's older siblings who were hell-bent on protecting their sister.

Anna stepped in front of him as if she were his protector, but Heath remedied that. He stepped in front of her. But that only prompted her to attempt another stepping in front of him, and Heath put a stop to it. He dropped a kiss on her mouth, a chaste one this time hoping it would get her to cooperate.

"I need to talk to your brother alone," Heath told her.

"No way. He's here to browbeat you, and he's got a shovel."

Lucky shrugged. Propped the shovel against the wall. "Riley said I should bring it and do my part to remind Heath that he should keep his jeans zipped around you." He shrugged again when he glanced at the front of Heath's jeans. "The zipper's still up, so my work here is done."

Lucky turned to walk away.

"That's really all you've got to say?" Anna asked.

Her brother stopped, smiled in that lazy way that Lucky had about him. Heath knew Lucky loved his sister, but he'd never been as Attila the Hun as Riley and Logan. Heath suspected that's because Lucky got out all his restless energy by riding rodeo bulls. And having lots of sex.

"Should I ask you two to stay away from each other?" Lucky didn't wait for an answer though. "Wouldn't work. You two have the hots for each other, and there's only one way to cool that down." His gaze drifted to the hayloft before he turned again to leave.

Was Lucky really giving them his approval?

No.

This had to be some kind of trick.

Heath went after Lucky. Anna, too, and they caught up with him by the porch steps. However, before Heath could say anything else, the door opened, and Della stuck her head out.

"Anna, you got a call on the house phone. It's Claire."

Anna volleyed glances between Heath and her brother and then huffed. "Don't you dare say anything important before I get back."

She hurried inside. So did Lucky and Heath, but they stopped in the sunroom.

"Zippers and haylofts aside," Lucky said. "I don't want Anna hurt again. She sort of fell apart the last time you left."

"Yes. I heard about the crying from Logan." Heath paused. "Define *fell apart*."

"It wasn't just the crying." Lucky paused, too. "It was the pregnancy scare."

Heath felt as if all the air had just been sucked out of his lungs. Out of the entire planet. And if there was air on Pluto, it was also gone.

"Anna doesn't know that I know," Lucky went on. "No one does, and I'd like to keep it from my brothers. If Riley and Logan find out, they'd want to kick your ass. And mine since I didn't tell them. Then I'd have to kick theirs. If you don't mind, I'd rather not have to go through an ass-kicking free-for-all."

"Pregnancy?" Heath managed to ask. Considering there was still no air, he was doing good to get out that one word.

Lucky nodded. "A couple of weeks after you left, I went into Anna's bathroom to get some eye drops, and I saw the box for the pregnancy test in her trash can. She'd torn up the box, but I was able to piece it together to figure out what it was."

Heath managed another word. "Damn."

"Yeah. Two words for you—safe sex."

"I used a condom."

Lucky shrugged again. "Then, it must have worked because when I found the pee stick—it was in the way bottom of the trash can, by the way—it had a negative sign on it."

Heath heard the words. Felt the relief at that negative sign. Then managed another word.

"Hell."

Anna had gone through a scare like that, and she hadn't even told him.

"The only reason I dragged this up now was so that you'd understand why I'm protective of her," Lucky went on. "Now, go find her. Confront her about all of this. Then use a condom when you have makeup sex."

There'd be no makeup sex. Because Heath wasn't touching her again. Hell. She could have had his kid.

Heath went looking for Anna, and when he didn't find her in the kitchen or any of the living areas, he went to her bedroom. Of course she was there. The one room in the house where he shouldn't be alone with her. The door was open, and she was still on the phone, but she motioned for him to come in. He did, but only because he wanted answers and didn't want to wait for them.

But he had to wait anyway.

He listened to Anna talk niceties with Claire. Several "you're welcomes" later, she finally ended the call and looked at him. The smile that was forming froze on her mouth though when she saw his expression.

Heath shut the door just as he blurted out, "You had a pee stick in the bottom of your trash can."

Anna gave him a blank look.

"The pregnancy test from nine and a half years ago," he clarified. "Lucky found it and just told me about it. I'm wondering why I had to hear it from him."

She laughed. Hardly the reaction he'd expected. "It wasn't my pee on that stick. It belonged to Kristy Welker. I bought it for her so her folks wouldn't find out, and she did the test here."

Heath had vague memories of this Kristy. Anna and she had been friends, and Kristy had come over a couple of times that summer.

Anna's laughter quickly stopped. "What the heck was Lucky doing in my bathroom?"

She was using her sister voice now, and it wouldn't have surprised Heath if she'd gone running out of there to confront her brother about it. She might have done that if Heath hadn't done something so unmanly as having to catch on to the wall to steady himself.

"Whoa. Are you all right?" She slipped her arm around his waist, led him to the bed.

Heath didn't even try to say he didn't need to sit down. He did. "I thought... Well, I thought..."

"Trust me, if you had knocked me up, I would have told you about it."

Of course she would have. But it might take a year or two for his heart rate to settle down.

She gave his arm another rub like the one she had in the barn. "Relax. You were my first, but I wasn't totally clueless." She stopped, paused. "I wasn't your first though, and that's why you knew to bring a condom to the hayloft."

Even though Heath was still coming down from the shock-relief whammy, he heard her loud and clear. She'd given him something that a girl could only give once. Her virginity. That upped the encounter a significant notch, and maybe she was looking for some kind of assurance that she'd given it to the right guy.

"You were the first one that mattered," he said. "I risked being hit by a shovel to be with you. That should have told you something."

No smile. No more arm rub, either. "And yet you left."

He nodded, tried to ignore the sting of that reminder. "I was leaving for basic training, and you were barely eighteen."

Anna waved that off. "I know where this is going. We were too young for it to have been real love."

"No, we weren't too young."

Okay, he hadn't meant to say that, and it was another opened box with contents that Anna was clearly waiting to be spilled.

"What I felt for you was real," Heath said. And strong.

He hadn't cried as Anna had done, but leaving her had left a hole in his heart. Best not to mention that, especially since he would be leaving again soon.

"I knew I couldn't give you a good life," he added. "Not when I was still trying to figure out my own life."

She stayed quiet a couple of seconds. "Fair enough. And if you'd stayed, you would have resented me because you gave up your dream of being in the military. Your wanderlust and need for an adrenaline fix would have come into play. We would have fought, broken up, and all these years later we would have cursed the mere mention of each other's names."

Heath frowned. He didn't like that version of what could have been, but she was probably right. Probably. Now he was cursing her name for a different reason. Because it reminded him of how much he wanted her.

"I still have the need for that adrenaline fix," he admitted. "The need to be…something. Somewhere. It's easier if I stay on the move."

"I get it." She motioned around the room. "That's why it's hard for me to be at the ranch sometimes."

He was pretty sure they were talking about her parents now, about the hole in her heart that their deaths had no doubt left. "Are the memories of your folks harder to deal with while you're here?"

"Every now and then. But sometimes it's hard no matter where I am. Sometimes, I wake up, and I can't remember what they looked like. That sends me into a panic. So I run to grab one of the photo albums just to remember their faces."

"It's your way of keeping them in your life," Heath said around the lump in his throat.

"Yes. The past has a way of staying with you like that." Anna took a deep breath, then sighed. "And you can't run away from your past. I know, I've tried. It's like that little mole I have on my right butt cheek. It just goes with me everywhere." She looked at him. "I know what you're thinking."

Because he thought they could use some levity, Heath asked, "You have a little mole on your butt cheek?"

"All right, I didn't know what you were thinking after all. I thought you might be wondering if I was trying to outrun my past by transferring colleges."

That hadn't even crossed his mind, mainly because he wondered why he hadn't noticed that mole on her butt cheek. He was also wanting to see that mole. Clearly, he had a one-track mind here.

He shook his head. "I didn't think the transfer was about running, more like ulcer prevention. No need for you to have to face a daily dose of Mr. Wrong and his new family."

"Exactly." She smiled in a triumphant *I didn't think you'd get that* kind of way.

Heath got it all right. He got a lot of things when it came to Anna. A lot of things because of her, too. Like that tug below his belly that nudged him to kiss her again. That was his red-flag warning to get moving, and he would have done just that if he hadn't spotted the silver heart locket on her nightstand.

When she saw that he'd spotted it, she tried to put it in the drawer, but Heath took hold of her hand to stop her.

Yes, it was the locket he'd given her all right.

"After Della asked about it, I found it in my old jewelry box," she said. Then, she frowned. "All right, I wear it sometimes. Okay?"

She didn't sound especially happy about that, but it pleased Heath that she still had it. Pleased him even more than she occasionally wore it. What didn't please him was the reminder of the two words engraved on it.

"Be my." Anna ran her fingertips over it. "I wasn't sure what you were saying—be my heart, be my locket. Be my lay in the hay." She chuckled, poked him with her elbow.

"It was a fill-in-the-blank kind of thing," he joked, poking her back with his elbow.

"It sounds to me as if you didn't know what you wanted to say." No elbow poke that time.

"I was eighteen. I didn't know."

"And now?" she asked.

For two little words, it was a mighty big question. One that he didn't have to answer because there was a knock at the door, and the knocker didn't wait for an invitation to come in. The door opened.

Riley.

Well, at least Anna and he weren't in a butt-grabbing lip-lock as they'd been in the barn when Lucky had found them.

"I need to talk to you," Riley said, looking at Heath. Then his gaze swung to his sister. "And no, this isn't about you. It's business."

Damn it. That didn't sound good.

Anna must have thought so, too, because she gave Heath a sympathetic look as Riley and he headed out. They didn't go far, just into the foyer.

"I just found out that you're still trying to get out of your instructor assignment, that you put in a request to go on another deployment," Riley threw out there.

Heath cursed. He wasn't exactly keeping it from Riley. Okay, he was, but he didn't want to justify what he was trying to do.

"You've already had two back-to-back deployments

as an officer," Riley reminded him. "Before that, you had back-to-back-to-backs as a pararescuer."

"You're going on another one," Heath reminded him just as fast.

"I've had breaks in between. In the past ten years, the only time you've been stateside is for leave and training." He put his hand on Heath's shoulder. "You don't have anything to prove."

"No disrespect, *sir*, but I have everything to prove. To myself anyway."

Riley huffed. "You can prove it by being the best Air Force instructor you can be."

"That sounds like a recruitment pitch."

"It is." Riley took his hand from Heath's shoulder, and his index finger landed against Heath's chest. "And here's some more advice—sometimes life gives you crap, and you just have to make crappy lemonade out of it."

Heath frowned, thinking he might never again want another glass of lemonade. Or another lecture from Riley. Of course, there wouldn't be any more Riley lectures if Heath got stuck with that instructor job he didn't want. Then Riley would no longer be his boss.

Frowning, too, possibly over that bad lemonade analogy, Riley walked away. Heath would have, as well. He would have headed back to the pasture to do something, anything, to burn off some of this restless energy inside him.

Yeah, he needed an adrenaline fix *bad*.

He figured in that moment that his thought must have tempted fate, because his phone dinged with a text message. There was that old saying about when the gods

wanted to punish you, they gave you what you wanted.
Well, it wasn't from the gods.

It was from Anna.

And the text flashed like neon on his phone screen. A
sort of warning from the gods out to punish him.

Meet me in the hayloft in one hour.

Chapter Four

Anna figured she wasn't just going to be able to sneak out of the house without anyone seeing her.

And she was right.

As she was cutting through the sunroom, Della spotted her. Anna smiled, tried to look as if she weren't up to something, but that was sort of hard to do considering she had a six-pack of beer in a plastic grocery bag. A six-pack Anna had just scrounged from the fridge.

Della glanced at the bag and its distinctive shape. Then gave Anna no more than a mere glance.

"What are you up to?" Della asked.

Anna shrugged. "I'm considering playing with some fire. Running with scissors. Taking candy from some guy I don't know."

Falling hard for an old flame she shouldn't fall hard for was something Anna could add to that list of no-no's.

"So, you're going to the barn again with Heath," Della said. It wasn't a question.

"No. Yes," she admitted when Della gave her that liar-liar-pants-on-fire look. Anna huffed. "Don't give me a hard time about this. I'm tired of everyone babying me."

"They do that because you're the baby."

"Was the baby," Anna corrected. "I'm a grown woman now, but none of them can seem to accept it."

"They love you," Della pointed out.

"And I love them, but I want the key to my own chastity belt."

Della smiled that sly little smile of hers which meant she could be up to something. But she only kissed Anna on the cheek. "Honey, you've had that key for a long time now. Might be time to see if it works the way you want it to work."

Anna opened her mouth to respond, but she had nothing to say. Not a word. Instead, she returned the cheek kiss, tucked the beer under her arm so the bottles wouldn't jiggle and clang, and headed out the back.

No brothers in sight. No ranch hands, either.

But she also didn't see Heath.

Since it was—Anna checked the time on her phone— three minutes to rendezvous, she'd hoped she would see him waiting for her. He better not have blown her off. Except Heath wouldn't do that. Well, he might have done it with a text, call or chat, but he wouldn't do an unannounced blowing-off.

And he hadn't.

The moment she stepped in the barn, she saw him. Not in the hayloft, but standing by the steps that led up to the loft.

"You came," she said.

"Of course I came. I'm a guy and I'm not stupid. All right, maybe I am stupid, but the guy part's still true, and I've got the junk to prove it."

She smiled, chuckled. All nerves, and she hated the nerves because they didn't go well with this blistering attraction. "Yes, I got a glimpse of your junk. You're definitely a guy."

He smiled, too. "Beer?" he asked, tipping his head to the bag.

"I thought you might be thirsty. It was either this, milk or a questionable green smoothie."

"You made the right choice. I've already had my quota of milk and questionable green smoothies for a while."

He reached out, took her by the fingertips. That was it. The only part of her he touched. It was like being hit by a really big dose of pure, undiluted lust.

"You may have made the right choice with the beer," he added a heartbeat later. "But asking me to meet you here might fall into the stupid category."

"Might?" she repeated. Well, it was better than an out-and-out "this ain't gonna happen."

"Is this going to happen?" Anna came out and asked.

With only that teeny grip on her fingertips, he inched her closer. So close that when she breathed, she drew in his scent. Mixed with the hay and the crisp November air, it gave her another dose of lust.

"It shouldn't happen," Heath said. "I've tried to talk myself out of it."

"And?" She was still breathing, through her mouth now. Still taking in that scent. Still feeling him play with her fingers. "I hope you're really lousy at talking yourself out of things."

He closed his eyes a moment. Groaned. And, as if he were fighting—and losing—a fierce battle, he brought her another inch closer. She figured if the lust doses kept coming that she was going to launch herself into his arms.

"I'm leaving soon," he reminded her. "And I'm trying to do the right thing here."

She wanted to point out that unless he was leaving within the hour, then this could indeed happen, but that would just make her sound needy. Which she was. So very, very needy.

He let go of her fingertips, and she figured this was it. Heath would send her on her way. But he took the beer from her, and as if he had all the time in the world, he set the bag next to a hay bale.

"So, what now?" she asked.

Heath didn't answer her. Not with words. He reached out, and just when she thought she was going to get more fingertip foreplay, he took hold of her, snapped her to him and kissed the living daylights out of her.

Anna forgot all about the stupid argument that he was leaving soon. She forgot how to breathe. But other feelings took over, too. Probably because Heath didn't just kiss.

He touched.

He slipped his hand between them and ran his fingers over her right breast. Nice, but he double-whammied it with a neck kiss, and Anna felt herself moving. At first she thought it was just her body melting, but nope, she and Heath were walking.

"What are we doing?" she asked.

"Complicating the hell out of things."

"Good. I like complications." At the moment she would have agreed to a lobotomy.

Heath kept kissing her, kept moving. Not up the steps of the hayloft but rather toward the tack room. Maybe because it had a door. Maybe because it didn't require the coordination of step climbing with an erection. Maybe because it was just closer.

It was the erection thing, she decided, and since she could feel it against her stomach, Anna added some touching of her own. She worked her hand over his zipper and would have gotten that zipper down if Heath hadn't stopped her.

She heard herself make a whiny sound of protest, but then he put her against the back of the door that he'd just shut, and he lifted her. Until his hard junk was against her soft junk. Everything lined up just right to create a mind-blowing sensation.

"Let's play a game," he said. And yeah, he drawled.

Anna nodded. She would have agreed to a second lobotomy.

"On a scale of one to ten, rate the kisses, and then I'll know which parts to concentrate on."

She wasn't sure she could count to ten, much less rate kisses, but Heath jumped right into the game. He kissed her mouth.

"A ten," she said after he left her gasping for air and reaching for his zipper again.

He put his hand over hers to stop her, but Anna just used the pressure of his hand to add pressure to his erection.

"We'll play that particular game later," he promised.

Heath moved on to the next kiss. He placed one in the little area just below her ear, and he must have remembered that was a hot spot for her because it didn't seem like a lucky guess.

"Fifty," she blurted out. If Heath hadn't held her in place with his body, she would have dropped like a rock.

There were no muscles in her legs, and her feet had perhaps disappeared.

"I'll definitely put that on my playlist," he said and added a flick of his tongue in that very hot spot that needed no such licking to further arouse it.

She went after his zipper for a third time, and the only reason she failed, again, was because he pushed up her sweater, pushed down her bra and did that tongue-flicking thing over her nipples.

"A seventy," she managed to say.

"Scale of one to ten," he corrected.

"Ten plus sixty."

He chuckled, which made for some very interesting sensations since he still had his mouth on her nipple.

"And this one?" he asked. He went lower, kissed her stomach.

"Ten," she admitted, and she was about to pull him back to her to breast and neck.

Then he went down a few more inches.

Heath clearly had some experience in zipper lowering. *Fast* zipper lowering. He slid down, unzipping her and dragging her jeans just low enough so that he could plant the next kiss on her panties.

Anna threw back her head, hitting it against the door and perhaps giving herself a concussion. She didn't care if she did. That's because the only thing that mattered now was the pleasure. Such a puny word for the incredible things Heath was doing with his mouth.

"Your rating?" he asked, and mercy, he added some breath with that question.

"Six million," she managed to say.

He laughed.

"One more kiss," he said. "Then it'll be your turn."

Oh, she wanted a turn all right. Wanted it badly. Until he shimmied down her panties, put her knee on his shoulder and kissed her again. A special kiss.

Tongue flicks included.

After a couple of those flicks, Anna went into for-get mode again. The thought of taking her turn went right out of her head. Everything vanished. Except for the feeling that she was about to shatter. And fall. And shatter some more.

Heath made sure he gave her the *more* she needed for shattering. One last well-placed kiss. An equally well-placed tongue flick. And all she could do was fist her hand in his hair and let him shatter her.

She had to take a moment to gather her breath. Another moment to keep gathering it. But even with the ripples of the climax tingling through her, she wanted to get started on her turn. And she was going to torture the hell out of Heath and his junk.

"Damn," Heath growled.

It took her a moment to realize that he was reacting to something he heard.

A knock at the tack room door.

"Heath?" Riley called out.

Hell.

"Uh, Heath, I need to talk to you," Riley added. "It's important."

Unless the world was about to end and Heath could stop it, then it wasn't that important, but Anna conceded that was the lust talking.

"How important?" Heath asked.

"Very."

Heath and she both cursed.

"Anna's in here with me," Heath volunteered.

It took Riley several snail-crawling seconds to respond to that. "Yes, I figured that out. Didn't think you'd go into the tack room alone and close the door. But this isn't about Anna. It's about your assignment."

Heath groaned, stood back up, helping her fix her jeans and panties. "You can wait in here if you want," he offered.

"Not a chance," Anna argued. "Riley knows what we've been doing. Or rather what we started doing, and the assignment thing could be a ruse to draw us out so he can ambush you with a shovel."

He brushed a kiss on her mouth. "You've got a very active imagination." Though she knew there might be a grain of truth in her theory.

Heath went out ahead of her, and Riley was indeed right there. He was sitting on a hay bale, drinking one of the beers. She braced herself for him to say something snarky like had she been trying to get Heath drunk or why did she have this thing for barn sex?

He didn't.

Riley did give her a look that only a big brother could have managed, but it had some, well, sympathy mixed in with the brotherly snark. A strange combination.

"I just came from the base," Riley said to Heath. "They want to see you about your deployment request."

"Deployment request?" Anna repeated. "I thought Heath was going to Florida."

Riley remained quiet, clearly waiting for Heath to explain.

"I asked to be diverted from the instructor job to another deployment," Heath said.

Riley's arrival had been a killjoy in the sexual-pleasure department, but hearing about Heath's request was a different kind of killjoy. Although obviously not for Heath since this was something he wanted.

Very much.

After all, he'd told her that the instructor job made him feel washed up, and maybe now he wouldn't have to feel that way because he could go back to one of those classified sandy locations. Where people shot at him and where he could be hurt or killed.

Mercy.

That felt as if she'd been slammed with a truckload of bricks. And there was no reason for it, because this was Heath's job. No logical reason anyway. But Anna wasn't feeling very logical at the moment.

"They want to see you out at the base right away," Riley added.

Heath nodded, looked at her as if he needed to say something, but Anna let him off the hook. She smiled, brushed a kiss on his cheek.

"Go," she insisted, trying to keep that smile in place. "We can talk when you get back."

Heath hesitated, gave another nod and then walked toward the house. Anna managed to keep her smile in place until he was out of sight. Riley opened a bottle of beer and handed it to her.

"Will he get to come back here to the ranch if the deployment is approved?" Anna asked, though she was afraid to hear the answer. "Or will they send him out right away?"

"Hard to say."

Or maybe not. The next thing Anna saw was Heath leaving the house, carrying his gear. He put it in his rental car and drove off. Obviously, he was prepared to go.

Anna took a long swig of that beer and wished it was something a whole lot stronger.

"Best to forget him," Riley said as they watched Heath drive away. "Heath isn't the settling-down type."

If only that weren't true.

"It's just a fling," Riley added. "That's what it was nine and a half years ago, and that's what it is now."

If only that were *true.*

Chapter Five

The McCord brothers were waiting for Heath when he got back from the base, and they didn't even try to make it look like a friendly, casual meeting. They were in the living room just off the foyer, and the moment Heath stepped inside, they stood.

No shovels. Not physical ones anyway.

"Where's Anna?" Heath asked. "You didn't lock her in her room, did you?"

The joke didn't go over so well, but Heath didn't care. He was tired, frustrated and wanted to talk to Anna, not the kid-sister police.

"Anna's Christmas shopping in San Antonio," Logan answered. "She'll be back any minute now."

Good. Well, sort of good. Heath definitely wanted to see her even if she probably hadn't liked his news. Hell, he hadn't liked it much, either.

"My request for deployment was denied," Heath explained. "The Air Force wants me to report to the base in Florida day after tomorrow so I'll have to cut my visit here short."

He expected them to jump for joy. Or at least smile. They didn't.

Riley immediately shook his head. "I didn't have anything to do with that."

Heath nearly snapped out "Right," but he knew in his gut that Riley was telling the truth. He wouldn't do anything like that even if it meant saving his sister from having sex with a guy Riley didn't think was right for her.

And Riley was spot-on.

Heath wasn't right for her. End of subject.

"I'll leave tomorrow," Heath added. "I just want a chance to say goodbye to Anna first."

None of the brothers objected, and Heath wouldn't have cared if they did. Yeah, it was the pissed-off mood again, but he had to get something off his chest.

"I know you think I'm a jerk, that I'm here only to try to seduce Anna, but I do care about her. Always have. If I hadn't cared, I would have never had sex in the hayloft with her nine and a half years ago."

There. He'd said it. But they weren't saying anything back to him. Maybe because Riley and Logan hadn't known about the sex. Lucky had, of course, because of the pee stick discovery, but even Lucky might have been stunned to silence to hear the de-virgining had taken place in the barn.

"Anna cares about you, too," Lucky finally said.

"She'll cry a lot again when you leave," Logan added.

"She'll be hurt," Riley piped in.

Maybe. Probably, Heath silently amended. Yeah, he was a jerk all right, but he was a jerk on orders, and that meant leaving whether he wanted to or not.

And he did want to leave, Heath assured himself.

He did.

Silently repeating that, Heath went to the guest room so he could finish packing.

HER BROTHERS WERE waiting for Anna when she got home. Hard to miss them since they were on the sofa in the living room.

She so didn't have the energy to deal with them now.

"You're all grounded," Anna said, going on the offensive. "Now, go to your rooms."

Of course, they didn't budge. Well, except to stand, and judging from the somber looks on their faces they had something serious to tell her. But she had something to say, too.

"I already know about Heath's deployment being denied. He texted me right after he got the news. He was at the base and couldn't talk, but he wanted to let me know that he's leaving tomorrow."

They stared at her as if expecting her to sprout an extra nose or something. Then Riley's hawkeyed gaze moved to the Victoria's Secret bag she was holding.

"Yes, I bought it for Heath," Anna admitted. "For me to wear for Heath," she amended when their stares turned blank. "It's red and slutty, and if you don't quit staring at me like that, I'll give you lots of details about what I want Heath to do to me while I'm wearing it."

Logan's eyes narrowed. Riley's jaw tightened. Lucky shrugged and went to her. He pulled her into his arms despite the fact she was as stiff as a statue from the mini hissy fit she'd just thrown.

"I've got two words for you," Lucky whispered to her. "Condom."

She pulled back, looked at him. "That's one word."

"If you wear what's in that bag, you'll need two condoms. Three if you skip what's in the bag all together and just show up in your birthday suit. Either way, condoms."

In that moment he was her favorite brother. Lucky

had always been her champion and not judgmental. Most of the time anyway. Plus, he was the only brother who talked safe sex with her. Or any kind of sex for that matter. He wasn't just her brother, he was her friend.

Anna kissed his cheek. "Thanks."

He shrugged in that lazy but cool way that only Lucky or a Greek god could manage. It was as if he drawled his shrugs. And his life.

Lucky returned the cheek kiss and apparently considered his brotherly/friendly duties done because he strolled toward the door and headed out. Logan went to her next.

"I love you," Logan said. "And no matter what happens, I'll be here for you. You can cry on my shoulder all you need. Or if you prefer, I can kick Heath's ass for you. Your choice."

She had to fight a smile, but she didn't have to fight it too hard because the nonsmiling emotions were just below the surface. "I don't want his ass kicked, but I might need the shoulder."

Logan tapped first one shoulder, then the other. "Any time. They're reserved just for you, and I swear *I told you so* will never cross my lips or my mind. You're a grown woman, and if you want to wear what's in that bag, then you have my blessing."

In that moment she loved Logan best. Logan had been her father more than her brother, mainly because he'd been the one to step up after their folks died. He'd been the one to bust her chops when she needed it and had been a whiz helping with her math homework.

Logan would walk through fire for her and not once complain. Well, maybe he would complain, but he'd still do it.

He kissed her forehead and headed off, not out the door but to his old room. Since he lived in town and no longer spent many nights at the ranch, Logan must have wanted his shoulders to be nearby in the event of an impending crying spell.

Uh-oh.

It was Riley's turn.

"If Heath makes you cry again, I'm hitting him with the shovel," Riley growled. "And wear a robe with whatever's in that bag."

Anna sighed. The support of two out of three wasn't bad.

Riley sighed as well, and he pulled her into his arms. "FYI, Heath did some crying, too, after he left here that summer."

Anna wiggled out of his grip so she could see if he was serious or not. He was.

"I don't mean he actually shed tears," Riley went on, "but he cried in his own man kind of way."

"How do you know that?" she asked.

"Because I'm the one who drove him to his basic training." A muscle flickered in his jaw. A sign that he was remembering that day as unfondly as she was. Some of the anger returned. "Heath asked me to make sure you were okay. Can you believe it?"

"The bastard," Anna joked.

"He said it as if I needed to be reminded of it. I didn't. Not then, not now. If you need someone to make sure you're okay, I'll do it. As long as I don't have to hear any sex details. Or see what's in that bag. And I'll do that—minus the exceptions—because you're my sister."

Anna blinked back tears. In that moment, she loved Riley best. Yes, he was hardheaded, and they had a history of sibling squabbles. Plus, there was the time when he'd ruined all her dolls with camo paint and duct-tape combat boots, but still she loved every stubborn, camo-painting ounce of him.

Riley wasn't her father or her friend. He was her brother.

And sometimes, like now, that was exactly what a sister needed.

Chapter Six

Heath paced. Cursed. He figured this much debate hadn't gone into some battle plans, but a battle plan would have been easier than trying to figure out what to do about Anna.

Or better yet what to do *with* Anna.

If he went to her room, sex would happen. Then tomorrow he would leave—just as he'd done nine and a half years ago. That hadn't turned out so well, what with all the crying and her brothers wanting to shovel him.

If he didn't go to her room, sex wouldn't happen. But then he would have to leave things unsettled between them—again—as he'd apparently done before.

He was screwed either way, so Heath decided he might as well go for it. He threw open the door and nearly smacked right into some idiot wearing a hoodie and an army-green vinyl poncho.

Except this was no idiot. It was Anna, and in addition to the garb, she was also carrying a blue sock.

She practically pushed him back into his room and shut the door. "Shhh," she said. "Della and Stella's book club is meeting tonight."

He was still wrapping his mind around the fact that Anna was there, that she had come to him, and maybe that's why Heath couldn't quite wrap his mind around the book club or the poncho.

"There are six of them in the living room, and I had to sneak past them," Anna added when he gave her a blank look.

When Heath kept that blank look, Anna pulled off the poncho, and he saw the hoodie. No pants. No shoes.

Just a pair of really tiny devil-red panties.

He was sure his blank look disappeared because his mouth dropped open. This was the best kind of surprise.

"I didn't have a robe here at the ranch, and the plastic poncho felt sticky against my skin so I put on the hoodie," she explained. Then she unzipped it.

No top. No bra. Just the Be My heart locket dangling between her breasts. Heath thought maybe his tongue was doing some dangling, too.

"And the sock?" he asked.

She smiled and emptied the contents onto the bed. Condoms. At least a dozen of them.

"I took them from Lucky's bathroom," Anna explained. She was still whispering, but it had a giddiness to it. "The poncho and hoodie didn't have pockets so I put them in the sock. I only brought the normal-looking ones. Some had pictures on them and some were glow in the dark." Anna looked at him. "Why would a man need that?"

Heath didn't have a clue. He didn't need any illumination to find anything on Anna's body. His most vital organ agreed. In fact, it wanted to go on that particular search mission right now.

But there was a problem.

"You got my text saying I was leaving, right?" he asked.

She nodded. "Tomorrow. That's why I didn't want to wait until after the book club left. Sometimes they hang around until midnight if Della breaks out the tequila, and we don't have much time."

Not if they were planning on using all those condoms, they didn't, but Heath had to make sure that Anna was sure. She stripped off the hoodie, and he was sure she was sure.

At least he wanted her to be.

He wanted that even more when she slipped into his arms and kissed him. Heath was stupid and weak so it took him a moment to break the kiss.

"Anna, I don't want you hurt," he said.

She frowned. "I think that ship's sailed. I'll be hurt, but I'll get over it. And tonight you'll give me some really good memories to help me get over it, right?"

Yeah.

Whether they had sex or not, Anna would be hurt. Or at least she would be sad to see him go. Ditto for him being sad to leave her. But at least this way they'd have new memories, and they didn't need glow-in-the-dark condoms to do it.

Now that he had a clearly defined mission, Heath pulled her back to him to kiss her. One of those kisses that reached scorch level pretty darn fast. But Anna was aiming for fast, too, and not with just the kisses. She was already going after his zipper.

"We're going to play that scale-of-one-to-ten game," she insisted.

Maybe. But the way she was tugging at his zipper, it was possible she was also trying to finish this all way too fast. Tonight, he didn't want the kissing game, and he didn't want fast.

Heath stopped what she was doing by catching on to her wrists and putting her against the wall. He liked walls because it gave him some control...

Damn.

He had no control. Anna ground herself against him, sliding her leg up the outside of his so that the millimeter of red lace was right against his crotch. Apparently, the orgasm she'd had earlier in the barn hadn't done anything to take the edge off because she was going for another one very quickly.

Again, Heath tried to slow things down. With her leg still cradling his, he turned her, intending to put her against the dresser, but he tripped over the poncho and fell onto the bed.

With Anna on top of him.

"Let's play a game," she said. Definitely not a virginal tone or look. "I'll use just my tongue to find all your special spots. You don't have to give it a number rating. Just a grunt for pleasure. A groan for find another special spot that's more special."

"Men only have one special spot," he told her. Heath took her hand and put it over his sex.

She laughed. Not a humor kind of laugh but the sound of a woman who'd come to play. Or maybe give a little payback for the things he'd done to her in the tack room. Well, Heath wanted to play, too. After all, he had a nearly naked Anna straddling him, and her breasts were making his mouth water.

He managed a quick sample of her left nipple before she moved away. Anna didn't waste any time. With her hand still on his special spot, she went in search of others. His earlobe.

He grunted, but Heath didn't know if that was because, at the same time, she started lowering his zipper.

"That wasn't a loud enough grunt," she said and went after his neck.

Heath grunted. Again, mainly because she lowered the zipper, and when she did that, her breasts got closer to his mouth again. She didn't grunt when he kissed her there, but she did make that silky sound of pleasure that Heath would never tire of hearing.

He would have kept on kissing her breasts, but apparently it was special-spot search time again because she scooted lower and ran her tongue over his own left nipple.

Oh, yeah. He grunted.

Grunted some more when she circled his navel with her tongue. All that tonguing and circling though didn't stop her from getting his zipper all the way down, and as he had done to her earlier, she shimmied his jeans lower.

"You really do go commando," she said.

"Yep—"

He might have added more. Something clever or at least coherent, but her hands were on him. The condom, too. Heath wasn't sure when she'd opened one of the packets. Nor did he care. The woman had clever hands after all—

Hell.

He grunted loud enough to trigger an earthquake when she dropped down onto him. That's when he figured out really, really fast that the panties were crotchless and that he was in her warm and tight special place all the way to the hilt.

"That's not your tongue," he said through the grunts.

"So, I cheated."

The woman was evil. And damn good. Heath usually liked to be the alpha when it came to sex, but even more than that, he liked taking turns with Anna. Apparently, she was going to make the most of her turn, too. She had the whole *ride 'em, cowgirl* motion going on. So fast that Heath knew this would all end too soon.

Of course, sixteen hours was going to be too soon.

As if she'd read his mind, she slowed. Anna put her palm on his chest and, still moving against his erection, leaned down and kissed him.

"After this," she said, "I want you all the way naked."

Heath thought that was a stellar idea. He wanted those panties off her, too, even though they fell into the *why bother* category of women's undergarments.

The locket whacked him in the face, but even that didn't put a damper on the moment. Heath just pushed the locket aside, gathered her close and let his cowgirl screw his brains out.

Chapter Seven

Anna wished there were some kind of anticry shot she could take. Even one that worked for just an hour or so would do. She figured she'd do plenty of crying after Heath had left, but she didn't want any tears shed in front of him.

Or in front of her brothers.

She wanted Heath to remember her smiling. Or maybe naked, since that's how he'd seen her for a good portion of the night. It was certainly how she wanted to remember him.

With that reminder/pep talk still fresh in her mind, Anna left her bedroom and went in search of Heath so she could give him that smiling goodbye she'd practiced in the mirror. But he wasn't in his bedroom. Or the living room. Or the kitchen. In fact no one was, and she figured they'd all cleared out to give her a chance to have a private goodbye with Heath.

Or maybe they'd cleared out because Heath was already gone. She had several moments of panic when she sprinted to the back porch to make sure his rental car was still there.

It was.

And so was Heath.

He was at the fence pasture, looking at some cows that'd been delivered that morning. He made a picture standing there with his foot on the bottom rung of the fence, his cream-colored cowboy hat slung low on his face.

He must have heard her approaching because he turned, smiling. It looked about as genuine as the one she was trying to keep on her face. Until he reached out, pulled her to him and kissed her.

Then the smiles were real.

"How soon before you leave?" she asked.

"Soon."

That reminder made her smile waver. Anna wasn't sure how far to push this part of the conversation, but there was something she had to know. "Are you feeling any better about the instructor job?"

"I've accepted it. Sometimes, that's the best you can do with crappy lemonade. Sorry," Heath added when she frowned. "It was just something Riley said. An analogy of sorts."

Riley not only needed a new threat, he needed new analogies, as well.

Since their time together was about to end, Anna reached into her pocket and took out the "gift" she'd gotten him on her shopping trip the day before. She hadn't wanted it to be a big gift because that would have made this goodbye seem, well, big.

Which it was.

But she didn't want it to feel big to him.

She took his hand and dropped the smashed penny in it. "It reminded me of your dog tags, and it's supposed to be good luck."

He stared at it, gave a slight smile. "Thanks."

"I was going to give you the red panties," she added, "but I thought it would look strange if the TSA went through your luggage."

Now she got the reaction she wanted. A bigger smile. A bigger kiss, too.

"I have something for you," he said. He took out a silver heart locket. It was similar to the other one he'd given her nine and a half years ago. Very similar.

Right down to the Be My engraving.

Anna checked to make sure she had on the original one. She did. And she was shaking her head until Heath opened it, and she saw what was inside. Not pictures of him and her.

But of her parents. Her dad on one side of the heart. Her mother on the other.

"Della got the pictures for me," he explained. "You said sometimes you forget their faces, and this way you won't forget."

Oh, God.

She was going to cry.

No matter how hard she blinked, the tears came, and they just kept coming.

"I'm sorry." Heath pulled her back in his arms. "I didn't know it would upset you."

"It doesn't," she said, sobbing. "It's a good kind of upset." Still sobbing. "Thank you, Heath, thank you."

He held her while she sobbed, and it took Anna several long moments to stop.

"I got you something else," he added.

Anna couldn't imagine getting anything better than the second locket. It was even more precious to her than the first one. But Heath must have thought "the more the better" because he took out a wad of lockets from his coat pocket.

"I went to the jewelry store this morning and bought every locket they had."

She had no doubts about that—none. There was another silver one, one gold and another in the shape of a cat's head.

"They're, uh, beautiful." Though she couldn't imagine needing that many lockets. Or the ugly one with the cat's head.

"I had them engraved," he added, "and this time I watched to make sure they did it right. You can choose which one you want."

It took her a second to realize he'd finished his sentence. Not "which one you want *to wear.*" Not "which one you want *to keep.*" Not "which one you want *to remember me by.*"

Heath turned over one of the silver ones, and she saw the engraving there. One word.

Lover.

He put the Be My locket next to it, and she got the message then. Be my lover.

She laughed. "Does this mean you want to see more of me?"

"Well, I've already seen more, but I'd like to see more of you more often."

That dried any remnants of her tears, and she blurted out an idea she'd been toying with for days. "I could look into transferring to a law school in Florida." And she held her breath.

No smile from him. "I don't want you to sacrifice going to a school that maybe doesn't have as good of a reputation as the one you're in now."

"No sacrifice. There are a couple of really good ones. And besides, I was transferring anyway. Might as well transfer so you can—" she held up the two lockets to finish that thought "—Be My Lover."

Anna tested his neck again with a kiss. And her tongue.

"Keep that up, and you'll be my lover again right now," he grumbled.

"If that's supposed to make me behave, then it won't work. Not with the hayloft so close. How much time do you have before you need to leave for your flight?"

"Not enough time for the hayloft."

She kissed him again, and he seemed to change his mind about that. He started leading her in that direction.

"Not enough time for the hayloft unless we hurry," Heath amended.

Good. The kisses were working.

Since she'd already put her heart on the line, Anna put the rest of herself out there, too. "I don't want a fling."

"Good. Flings are overrated." He kissed her again. "And temporary."

She released the breath she didn't even know she'd been holding. Heath didn't want temporary. Nor a fling. He wanted sex.

That was a solid start since she wanted that, too.

"I'm not done," he said. "Remember, you pick the locket you want." He held up the next one, the gold one, and it also had a single word engraved on it.

Woman.

As in Be My Woman.

Yes, they were so going to that hayloft, and then she was going to the university to start that transfer to Florida.

"Can I wear both the *Lover* and *Woman*?" she asked. Because she wanted both.

"You haven't seen the third one yet."

And she probably couldn't see it before the next kiss crossed her eyes. Along with singeing her eyelashes.

Still, he put the locket in her hand just as her butt landed against the ladder. Anna backed up one step at a time, which wasn't easy to do with Heath kissing her like that. And he kept on kissing her until they made it all the way to the top of the hayloft.

But Anna froze when she saw what was engraved on the tacky cat's head locket.

Love.

"Be My Love," she said, putting the words together.

Putting *everything* together.

"The *L* word?" she asked.

Heath nodded. "Sometimes it's the only word that works. What about you? Does the *L* word work for you?"

Anna had to catch her breath just so she could speak. "It works perfectly for me." She kissed him. "Does this mean we're going steady?"

"Oh, yeah," Heath confirmed. "That, and a whole lot more."

* * * * *

#1629 TROUBLE WITH A BADGE
Appaloosa Pass Ranch • by Delores Fossen
Lawman Levi Crockett would never turn his back on PI Alexa Dearborn and the baby girl in her care. But as a serial killer stalks them, Levi must fight a powerful enemy—the desire between them.

#1630 DECEPTIONS
The Battling McGuire Boys • by Cynthia Eden
Secrets from their pasts threaten Elizabeth Snow and Mac McGuire—as much as the killer who seems to know their every move. Can they trust each other again? Or will a shocking truth prove fatal?

#1631 NAVY SEAL CAPTIVE
SEAL of My Own • by Elle James
Being abducted wasn't part of Sawyer Houston's R & R mission. Jenna Broyles claims she's rescuing the navy SEAL from unknown assailants. Only, it's her life on the line when the jilted bride becomes a target.

#1632 HEAVY ARTILLERY HUSBAND
Colby Agency: Family Secrets • by Debra Webb & Regan Black
When someone tries to kill security expert Sophia Leone, she's rescued by her husband, Frank—an army general she *thought* died a year ago. Now Sophia must trust her life to the man she married...the man she never stopped loving.

#1633 TEXAN'S BABY
Mason Ridge • by Barb Han
Bodyguard Dawson Hill is committed to protecting the woman who left him two years ago. Melanie Dixon has returned to Mason Ridge...with his son. Now a madman is threatening the family Dawson never dreamed he could have.

#1634 FULL FORCE FATHERHOOD
Orion Security • by Tyler Anne Snell
Fatherhood was never in the cards for Mark Tranton, until widow Kelli Crane and her daughter wrapped themselves around his heart. But digging into their past riles someone who won't rest until Kelli pays the ultimate price...

HICNM0316

REQUEST YOUR FREE BOOKS!
2 FREE NOVELS PLUS 2 FREE GIFTS!

ⓗ HARLEQUIN®

INTRIGUE

BREATHTAKING ROMANTIC SUSPENSE

YES! Please send me 2 FREE Harlequin® Intrigue novels and my 2 FREE gifts (gifts are worth about $10). After receiving them, if I don't wish to receive any more books, I can return the shipping statement marked "cancel." If I don't cancel, I will receive 6 brand-new novels every month and be billed just $4.74 per book in the U.S. or $5.49 per book in Canada. That's a savings of at least 12% off the cover price! It's quite a bargain! Shipping and handling is just 50¢ per book in the U.S. and 75¢ per book in Canada.* I understand that accepting the 2 free books and gifts places me under no obligation to buy anything. I can always return a shipment and cancel at any time. Even if I never buy another book, the two free books and gifts are mine to keep forever.

182/382 HDN GH3D

Name _____ (PLEASE PRINT) _____

Address _____ Apt. # _____

City _____ State/Prov. _____ Zip/Postal Code _____

Signature (if under 18, a parent or guardian must sign)

Mail to the **Reader Service:**
IN U.S.A.: P.O. Box 1867, Buffalo, NY 14240-1867
IN CANADA: P.O. Box 609, Fort Erie, Ontario L2A 5X3
**Are you a subscriber to Harlequin® Intrigue books
and want to receive the larger-print edition?
Call 1-800-873-8635 or visit www.ReaderService.com.**

* Terms and prices subject to change without notice. Prices do not include applicable taxes. Sales tax applicable in N.Y. Canadian residents will be charged applicable taxes. Offer not valid in Quebec. This offer is limited to one order per household. Not valid for current subscribers to Harlequin Intrigue books. All orders subject to credit approval. Credit or debit balances in a customer's account(s) may be offset by any other outstanding balance owed by or to the customer. Please allow 4 to 6 weeks for delivery. Offer available while quantities last.

Your Privacy—The Reader Service is committed to protecting your privacy. Our Privacy Policy is available online at www.ReaderService.com or upon request from the Reader Service.

We make a portion of our mailing list available to reputable third parties that offer products we believe may interest you. If you prefer that we not exchange your name with third parties, or if you wish to clarify or modify your communication preferences, please visit us at www.ReaderService.com/consumerchoice or write to us at Reader Service Preference Service, P.O. Box 9062, Buffalo, NY 14240-9062. Include your complete name and address.

HI15

Levi eased into the shadows away from the pulsing neon
bar lights, and he listened. Waiting. It was hard, though,
to pick through the sounds of the crackling lights, the
wind and his own heartbeat drumming in his ears.

But somewhere there was the sound of an engine
running.

Because the driver had the headlights off, it took Levi
a moment to realize the car wasn't approaching from
the street but rather from the back of the bar. No road
there, just a parklike area that the local teenagers used for
making out. It could also be the very route a killer would
likely take.

Before the car eased to a stop, Levi whipped out his
gun and took aim. He froze. And not because of the
weather.

The person stepped out from the car, the watery lights
just enough for him to see her face. Not the Moonlight

Strangler but someone he did recognize. The pale blond hair. The willowy build.

Alexa.

Of all the people that Levi thought he might run into tonight, Alexa Dearborn wasn't anywhere on his radar. Heck, she shouldn't be anywhere near him, this bar or the town of Appaloosa Pass.

Because she had a bounty on her head.

Word on the street was that the hired guns who were after her had orders to shoot to kill.

It'd been five months since Levi had seen her, as the marshals had whisked her away into WITSEC to an unnamed place. A change of name, too. But five months wasn't nearly long enough for the memories to fade.

Don't miss
TROUBLE WITH A BADGE
by USA TODAY *bestselling author Delores Fossen,*
available in April 2016 wherever
Harlequin® Intrigue books and ebooks are sold.

www.Harlequin.com